LEAVING CUB CREEK

Cub Creek #2

A Virginia Country Roads Novel

LEAVING CUB CREEK

by

Grace Greene

Cub Creek #2
(Sequel: Leaving Cub Creek)

A Virginia Country Roads Novel

Kersey Creek Books
P.O. Box 6054
Ashland, VA 23005

Leaving Cub Creek
Copyright © 2014 Grace Greene
All rights reserved.

Virginia Country Roads (series name)
Copyright © 2014 Grace Greene
All rights reserved.

Cover Design by Grace Greene

Trade Paperback Release: December 2015
ISBN-13: 978-0-9968756-2-2
Digital Release: December 2015
ISBN-13: 978-0-9968756-3-9
Large Print Edition Release: November 2017
ISBN-13: 978-0-9996180-2-8

DEDICATION

Leaving Cub Creek is dedicated to my mother who, during the time I've been writing this book, has struggled and endured through valleys she no longer fully understands or recognizes, but whose sweet nature, courage and essential loving kindness have never been lost.

ACKNOWLEDGEMENT

My love and sincere appreciation to my husband, family and friends for their encouragement and support.

Definition from Wikipedia: Synesthesia is a neurological phenomenon in which stimulation of one sensory or cognitive pathway leads to automatic, involuntary experiences in a second sensory or cognitive pathway. [April 2014]

Books by Grace Greene

Stories of heart and hope ~ from the Outer Banks to the Blue Ridge

Emerald Isle, NC Stories
Love. Suspense. Inspiration.

BEACH RENTAL (Emerald Isle novel #1)
BEACH WINDS (Emerald Isle novel #2)
BEACH WEDDING (Emerald Isle novel #3)
BEACH TOWEL (short story)
BEACH WALK (A Christmas novella)
BEACH CHRISTMAS (A Christmas novella)
CLAIR: BEACH BRIDES SERIES (novella)

Virginia Country Roads Novels
Love. Mystery. Suspense.

KINCAID'S HOPE
A STRANGER IN WYNNEDOWER
CUB CREEK (Cub Creek series #1)
LEAVING CUB CREEK (Cub Creek series #2)

Single Titles from Lake Union Publishing

THE HAPPINESS IN BETWEEN
THE MEMORY OF BUTTERFLIES

www.gracegreene.com

LEAVING CUB CREEK

In the heart of Virginia, where the forests hide secrets and the creeks run strong and deep ~

Libbie Havens never fit in. She bought the old Carson place on Cub Creek and moved to the Virginia countryside to prove she could live on her own terms. In the process, she learned some truths about herself and found love ~ but love, acceptance and belonging can be easier to find than to keep.

While on a trip to Slcily with Libbie, Jim Mitchell must leave suddenly because his son is injured in an accident in California. Now alone, Libbie is surprised by an old friend, Dr. Barry Raymond, but Dr. Raymond is a reminder of her troubled past and she's glad to see the last of him when she leaves Sicily ~ until he shows up at her house on Cub Creek.

Years before, Dr. Raymond told Libbie that if troubles weren't dealt with, they'd keep coming back. With Jim still away helping his son, Libbie's troubles are returning in force and wreaking havoc on her confidence and their relationship.

Libbie would rather hide than risk rejection, but she must face down the past and fight for what she wants, or the troubles that haunt her past and present will forever doom her future.

LEAVING CUB CREEK

Chapter One

Libbie Havens flinched at the bright light and raised her hand to shield her eyes. The Mediterranean sun, magnified by the reflection of nearby whitewashed walls, suddenly seemed sharp and blinding. The light, the sounds of Taormina, Sicily, the jostling of the crowd at the curb as they waited to cross the street—it was lively, but disconcerting, too. Libbie and Jim were caught up in a mash of tourists and locals. The tourists were trying to stay in a group. The locals wanted to get around or through them.

Jim Mitchell carried the large camera backpack with the strap slung over his shoulder. Libbie kept her hand on his arm until a man pushed between. She struggled to stay close, but someone in the back shouted and the mass of people surged forward taking Jim with them. The crowd parted briefly, and she caught sight of him. He'd paused in the street and turned back, seeking her. Their eyes met. As he started to smile, they heard the heavy sound of a car's accelerating engine. In the next instant brakes squealed and Jim fell. She lost sight of him. A woman screamed, tires burned against the cobbled street, and then the car kicked into gear and surged forward and away.

It happened fast and just as quickly Libbie heard Aunt Margaret's voice in her head saying, "How many people who cared about you are still alive?"

Libbie shoved through the people. She stumbled over the curb, falling and scraping her knee, then she was up again and moving. Those few feet seemed an eternity. Others rushed toward Jim. She pushed them aside saying over and over, "Move, move, move," until she finally broke through.

A man was bending over Jim with his hand on Jim's shoulder, asking, "You okay?"

Jim nodded.

"Okay. He's okay." Then the man mumbled words Libbie didn't understand. It sounded like disgust and she presumed it was about driving skills, or maybe it was about crazy, foolish tourists who stopped in the middle of the street.

He helped Jim to his feet, then moved on with the rest of the crowd. Show over.

Jim reached out to her, his hand unsteady, his face pale. He asked, "You alright?"

Horns, from both cars and motor bikes, honked. Strangers streamed around them, their eyes touching Jim and Libbie as the two stood in the street, then their gazes slipped past, dismissing them, as their own plans eclipsed their curiosity. Their voices were international. They filled the air with words that were mostly unintelligible to Libbie.

She tugged at Jim's arm. "Let's get out of the street."

With Jim securely at her side, they made their way to a quieter spot. Libbie needed open space, and a moment to sit and breathe. Wide steps in front of a nearby building offered the chance to do both. She pushed at Jim to sit and as soon as he did, her own knees, shaky, folded. She joined him on the steps a little more abruptly than intended.

He steadied her as she leaned against him. She closed her eyes, feeling the fabric of his shirt against her cheek, smelling his scent and hugging his warmth, drawing from it, until the air around them shifted, enough that she felt stable. Safe again. Almost. The sky was again a pure, clear blue, and bright but without the painful starkness from before the accident.

She should've realized. If she'd recognized the altered light, she might have been more watchful, more careful.

"You're okay, right?" Libbie touched his cheek and stared into his hazel eyes. "Are you sure you're not hurt?"

He put his hand on her leg. "I'm fine. I was hardly touched. I lost my balance, that's all. What about you? Your knee is bleeding."

He was right. She was wearing knee-length shorts. A thin dribble of blood marked her knee and shin. She pulled a tissue from her tote bag and dabbed at it. "It's nothing."

"I doubt these streets have less germs and bacteria than the ones back home. The cut needs to be washed and treated."

"I have adhesive bandages here in my tote. Antibiotic ointment, too."

"Your magic tote." Jim laughed. "Let's go back to the hotel and regroup. You can wash it properly and I want to check the camera. Sorry, but I heard something crack."

"I don't care about the camera."

He smiled, pulled her closer, and kissed her temple. They stayed like that for a few long seconds, then Jim stood and offered his arm. He helped her to her feet and picked up the backpack.

Back at the hotel Libbie washed the wound. A few scratches. She applied the ointment and a bandage, then came back into the room saying, "Good as new."

Jim looked grim. "Sorry to say the news isn't as happy for your camera."

He handed it to her. She held it and stared at it, but she wasn't seeing the camera. The danger was past, but the memory of Jim disappearing into the crowd to the tune of a revving engine threatened to overwhelm her again. That look in his beautiful eyes in the moment before he was hit.... She shivered.

He hugged her with great gentleness and kissed her forehead. "Listen. Let's take a break. You could use a few minutes to relax anyway."

"I'm fine."

"Well, to be honest, I have to reply to some emails. I was going to do it later, but I just received a couple of new ones from the bookkeeper and the nursery manager." He half-grinned, apologetic. "I'll meet with them now while they're still up, get it done, and then we'll be free and ready to tackle Taormina again." He tightened his hug and whispered in her hair, "I love you."

Libbie wrapped her arms around him. She closed her eyes and saw the near-disaster replay in her head, accompanied by Aunt Margaret's words like a voice over.

"Hey, are you okay?" He put a finger below her chin and lifted her face. "Or is it the work?"

"No, of course not." She forced a smile. "In fact, you've done remarkably little of that on the trip."

"Then what? The headache from this morning?"

She wanted to answer, but couldn't. Aunt

Margaret's voice had lodged in the front of her brain, blocking a reasonable response.

She could tell him. He'd understand about her aunt…and the rest. He already knew some of it. But to say it aloud was like inviting the ugliness to travel with them. She wasn't going to make her past Jim's problem, too. On the other hand, what about honesty and trust?

Libbie pulled back her words. She was a grown woman, thirty-three and independent. She would not be ruled by the past, nor would she allow nasty people like her aunt to haunt her.

He stared at her, examining her face. "You look pale. Lie down and rest while I boot up the computer. Once I get the call started, the meeting should only take a few minutes."

She picked up his phone. "The computer for the meeting, not the phone?" She wanted to say something funny, anything to break the heaviness that seemed to be trying to settle in over them. She waved the phone at him, saying, "And I don't need a camera for photos. Just a phone and a selfie stick."

"The camera on your phone isn't quite the same as that expensive camera you carry. I'm sorry yours broke. You are an amazing photographer."

In handling the phone, she must've touched the phone log because suddenly a list of calls came up. Stunned, she asked, "What's this?"

Jim took the phone and looked.

She watched his face as he recognized Liz's number on the screen. A frown briefly crossed his face, then he smiled.

"She called. She wanted to know how you were doing."

"Liz cut me out of her life. What do you mean she wanted to know how I was? Why on earth didn't you tell me she called?"

He came close and touched her cheek, her hair. "That's why I didn't tell you. I'm sure your cousin meant well, but she had nothing to say that was worth stressing you out over. The only reason I took her call was in case something important had happened back home with her or Josh, or the children. It hadn't. Forget Liz for now. Worry about her when you're back home. For now, relax and enjoy yourself."

Still uneasy, but determined to shake Liz and other unpleasant memories, including their own excitement that morning, Libbie forced a smile and went through the open connecting door into her own room.

"Are you okay?" Jim asked.

"I am." She picked up a book from the nightstand. "You take care of business now, and then we can enjoy the town after, okay?" She smiled.

Jim nodded. He initiated the call on his

computer and soon the nursery manager's face was right there, practically in the room with them. Libbie tried to read, but couldn't concentrate with the conversation going on and she felt Jim's distraction, too. Finally, she stood in the doorway, waved her book at him, and mouthed, "Yell when you're done," then went out the French doors to the terrace.

Jim was right about Liz. He should've told her, but she also understood his reasons. She wouldn't allow her cousin Liz to intrude in, ruin, this trip. A few months ago, Liz had asked how she, Libbie, could stand being alone most of the time? Libbie enjoyed solitude and had made a flip remark in response, but that was before she and Jim had become a couple. Since Jim, Libbie had discovered she liked solitude better as a treat, not as regular fare. Maybe the difference was in who you were sharing the time with.

Up here, above the bustle of the city—a tourist mecca for anyone visiting Sicily—the high blue sky and the scents of gardens and the Mediterranean reigned. She found a bench in the shade of a small tree, and opened her book. She couldn't focus on the words. She kept seeing Jim's face and his calm confidence. She'd almost lost him.

No, she told herself, it hadn't been that close.

It could have been deadly.

She pressed her fingers against her temples. *Focus, Libbie, focus. Shake it off.*

Jim owned his own business, a long-time family concern with a large nursery as well as a landscaping and lawn care business. A lot of people, including family, employees and customers, were depending upon him to pay attention to business. Libbie didn't mind about the business calls. Without his encouragement, she would never have attempted this trip at all.

****

Libbie soaked in the beauty of the garden for a while, but Jim's meeting must be running longer than expected and the bench had grown hard. She closed her book and wandered along the terrace, her hand sliding along the railing, and then descended the stone steps enjoying the view.

When she returned to the terrace outside their rooms, Jim was standing at the door, the phone to his ear. He motioned for her to come in. She walked into the room and saw that everything had changed.

His jacket was folded on the coverlet and his suitcase was open on the bed. He dropped his cell phone beside it.

"Mom called while I was talking to Walt. Matthew's hurt. Car accident. It's serious."

"Serious? How serious?"

"Very. I have to leave immediately."

"California?"

"Yes."

"His mother is with him, right?"

"She was driving. She's injured, too."

"I see." Libbie turned away thinking of next steps. "Well, you need to be with your son. We'll leave now." She began pulling out their travel info and looking for a phone number. "I'll call the airline."

Jim touched her hands to slow them. She stopped and looked into his eyes.

"I've contacted them. I was able to secure a seat. Only one. Plus, I had to change my connection at Dulles to get to California." He stopped to let it sink in.

"You're leaving me." In her head, the words here and alone echoed. She cringed, realizing that fear was pushing her instantly back in old habits where bad emotions were ruled by fear and feeling unloved. Yet, Jim had done this, made these changes in their plans, without her. She shook her head trying to stop the negative blowback from the past.

Jim rushed his arms around her and breathed words into her hair. "Not by choice. I need to get there as soon as possible."

She pressed her face against his shirt. She was stronger now. She could do this. "I understand."

"Libbie. I'm sorry."

She eased out of the circle of his arms and pushed at him gently. "Finish packing. Should I ask the hotel to summon a taxi, or have you already done that, too?" The hint of petulance was unmistakable. She hated it.

Jim frowned and pulled her close again. "Can you manage on your own?"

"I can. I'll be fine." She put her hands on his chest. "Travel safely, Jim. I can manage on my own, but I've grown accustomed to your company and I'm not willing to do without it for long."

"You've never done much traveling. This is a long way from Cub Creek."

"Don't worry. Take care of yourself and your son."

Jim zipped the case closed. "Mom will meet you at the airport when you arrive in Richmond. Or my sister, or someone from the nursery, if she can't."

"No need. I'll be fine."

"We should have driven ourselves to the airport. My car would've been there waiting for you to use."

"I told you, Jim. Go and don't worry. I'll be fine. Call me when you know more."

She leaned against him and he kissed her. She welcomed the feel of his lips on hers, on her neck. For a minute she could pretend everything was okay. As his arms eased away from her and the kiss ended, it occurred to her that if Aunt Margaret was right, maybe Jim would be safer on the far side of the Atlantic, and even safer on the far side of the US. Wherever Libbie wasn't.

She took a deep breath, then said, "I'll walk you down. What can I carry?"

****

Libbie waved at the back window of the taxi that drove Jim away.

Weird. Unsettling. She wasn't waving goodbye from her own porch, surrounded by tall pines and wide-spreading oaks, but from the stone steps of a hotel in a foreign place. The city, the island, were beautiful, and the people were pleasant, but without Jim beside her it felt more than foreign. Crowded. Loud. Alien.

Jim was right. She was no traveler. Suddenly, and not for the first time on this trip, she missed home. She missed Cub Creek.

In a few days, she'd be back where she belonged. And she could get there on her own.

For now, except for a whispered prayer of recovery for Matthew and safe traveling for Jim, there was nothing she could do for either of them.

For herself, she could make a choice. She

could wait out the remaining days in her room until it was time for her to fly home, or she could use them well. Her tote bag was filled with everything a traveler needed and more. Among people she didn't know and whom she'd never see again, if she messed up or made a fool of herself, what would it matter?

The tote was roomy. She had the guidebook she'd carried with her since leaving home. There was no room for the big camera, and it was damaged anyway. Despite the protection of the backpack, the lens threading had jammed onto the attachment ring. Clearly, the camera and lens had taken a big hit.

It could've been Jim.

No. No more of that. She cut off the voice, unwilling to get caught up in the what-ifs again.

Libbie walked the narrow streets lined with shops, mixing in with the other tourists. She lingered in the shops longer than she had when she was being considerate of Jim, but she missed the strength of his hand in hers or his arm around her waist. A shared laugh or his breath against her neck as he leaned close....

"Excuse me."

"Pardon."

Tourists. She was blocking the walkway. She didn't bother to apologize. They were already past with their shopping bags and backpacks. From behind, most of them looked alike. She wished she could tell Jim, whisper it to him, that perhaps they needed to check their own rear images. She resumed walking with a destination in mind. Despite her joke about the phone camera and selfie sticks—they weren't for her. She needed more. At least something with a viewfinder, some minimal controls and a decent zoom—electronics she was more familiar with.

Libbie hugged her tote bag closer and moved on.

She found a camera store where she purchased a small mirrorless camera and a small prime lens and a slim zoom. They would fit easily into the tote. Important now that Jim wasn't here to carry the backpack.

Libbie decided to eat at the trattoria between the lunch and supper crowds because it would be less hectic. The café—correction—this trattoria was their place. In fact, it was the same trattoria they'd eaten breakfast at that morning. The table in the corner, nearest to the building, was their favorite. She moved Jim's chair closer to hers and placed her tote on it. The light, broken by the wooden framework overhead and the vines growing around and through it, created points of light on the table top. At first, it reminded her of her dining room ceiling, which she hadn't ever quite finished, which then made her think of her terrace.

Jim's crew had built her a terrace, but she didn't have this overhead framework. She dismissed the idea as quickly as she considered it. Her backyard was too shady.

"Signorina? Your friend, he is coming?"

Their waiter. Tony. Dark curly hair and long lashes over deep brown eyes. She shook her head. "Not this time. Only me."

He brought a glass of wine and she placed her order, then pulled out the camera's instruction sheet to read while she waited. Nowadays, the full manuals were online, not in the box. She sensed no one approaching until hands touched the back of her chair and a man leaned close, saying, "Libbie? Is it really you?"

Startled, she turned in her seat.

The man said, "It is you. I can't believe it. Here you are, sitting in a trattoria in Sicily."

Her wine glass tipped, and he grabbed it while she sat, stunned. He set the glass back on the table.

"Dr. Raymond," she said.

"Did I frighten you? I hope not. I saw you sitting here. I thought...I thought this is impossible. This cannot be, and yet here you are, and as beautiful as ever."

He laughed, and she stood. She touched his arm. He was real. Of course, he was.

"It's okay to hug an old friend, I hope." He wrapped his arms around her, but only for a heartbeat or two, and then he released her.

His goatee was gone. His thinning hair was laced with gray. He'd always worn a dark suit and red silk tie back when they'd known each other. Now, he was in a loose cotton shirt, khaki slacks and leather sandals. His skin was tanned. The casual look seemed much more at home on him than the office pallor she remembered.

Dr. Raymond pointed to Jim's chair. "May I join you?"

"Of course." Her response was automatic. She struggled to find the right words as she moved her tote from the chair and set it at her feet.

He continued, "Are you alone? How long have you been in Sicily?"

"It's been how many years?" Libbie shook her head. "Sorry, it's hard to believe you're here and just happened to...." She forced a smile. "When you left your practice, you said you were going away. Italy, right? And I did receive postcards from you early on, but that was a long time ago."

The waiter returned with her drink. He stared at Dr. Raymond who obviously wasn't Jim.

She felt compelled to explain. "This is an old friend of mine. Can you imagine us running into each other here? What are the odds?"

Dr. Raymond said, "I don't believe in

coincidence, Libbie."

Tony asked, "Would the gentleman like to order?"

He looked at Libbie. "May I join you for lunch?"

"Certainly. Unless you don't have time? You may have somewhere you need to be?"

"I would never insult fate, or you, by ignoring where it has led me. This meeting, Libbie, is a gift."

Libbie shook her head, "I'm sorry. I don't know what to call you. You were Dr. Raymond back then, but I'm no longer your patient."

"Barry, of course. What else would you call me? We were always more friends than doctor-patient."

"I always felt we were friends, but it has been a while." An old familiar uneasiness shifted inside her and a little voice whispered in her head that a close relationship is not unusual when a person is receiving therapy, not for the patient, anyway. And not entirely appropriate. She reached for her drink and took a sip forcing her attention back to Dr. Raymond. Barry.

"Did you resume your practice? Or stay retired?" Her words came out sharper than intended. She tried to soften them. "Is there a Mrs. Raymond? Perhaps an elegant Italian lady?"

"No wife. I did stay retired. I've enjoyed

myself." He shrugged. "I've traveled here and there. Took up painting for a while, but," he laughed, "I have no talent. I wrote a few professional papers." He spread his hands. "Aside from an occasional consultation, I've become a bum, I'm afraid."

"If you're happy and you can afford it, then good for you. Not many find that kind of contentment."

"And you, Libbie. You look amazing. I believe you have found peace."

"Thank you." She fidgeted. She appreciated the compliment, but this could only be a reference to past tragedies. Long past. At least as far in the past as Barry Raymond himself had been. They should stay there.

The food delivery seemed to be lagging. She looked toward the restaurant, but resisted checking the time on her phone.

He reached across the table and touched her hand. "Is something wrong?"

She shook her head. "No. The food service seems slow today."

"Worth waiting for, especially with you sitting across from me." He paused, then said, "Perhaps you need to be somewhere and I'm holding you up?"

"No, really. It's fine."

"What have you been up to, Libbie? You talked about doing many things. Which path did you choose?"

Paths? Choices? She straightened the knife and fork, and smoothed the napkin in her lap. "That seems so long ago. I hardly recall what we discussed." Not true, though she would've liked it to be. "I've been doing some renovating and redecoration. Lots of photography."

"All creative occupations. I'm not surprised." He smiled as if they shared a secret.

Libbie was still trying to puzzle it out, and wondering why she had to, when he said, "I believe our food is here."

The waiter brought both food orders. "Sì, signorina. I held yours back, so they'd be ready about the same time. I hope that was satisfactory."

"Of course. Thank you."

Again, the waiter cast a quick look at her companion. He'd always joked with Jim. Jim was the kind of guy people wanted to be with. He was just that way—authentic through and through.

Dr. Raymond asked, "Are you here on holiday? How long?"

She thought of Jim, their trip and his sudden departure. She didn't want to discuss Jim with Barry Raymond. "Holiday, yes, but my trip is almost over."

"Well, then, what are your plans? Perhaps we can spend some time together before you leave?"

She searched for the right words. "I don't want to inconvenience you."

What was wrong with her? Dr. Raymond—Barry—was an old acquaintance. A friend, really.

"You're staying nearby?" he asked.

Libbie answered between bites. "Over there." She pointed up the street in the general direction of the hotel. "Past the white building."

"Castello Alcantara? I'm familiar with it. It's very nice."

"It's lovely. The staff are friendly, and the rooms open directly onto the terrace and gardens. I could sit there all day enjoying the view."

"I'm glad you didn't do that, or I wouldn't have found you."

"Were you looking for me?" She meant it as a quip. A play on his words. She saw by his expression that it went astray, or hit some sort of mark.

"I—" He stopped and sipped his wine, seeming to regroup his thoughts. "What are you planning for this afternoon? I'm happy to take you around." He reached across to touch her hand. "I can't believe you're here."

"I feel the same, but I already have plans. Some things to take care of." She said it in a tone that didn't invite questions.

"Then dinner," he said. "Join me this evening. Wherever you'd like. Or I'll choose. I know some excellent restaurants."

The waiter brought the check and Libbie opened her tote bag to find her wallet.

"This is my treat," he said.

"No, I'll pay for my lunch."

He went silent and gave her a considering look. "Still independent and determined." He shrugged. "I agree so long as tonight is on me."

Libbie nodded. "Fine. Where will we go?"

He reached into his pocket and pulled out his wallet, along with a loose coin. The coin went back into his pocket and he slipped some cash out of his wallet. He added it to hers for the waiter.

"I'll surprise you. Shall I pick you up at 6? What's your room number?"

She paused. "I'll meet you in the lobby."

He stared, as if assessing her motivation. "Am I pushing in, interfering? I am so happy to see you, but if I've over-stepped...."

Now she was embarrassed, and for no reason. "There's a lot going on in here." Libbie tapped her head. "You probably remember that about me."

His look changed from considering to benevolent. "I'll see you at six. In the lobby."

She stayed seated as he stood. She waited for him to walk away before rising. It should have been fun to see Barry Raymond appear out of nowhere, and just when she was feeling a little lonely without Jim. She wished Jim had... No. In fact, she was grateful Jim and Barry hadn't met. Maybe that was the core of her uneasiness.

Libbie rose, picked up her tote bag and pushed her chair under the table. The iron feet scraped against the stone surface, reminding her of her wrought iron set, and even her grandmother's set...and that brought her thoughts back around to Dr. Barry Raymond.

The core of the problem was what Barry Raymond represented, and what he knew, and how he'd told her secrets, however well-intentioned.

Instead of sharing a meal with him, she should be confronting him. That was still an option, but in the end, did it matter?

She set off in the opposite direction. Buildings rose on either side casting the street into shadow. People passed alone and in groups, but all afoot. The corners were impossibly sharp for cars. No wonder Vespa's were so popular. Libbie was accustomed to the uneven stone surface beneath her feet by now, but she missed Jim's arm in hers. She missed their clasped hands. She missed the approving looks strangers gave them as they passed, something she rarely won on her own.

Finally reaching the broader thoroughfare, Libbie stood at the corner, the same corner where Jim had been hit. She paused there, waiting to cross.

Dr. Raymond represented a dreadful time in her life, the culmination of years of neglect and occasional abuse by her grandmother, her grandmother's death, and then her own breakdown. Jim knew some of the tale and that was enough. She didn't want her history, ugly and real, in their relationship. As amazing as it had been to see Barry Raymond so unexpectedly, and after so many years, she didn't want to re-live her past, not even as memories.

Libbie wandered downhill, over the cracked, uneven pavement to the small harbor. Because of the news about Matthew, she and Jim hadn't been able to make the trip back down here. The near accident, she corrected herself.

Spare cameras were easy to come by. She didn't have a spare Jim.

Jim gave her support and encouragement without strings and she trusted him absolutely. Barry, as Dr. Raymond, deserved credit for helping her through tough times, but that was a decade ago, and she hadn't seen him or heard from him in five years.

So long ago. She'd put it aside and moved on. She forgave Barry as she'd forgiven her grandmother, and herself, too, because she was far from perfect, but the memories couldn't be erased. Her goal was not to allow them to be part of her present. So, no confrontation or recriminations.

Down at the sea wall, she took a few photos of the water, of nearby vessels, then turned and snapped photos of the street winding up, narrowing between the broad planes of colorful walls which were broken by bright bursts of color from Bougainvillea or colorful pottery or overhanging balconies. High, rough cliffs rose to her left and right, with the Mediterranean Sea lapping at their base.

Jim. He was somewhere over the Atlantic. California was still ahead of him. Libbie hoped he'd get there and find that the trip, the urgency, hadn't been necessary. Bad enough that he'd had to leave. Far worse, if his son was as seriously injured as Jim feared. But then he only knew what he'd been told. People could exaggerate, especially early in a crisis.

Matthew had made a recent and sudden decision to live with his mother for his senior year of high school. New school, new state. It was a decision Jim hadn't discussed with her, but the obvious reasons for Matt making that decision lurked in the background.

Some things, especially relationships, took time. She'd met Matthew a couple of times, both meetings were at Jim's house. They hadn't exchanged more than a few words. She and Jim had been a couple for such a short time, really. Things had moved swiftly for them.

As she rested against the seawall, people walked past. She was a tourist, and not one who appeared approachable. She did her best to keep it that way. Two children skipped by, their voices high and soft. Somewhere nearby girls giggled. Other feet shuffled past that weren't as easily seen, but that walked with history—with the weight of old history. She felt pressure against her chest and suspected that if she wasn't careful, she might see an ancient Greek, an Arab, or a Crusader amble by. It was tempting to try.

Under this press of history, no one would care, not one little bit, about Grandmother, about Tommy, or countless other lesser regrets that plagued her. Time would dismiss them. Surely, she could.

Finally, knowing she'd sat in one place too long, she stood and followed the road that bordered the harbor and the sea. It was a beautiful stroll, but without Jim, it was scenery and nothing more.

****

If she'd had a way to contact him, Libbie would've called off the dinner plans with Barry.

The unexpectedness of meeting him today still unsettled her. She put on a nice, dark blue dress and fixed her hair and makeup because she owed something to the old relationship. In fact, this whole trip could be traced back to him. Dr. Raymond had planted the idea of Italy in her brain all those years ago when he'd quit practicing psychology and went away. He'd mentioned Sicily in a postcard. The first one he'd sent? Or maybe that last one two years ago. She didn't remember.

Sicily. Like a small seed, the concept of it had taken root in her head. Sun, lush landscape, laughing people and good wine and good food—an aura of happiness—was what it had represented to her over the years between. It hadn't represented Barry Raymond.

After Liz had brutally cut Libbie out of her life about a month ago, running away to sunny anonymity became appealing. No past, no future, just living the now. Jim, accompanying her on the trip, had been a wonderful bonus.

Libbie went down to the lobby early. Barry was already there, standing by a decorative pillar wearing a suit and dress shoes. He came directly across to Libbie as she stepped out of the elevator. He touched her arm slightly above her elbow.

"You are lovely." He smiled.

"As are you." Stupid. "You look

distinguished," she amended.

He had a car waiting. The hotel already seemed far above the Mediterranean, but the car climbed still higher until it felt like they were at the top of the world. Barry assisted her from the car and the driver pulled off.

The restaurant was a shiny place. Gilt frames and glittering candles and creamy tablecloths. The maître'd led them through the main dining room to the balcony. Libbie stopped, stunned by the lights of the town below and down and around, appearing almost disconnected from the land. Out to sea, the lights of ships, cruise liners and yachts were specks crossing the distance to the horizon, and arching over all were the stars. It was as if she was suspended amid the brilliant and twinkling lights. She walked forward, passing her escort.

"Libbie?"

She stood at the railing, grasping the black iron, unwilling to be drawn away. When Barry touched her arm, she turned and saw people were staring. Not with unkind eyes. Just noticing. She nodded and followed Barry to the table, but made sure her chair was turned such that her view was unobstructed.

"This is amazing."

"I knew you'd love it. This table has the best view in Sicily."

"I wish...."

Barry smiled. "What do you wish?"

She shook her head and looked down. She couldn't tell him that she wished someone else was sitting in his place.

They arranged the napkins in their laps. The waiter arrived with a bottle of wine Barry had evidently ordered while she was stargazing.

It was a fine meal, a lovely evening. How could it be otherwise with an exquisite view, perfect weather, excellent food and service, and a friendly, congenial companion? He wasn't Jim, but perhaps it was nice not to be alone in such a place, after all. In fact, had she been alone, she would likely be dining in her room at her lovely, now lonely, hotel.

"What shall we do tomorrow?" he asked.

"Tomorrow?" Libbie shook her head and lied. "I'm leaving tomorrow."

He frowned. After a pause, he said, "I see. Are you flying out of Rome?"

She nodded. "Yes. I'll travel to Rome tomorrow and fly out of there."

"I could go along. I'd be happy to assist with the travel and baggage and anything else you need."

Deep breath. Having begun the lie, she was committed. "No thanks. That's all arranged. All handled." She repeated, "Thanks, anyway. I appreciate the thought, but I'm all set."

"Well," he said. "It's still early. What do you say we finish the evening with a walk? Perhaps drinks?"

Relieved, Libbie said, "A walk would be nice." She added, "But no drinks because I have an early start tomorrow and a long day and night of travel."

Lies. All lies. If she couldn't spend the last days in Sicily with Jim, then she preferred to be alone. Most definitely, she didn't want to make more memories with Barry Raymond. In the end, how she spent her time wasn't anyone's business but hers. She didn't want to hurt him, so it was better to tell a little lie.

They walked together along a quiet street and through a piazza. They lingered by a baroque fountain as the water flowed and pattered, making its own special music. Libbie, as before, was struck by the age of the buildings, their surroundings. Here and there were new, updated shops, but new or old, it was all in use.

The walk was pleasant enough, but Libbie was calculating how quickly she could excuse herself and return to the hotel when he tried to slide his arm around her waist. She moved away.

Barry pulled his arm back awkwardly. "I remember that young woman, hardly more than a teenager, who was lost, locked away in her grandmother's house. The deceased grandmother by that time." He stopped and touched her arm. "You were so torn with grief, anger and guilt that you shut yourself off from the world. Now I see a different person. A confident woman. A woman who made peace with the past."

Libbie stepped back and turned away, walking toward the low stone wall that bordered the walkway.

He said, "Not entirely at peace? I'm sorry if I hit a tender spot?"

"No, not tender, but definitely long ago. Why must you bring up the past? I've dealt with it, and I've forgiven as much as I ever will, but that doesn't make the memories any sweeter."

"Are you angry? With me?"

His expression, by the light of the streetlamp, was hard to read. Libbie waited.

He said, "I wanted to point out how wonderful you are. How far you've come. One way to understand that is by looking back at where we started."

"I'm done with looking back. Done with re-living the past. I found a home that I love. I've moved on. Plus, I'm in love with a wonderful man who loves me, too."

His mouth hung open for a brief moment, before he took her hand. "I'm happy for you. Who is he? I'd like to meet him, to give him my congratulations and tell him what a special lady you are."

He looked at her fingers and then at her. He was making a point, she knew. She refused to acknowledge the lack of an engagement ring. She pulled her hand back.

"He already knows."

"Then I'm happy for you, as I said, but I do wonder."

"About what?"

"You are doing so well on your own, yet I sense defensiveness. Tell me, Libbie, do you still hear the voices? See the colors?"

Her blood turned to ice in her veins. Her face felt numb. Was this, in part, what she'd feared from Barry Raymond? But as quickly as she felt his betrayal, calm followed, uneasy, but there.

She faced him. "You ask that after all these years?"

"I didn't mean to imply.... Of course, much of it was...your perceptions...due to the synesthesia. Natural and normal. It's rare, and your case, complicated by the dysfunction of your childhood, was all the more interesting."

Her hand moved before she was aware it was happening. But he was quicker. He grabbed her hand as it neared his cheek and firmly held it in his.

"I am not a science experiment."

"Forgive me. I expressed myself poorly. My

interest is not entirely scientific." He released her hand. "You said you are happy and you are moving into a serious relationship, which, at best, are fraught with ups and downs, misunderstandings, anger. Be sure that's what you truly want and are ready for."

She felt a tremor inside, but she smiled broadly and said, "I don't have a single doubt." She stepped away. "Good night, Barry. It was so unexpected meeting you here and I'm glad to see you are well. Thank you for the evening, but it's time I returned to the hotel."

Libbie turned and climbed the steep narrow stairs to the road. Barry followed close behind her and as they reached the top that shiny black car pulled up.

The car must have been discretely keeping pace with them. Nothing like convenience.

Barry opened the car door for her. He climbed in on the other side, but she kept distance between them. It was a quiet ride back to the hotel. Her 'goodnight' was perfunctory. As she left the car and walked to the hotel entrance, he stayed by the car. He raised his hand in a wave as she turned to go inside.

Back when they were doctor-patient they'd been friendly, but she'd never had romantic feelings. Now, older and wiser, and with the benefit of retrospection, she realized he might have felt more. Perhaps that had interfered with his objectivity back then. She'd forgiven him in her heart for the betrayal all those years ago, and she wished him well, but having left him behind, she felt like a weight had been lifted.

She was perfectly content never to see Dr. Barry Raymond again.

Chapter Two

Home. She was so grateful to be back on Virginia soil. Never mind the exhaustion of the long journey, or the nuisance of traveling. The reward was priceless. Home.

Libbie was missing Jim big time, including in a practical way. The large suitcase weighed a ton. There were porters with baggage carts, but they were strangers and she could handle it herself.

Going on a trip held all the possibilities. Returning involved careless packing and dirty clothing. But, for Libbie, there was great satisfaction in knowing she'd be home in a little more than an hour or so. She secured the smaller items to the suitcase handle, and carried the tote bag over her shoulder.

Jim had called when he landed in California. Given that he'd had to travel such a distance and was so worried about his son, even that brief conversation was a gift. On top of everything he was dealing with, he had still arranged for her car to be left at the airport and had the driver text a picture of the parking spot with its number. Jim thought of everything. She envied him his ability to live in the present. One day, she'd be able to do that, too, and not get dragged back into the past, or worry over the future.

The Richmond airport was a convenient size and she walked across to the parking deck, towing all her paraphernalia along with her. She found her car and with a little effort, got her suitcase loaded. She wasn't an experienced traveler, but she was accustomed to taking care of herself.

About thirty minutes later, she left interstate 295 behind and headed west on I-64. The city and suburbs gave way to forest. She relaxed.

Cross County Road. Winding miles of up and down and around—with occasional glimpses of the distant, rounded peaks of the Blue Ridge Mountains beyond the rolling hills and forests. The voice in her head whispered reminders to ignore the scenery and watch for deer, dogs and cats, perhaps even a person walking on the barely-there shoulder. A few insects splattered on her windshield, but the weather was fine and the way was clear, and nothing slowed her down.

Cub Creek Loop. Less than a year ago, she'd taken a wrong turn on a country road and found her home, the old Carson Place, now the Libbie Havens' place. More than a house. It was truly her home. She'd hung a sign by the road that said "Cub Creek." As she slowed and turned into her long, sloping driveway, she noted the dried leaves, brown and yellow, scattered across the broad slope of the lawn. It wasn't officially autumn yet, but the season was on the cusp of changing. She liked the way the leaves looked, clean and crisp, highlighted against the green grass.

She dropped her bags on the porch, unlocked the door and stepped inside. She pressed her hands flat against the foyer wall. Warmth touched her palms and beigey tones of happiness rushed up her arms. Welcome. The message, and her ability to receive it, told her all was well.

From the time she'd first crossed the threshold of the house on Cub Creek, this had been its message to her. Happiness. She'd been willing to settle for peace. Peace of mind, peace in her life. As for the rest of the world? Well, she had never fit in.

Although, with Jim at her side, she came close.

Jim didn't know she had this special sense. She'd discussed it with Barry Raymond back when he'd been her therapist, but that was it. If not for the Dr. Raymond's big mouth, that would still be the case.

The study was to the left of the foyer. Libbie

turned right and walked through the living room. The rows and columns of framed photographs filled the walls like a grid. The Road collection. The Train Tracks. But also, the photographs of Audrey and Adam, Liz's kids, smiling and glowing. Those hurt her heart.

A slight odor of charred wood hung in the air and grew stronger as she entered the kitchen. The garage. She opened the back door and pushed the storm door wide.

The concrete pad of the detached garage was still there but the building was gone. She stood on the back stoop and gripped the handrail. Not only had the garage burned, but someone had cleared away the worst of the coal-black debris. The smell stung her nose. It wasn't an unpleasant smell, only an unaccustomed one.

It was Jim who'd told her the news after a call from home. "The garage is gone," he'd said. "The house is fine."

"How?" she'd asked.

"Fire. Under investigation. Looks accidental."

"Really? Seriously? Did the tank.... I left it in the garage, I think."

Jim shrugged.

"Could it have ignited on its own?" She was horrified. Her house could've burned due to her carelessness, her self-absorbed negligence.

"Hey, it's okay." Jim touched her shoulders in reassurance. "Dan found it. He took care of it."

There was something in the quirk of Jim's smile and the glint of his eyes that made Libbie suspicious. Then it hit her. A double-entendre?

Dan took care of it.

Libbie was grateful. Maybe her friends, or rather Jim's, had helped her out.

So, the garage was gone. Whatever unpleasantness it had represented to her was gone with it. She was pretty sure the answer lay in her childhood memories of dark places and dark days—the memories that had followed her into adulthood. The garage had been a sacrifice to ease her mind. Reasons and practicality didn't matter. As Jim had said, her reasons were her own and it was no one's business but hers. She'd tried to destroy it, but failed. The deed had been done for her. The how or who didn't matter, and was best left unremarked.

Some of the lower leaves on the old oak were singed. Libbie stepped down to the terrace and examined the back of the house. No marks. No damage. She touched the old, painted boards. A trace of soot maybe. She'd hire someone to give the house exterior a gentle wash.

The back stoop was gray-painted concrete. The screened porch was farther from the garage, opening off of the dining room, and was untouched. The swing on the porch beckoned, but she had no energy for even a peaceful swing today.

It was too late to pick up Max this afternoon. She'd get him first thing in the morning. For now, she returned to the front porch, dragged her suitcase over the threshold and opened it in the foyer.

Libbie emptied some things from the big suitcase before attempting to carry it upstairs. In fact, the dirty laundry went directly into the laundry room next to the kitchen. The camera equipment went on the desk in the study. Jim's sweater that he'd missed in his rush to leave the hotel, she folded and set aside.

The odds and ends, like the guidebook, maps, and ticket stubs, she put in her desk drawer. She'd scan the bits and pieces into jpegs and mix them with the Sicily photos for the picture book of their trip, the first of many trips they would take together.

She checked in the cupboards and fridge and settled for a can of chicken and dumplings. She needed to start a grocery list. Libbie emptied the can, heated the contents, and took the plate into the living room. She set it next to the sofa and was reaching to turn the lamp on when she noticed the police cruiser. It was parked in the driveway, but down near the road.

With the daylight fading, she couldn't identify the driver.

Dan?

A knock on the door. She nearly dropped her dish. She sat it on the end table and went to the door.

"Officer Hoskins?"

The young deputy grinned. "Yes, ma'am. Nice to see you."

Someone had stayed in the car. The light was failing, and she couldn't tell who it was, not for sure anyway.

"What brings you by? Surely not to welcome me home."

"Well, yes, ma'am. That's exactly it. Jim Mitchell asked us to check to make sure you were home and okay."

Libbie smiled. "You'd think he had enough to worry about without wondering if I made it into the house."

"Yes, ma'am, I'm sure. I won't keep you. When you speak to him, please let him know we all send our regards." He nodded and stepped back.

"Thank you."

"Yes, ma'am."

Ma'am, ma'am, ma'am.... Made her feel old. Or maybe it was the hours spent in that airplane. If she'd known she would be traveling alone, she would've flown first class. Jim, however, had balked at the idea when they were purchasing the tickets, so.... She respected how he felt. Now, despite being in different time zones and being tied up with his son, he was still thinking of her. He'd texted a few updates on Matthew's condition who was out of danger, but far from well and would need surgery and therapy. Jim wrote that he'd tell her more when he called.

Her heart ached for him. Aside from his obvious worry over his son, Jim had spent time away from his business while traveling with her, and now this with Matthew. Life was unpredictable. No one would dispute that. It paid to have patience and enjoy each day.

For her part, she was suddenly exhausted and wanted nothing more than to eat her food, take a soothing bath, and then fall into bed. She needed her rest before tackling Max and Joyce in the morning.

****

The sun rose, the light streaming in through the rear windows. As Libbie walked into the kitchen, she stretched her arms and yawned, enjoying the feel of being home. She opened the back door and saw that the day was beautiful. She left the door open to allow some fresh air in while she checked through her cabinets and fridge for something to nibble on.

It was a perfunctory check. She knew what was on each shelf. Her memory was too perfect.

Except for remembering to stop by the grocery store on the way home yesterday.

But there was coffee, and that would be sufficient to get her to the store to grab some groceries, and then on to pick up Max at the vet's office.

****

Max was a vision of exuberant doggy joy as his stubby tail wagged his lean, long-legged body. She could see it in his eyes that he wanted to jump up into her arms. But he was a large dog, a Weimaraner. The vet tech soothed him, running calming hands along his back and around his ears.

"Stay, Max," the girl said.

He did, but barely. She held out the leash for Libbie to grasp.

"Thanks." Libbie accepted the leash but knew Max would set the pace.

Straight to the door he went and Libbie followed. The leash was unnecessary. Max's first goal was the car.

Once inside the car, he bounded from window to window as if the view might differ. Libbie knew what he wanted. Home. She climbed into the car and he settled down. He sat in the front passenger seat, nose forward, ready to roll. She sensed the tension in his body, a low humming expectation. She eyed his seatbelt. Groan. She reached across to pull it around his body and he washed her face. Disgusting.

Home. Joy. Joy. Joy. Max dashed around the yard, rolled in the grass, and sniffed the tree trunks— all within seconds as she unlocked the front door. He beat her inside, nearly knocking her feet from under her, and raced to the kitchen and the food and water dish. He came to a sliding halt on the linoleum and barked twice.

"Hush, Max. They didn't starve you. Those people treat you like a prince." Libbie poured some food in his dish anyway and put fresh water in the other. This was Max's welcome home, too. A celebration for both of them.

He had places to go and territory to patrol, so when he asked at the door, very politely, to go out, she let him. He dashed across the yard and vanished into the woods amid the shadows.

Max would have the run of Libbie's fifteen acres of woods while she visited Joyce.

****

Ethel's Home for Adults sat back from the main road, less than a mile from Libbie's house by way of the path through the woods. Joyce's path as far as Libbie was concerned. Joyce had traveled that path for many years, but she was elderly now and it was dangerous for her. Joyce had promised not to walk the path again to visit Libbie, but Joyce's promise was probably as convenient as her memory. By road—down Cub Creek Loop, then back up the main road— it was close to two miles. A longer trip distance-wise, but still a quick drive. Libbie timed her visit to arrive toward the end of lunch, but before Joyce could drift off into her post-meal nap.

Libbie was a little late. Messy plates and crumpled napkins were on the tables in the dining room. The aide who answered the doorbell allowed her in, led her down the hall and pointed to the sunroom.

"In there, Ms. Havens. Welcome back from your trip."

The aide waved Libbie off. She was busy and Libbie was known around here. It was generally accepted, thanks to Joyce, that Libbie was her niece. She wasn't, but who was she to turn down an honorary title? She walked through the TV room where the recliners were lined up and filled with nappers. A movie was playing, but the sound was turned down low. A few eyes were focused on the screen, but most were closed and several ladies were lightly snoring.

Joyce was alone in the sun room. She

tended to hold herself apart from the other residents but, apart or not, she, too, was dozing.

"Joyce?" Libbie spoke softly and touched her arm.

The woman's eyes opened. They were a soft, faded blue, but sharp in their own way as she fixed them on Libbie. "About time," Joyce said.

Libbie took the chair next to her and angled it toward her so they could chat. "I was in Sicily, remember?"

Joyce gave a disgusted grunt and scratched her cheek. "I got the postcards."

"Thank you for speaking to the press for me about the garage and the fire and all that. Jim's mother told him about the newspaper article, but I haven't seen it yet. How did you know about the fire? Did Dan tell you?"

"One of the gals here mentioned seeing and smelling the smoke. Had to wait 'til the morning, but then I walked over to check on your house. I did that because we were friends. So I thought. The reporter came along asking questions. Then Dan came along looking for me. Cain't hardly take a breath around here without someone making a big deal about it."

"You promised you wouldn't walk the path again."

Another rude grunt. "Don't be acting like you

rushed over here from the airport to say hello 'cause I know better."

"You know? What do you know? I got home yesterday. Late yesterday."

"That so? Seems like longer."

Libbie relaxed and smiled. "You missed me."

"Well, 'course I did. Nothing interesting happens around here. You're my entertainment."

"That hurts. I thought we were friends."

"It's nice to have entertaining friends. Gives you something to talk about." Joyce tugged at her sleeve. "Got pictures?"

"Photographs? Sure, but nothing I can show you today. I'll bring you over for lunch soon and we'll watch the slideshow on my computer."

"Don't you have real pictures? The kind on paper?"

"Trust me, you'll enjoy it."

Joyce looked doubtful, but moved on. "How'd Max do?"

Libbie laughed. "They adore him at the vet's office. They keep him happy."

"How about you and Jim Mitchell? How's that going?"

"Fine. He's with his son right now."

"I hear he left you over there. On your own. Took off on you, so to speak."

Surprised, Libbie said, "Not at all. No. He left, but it was because his son was in an accident. We couldn't get two seats on a flight out at the last minute. He was lucky to get the one." She paused before continuing. "Joyce, this feels like an inquisition. Do you think something's wrong between me and Jim?"

Joyce stared at a window across the room. The light filtered in. It created a barely perceptible halo around the edges of her hair and her pale pink shirt. She looked frail.

Libbie repeated, "Do you think something's wrong between me and Jim?"

"Not Jim. Nothing wrong with him. I'm having trouble picturing you leaving that house."

Libbie forced a laugh. Joyce was more on target than she could know, but Libbie reassured her, "Jim and I are fine. And why would I leave Cub Creek?"

Joyce coughed dramatically.

Libbie leaned toward her and spoke directly, "We have only been dating a couple of months. Let's not rush anything. The subject of me leaving Cub Creek hasn't come up yet, so no need to worry."

With a little pout Joyce added, "Maybe I don't want my entertainment moving to the far side of the county." She patted her pocket, then reached her thin fingers in and pulled out a folded piece of newsprint. "Almost forgot I had it. This is for you."

Libbie leaned forward and took it from her.

"What is it?" She unfolded it. "Oh, the newspaper article." Silently, she read the account of the garage fire until she reached Joyce's quote at the end. Libbie froze, her mouth agape. She stared at the article, then at Joyce.

LOCAL GARAGE EXPLODES - An evening blaze in a detached garage on Cub Creek Loop in Louisa County destroyed the building, but the residence suffered only minor damage. Sgt. Dan Wheeler and Cpl. A. W. Hoskins of the sheriff's office were first responders to the report called in by an unidentified passing motorist who noticed flames in the branches of a large oak over the engulfed garage. It is believed the fire was connected to a loud explosion heard by nearby residents. The Volunteer Fire Department arrived on scene shortly after Officers Wheeler and Hoskins and prevented significant damage to the home. The Emergency Services Coordinator was unable to positively identify the cause of the explosion, but suspected it was related to a propane tank found in the ashes. It is believed the propane tank had been removed from a gas grill on the patio behind the main residence and left in the garage. It is not known who placed the tank in the garage or when. There were no injuries and no one was in residence at the time. A family friend, Mrs. Joyce Inman of Louisa County, reported the garage had recently been in the process of renovation and that the owner, Ms. Libbie Havens, was on vacation with her fiancé, Jim Mitchell, in Sicily at the time of the incident.

Joyce pointed her finger at Libbie. "No need to get mad at me, young lady."

Libbie shook the square of newsprint at her. "It says I'm in Sicily with my fiancé. Did you tell the reporter that?"

"You can thank me later when you remember how to be grateful."

"Really? Really?" She stammered. "Joyce, how could you? When Jim sees this...."

"Jim's a big boy. Besides, he surely knows. Didn't you say his mama told him about the article? Well, I guess he didn't pass that bit about the engagement on to you?"

"Joyce. Why would you lie to the reporter? Everyone knows the Mitchell's. They're going to have to explain to a lot of people that Jim isn't engaged."

"Your reputation, missy."

"What about my reputation?"

"You went off with a man, a handsome man, to a foreign country without a care for how it made you two look. Especially you. Call me old-fashioned, but a tiny white lie at least makes it look a little less, less...."

"It's no one's business."

"When did that ever stop folks from talking?"

"Joyce. I don't care what people think. I never have."

Her eyes, a faded blue, fastened on Libbie. "Oh, but you do. Even if you didn't, what about Jim's people? What about that boy of his? A minute ago, you were all in a tizzy about them explaining an engagement."

Joyce shook her head. "People should have some dignity, that's how I figure it." She massaged her fingers. A couple of the knuckles looked red and swollen. "Besides, we both know I only got a little ahead of the truth. He's gonna propose."

Libbie's heart stilled. "Maybe." She shook her head and forced some certainty into her voice. "It's too soon. We've only been dating a few weeks."

"Uh huh. But it weren't too early to travel to Europe with him."

She didn't try to answer that one. Joyce was in one of those moods. She'd fired her best shot and was done. Now her attention had drifted away, and her gaze was slightly unfocused. Libbie decided they were both done with this visit. She tucked the news clipping into her purse.

"I'll let you get on with your nap."

"Nap? I don't nap." Joyce smoothed the front

of her blouse. Her fingers were long and bony. She was so thin. "Might close my eyes for a minute though."

"You do that." Libbie half-rose.

"How's Alice's dog? What's his name?"

Libbie stared. "Max. And he's fine."

"Glad to hear it. Alice asked me about him the other day. Guess 'cause he wasn't at the house. I told her you were gone on a trip."

Alice. It stole Libbie's breath. She sat, no longer anxious to leave Joyce. A chill wrapped around her heart. She wouldn't say it aloud though. She wouldn't correct Joyce and remind her that they had already discussed Max and that Alice was dead. It was Alice's death that had made the house and property on Cub Creek available for Libbie to buy.

She touched Joyce's arm. "Max is fine. They always spoil him at the vet's office."

Joyce patted Libbie's hand with her own. "That's good then." She yawned and the eyelids dipped again.

"Bye." Libbie tried to breathe deeply and pull herself together. She stood, almost reluctantly, and turned away slowly.

Joyce called after her, "You wait too long, and I may not be able to make it."

Libbie paused in the doorway. "To come over for lunch and see the photos from Sicily? We'll do it soon."

"For that or the wedding. You could maybe speed that along. The nuptials." She grinned. "Make everybody happy."

Libbie paused in the doorway and took a long look at her friend. Had that moment of confusion been genuine? Joyce wouldn't scruple at manipulation, but she wouldn't feign dementia.

Maybe it came down to a simple truth. Days in Joyce's life were getting more precious than a youngster like Libbie could understand—until one realized how easily a person's grip could loosen on life and begin to lose touch with the reality that most people shared.

When Libbie returned home, she found a vase of flowers on the porch. Max was dozing nearby, under the settee. The card read, "Jim". The flowers helped chase away the lingering unease from her visit with Joyce. Libbie put her face close to the bouquet and inhaled. Roses. Red and white. They were glorious, smelled like heaven, and would look perfect on her coffee table.

Joyce was right. Jim was going to ask. He'd hinted more than once. They'd only been dating a few weeks, but they'd known each other since she moved here. She'd always known that he…well, he was interested in her. The dating seemed almost predestined after she and Dan broke up.

Except. A big except for Libbie. Had he known about Joyce telling the reporter that they were engaged? Surely, he had, but he'd kept that part to himself.

Why? Maybe he knew she was apprehensive about commitment? Or maybe he still had doubts, too, and she was misreading him.

There was no rush. They weren't kids. Thirty-something was just getting into the prime of it all—the best of life. Jim was a little older, but he was still on the shy side of forty. They had time to figure it out.

****

Max went back outside that afternoon, excited and barking. He dashed off into the woods. Libbie set off on a stroll of her own.

She went to the clearing where the Lady's Slippers grew. Had grown, rather. It was long past their season and they weren't likely to return. That was the nature of Lady's Slippers in the wild, as Jim had explained to her. They didn't cultivate easily, but required specific conditions that couldn't easily be replicated.

That day in the woods, she and Jim had sat and talked in the midst of the pink orchids. Later, in Sicily, Jim had reached across the table—their table—and touched her cheek. She'd been staring at the brilliant light hitting the side of a whitewashed building. The blue of the sky beyond was intensified by the contrast. It was dazzling. She was fascinated, yet disappointed, because while she was skilled with a camera, she didn't possess the ability or the talent needed to capture the exquisite glory of that light. Maybe only God did. So, she admired the scene, but was also sad.

Jim had reached across the café table and touched her cheek to call her back from her fascination. She smiled and started to apologize, but he placed a finger gently on her lips.

"Remember the Lady's Slippers?" he asked.

She nodded, captured his finger and slipped her hand into his.

He said, "You are as rare and exquisite."

Okay. That was nice, but rather over the top. Her cheeks burned and she knew she was blushing. That wasn't the kind of compliment you could throw back, even if you were crazy enough to want to. "Thank you" felt inadequate. Libbie stared at his face, thinking she could pay him flowery compliments solely on the basis of his fine complexion. Or his eyes that changed color, his dark, perfect hair...but he was too masculine to compare to a flower. She was trying to think of a more apt comparison when he added, "I can't believe the good fortune that brought you to Cub Creek. If you hadn't moved there, we would never have met. What a tragedy that would have been."

Now, thinking back as she stood on the banks of Cub Creek where it marked the back line of her property, she realized he'd been more right than he'd known—or maybe he had known on a subconscious level. What did she have in common with a Lady's Slipper? She had rare, wonderful moments when life was so perfectly right that there was no more to be desired or dreamed of—and then it was done and gone. Beauty and happiness were unreliable. Not to be relied on, like Lady's Slippers that appeared unexpectedly, bloomed and died, and could not be counted upon to return. They couldn't be counted on at all.

Jim, I miss you, she thought, and hugged herself. Where are you right now? Why aren't you here beside me?

She closed her eyes and saw the music of Cub Creek. The water shimmered light and silvery with threads of steel blue streaming through it. With her eyes opened wide again, she looked at the dark brown water as it licked at the dirt clinging to the exposed roots of trees, the water rushing around and sometimes over the rocks near the banks, and the deep middle, so still and sly, the appearance was at odds with the sounds her brain heard. Things, like people, could have more than one aspect.

Two old boards spanned the creek. One was wide as boards went, and Libbie had carried it there herself with help from Jim. The other board was narrow and warped. The "bridge" was crossable, surely, as long as the boards held. Which they would and did. Libbie crossed them without much thought, paying more attention to the opposite bank. The far side of the creek was someone else's property. She didn't know whose and it didn't really matter unless they decided to knock down the trees. In fact, those trees wouldn't be any of her business if Jim did propose and she accepted. They would move to his house by the nursery. The other side of the county.

Move away from Cub Creek. The thought sent a chill through her. She pushed back at it, testing it.

This house, her house and property, would be sold.

It wouldn't be right to leave the house empty. Old, empty houses didn't fare well.

She could rent it out. No, she dismissed that idea as soon as it occurred. She'd drive renters crazy, or they'd drive her crazy.

Libbie walked up the low hill to the clearing. Once upon a time, only a few short months ago, she'd left her sweater here. She'd seen the wild orchids and had been in a hurry to fetch her camera. She'd been careless and ended up taking a dunk in the swift, dark waters of Cub Creek. She had returned the next day, this time with Jim. The sweater was gone, but she didn't care. The amazing, unusual abundance of Lady's Slippers had been the focus. She'd taken a ridiculous quantity of photos. Now their season was past.

Libbie and Jim—their season hadn't passed. So, why did that uncertain feeling keep edging in? Because when you really loved someone, you wanted the best for him. Libbie was afraid she might not be it. Aunt Margaret would surely agree. Good thing she didn't let Aunt Margaret rule her life.

Max was waiting on her side of the creek. He greeted her with a short bark. When she crossed the bridge, he walked beside her back to the house, a faithful companion when it suited him, or if he didn't have a more interesting offer.

****

After supper, the phone rang. Libbie seized it.

"Jim? Hello."

"I love hearing your voice," he said. "It reminds me of our trip, of spending time together, of us. Sorry I didn't call yesterday."

"Are you okay? Matthew? You sound...."

"I'm tired, that's all. With the trip to Sicily and

flying directly out here.... Between worry and frustration.... I'm not able to take care of my business or my personal life. Matthew is improving, thank God, but that's all relative. He's stable now, so surgery is planned for early tomorrow."

He sounded so sad. Libbie said, "I can fly out there first thing tomorrow. I can keep you company, maybe help with Matthew."

After a brief hesitation, he said, "Thanks, but we're okay here. It's just..."

"I understand." She did, too. He had enough to deal with. She'd be in the way. "Thank you for the flowers. The roses. They are beautiful."

His voice lightened a bit. "I wish I could've delivered them in person."

"I wish I could've thanked you in person."

A moment of silence, a shared moment, and then she asked, "Is there anything I can do to help here at home?"

"Thanks. They're managing without me at the nursery. You could do one thing, though."

"Sure, what's that?"

"Call my mother. Maybe go out to lunch with her or something."

After an awkward pause, she said, "Maybe we should wait until you're back so you can join us. I'm sure she'd enjoy it more with you there, too."

After an equally awkward pause, Jim said,

"I'm sorry. Sometimes I forget how shy you are."

She pictured his hazel eyes. She touched the wall and felt its warmth. Some of her own tension flowed through her arm, into the clean paint and cool plaster.

Jim said, "I feel like I've known you forever. It seems impossible that we met less than a year ago. I don't want to rush you."

"Do you remember?"

"The day we met?" He laughed softly. "The day I nearly ran into you with the truck and you fell into the ditch? I'm not likely to forget that."

Libbie smiled. "I'll never forget how gorgeous you looked when you stopped to rescue me. I didn't even mind the mud."

"Gorgeous? Not me. That was you. I couldn't keep my eyes off your hair, the way you carried yourself. I don't know how to describe it...but I knew the moment I saw you that I'd never met anyone like you."

And never likely to, thank goodness. The world was crazy enough as it was. But she didn't say that aloud. She said, "Yes, but not what I meant." She sank onto the sofa and pulled the rose throw across her legs. "I was thinking about when I first saw you. That first day, the day I saw this house and then you and Dan came around back. I saw you through the screening on the porch. I don't think you could really see me, and Dan did the talking, but what a day that was. What a life-altering day, Jim. Suppose I hadn't taken a wrong turn that day? Last February. And by March I'd moved in and a week after that you drove down Cub Creek Loop and introduced me to the ditch." This time she laughed aloud and Max came from the kitchen to see what he was missing.

There was a long pause before Jim responded. "Libbie." He said her name as if it meant something real. Another moment passed and he said, "My son needs me, the business and employees need me, but most of all, what I want is to get on with us."

"Me, too. Let me think about spending time with your mom. I know she's probably the loveliest mom ever to reside on earth…but you should know I don't have much luck with maternal-type figures. Moms, grandmother, aunts. But that's my problem and I need to get past it. Maybe I'll reach out. Maybe she will. For now, let's let it be natural."

A pause. His breath fell softly against the receiver. "Yes, ma'am. You make good sense. For what it's worth, you will love each other. You are both amazing people."

"Thank you, Jim. I'm glad you understand."

"Do one thing for me?"

"What's that?"

"Think about us, Libbie."

"I do."

"Our future."

Her heart skipped a quick beat. She took a deep breath, then answered, "Right now your focus is your son. We have lots of time ahead for us. In fact, if you think about it, we haven't been dating all that long and—"

"The nurse is here." His tone had changed. "I'll call you back."

"Sure. Go ahead."

He disconnected before she could finish her goodbye.

Libbie stretched out on the sofa. Max settled on the floor. She reached down and scratched his head.

Mothers. Families. Aunt Margaret.

That time in Sicily had been for the two of them. But life always intruded.

If only he hadn't had to leave Sicily early. And what about Barry Raymond showing up out of nowhere? How crazy had that been? And Liz—she'd called Jim in Sicily, but Libbie hadn't heard word one from her. So, forget Liz.

As for Jim? He'd had no choice. He had to go to California and stay there because his son....

She sat upright. Max jumped and snarled. She heard the words in her head as clearly as if Aunt Margaret had a pipeline straight into her brain.

Because his son was in a serious accident.

Jim. His son. Aunt Margaret was right. Who was next?

Libbie paced the house and Max followed. She heard the tap, tap, tap of his nails on the wood and tile floors. She told herself everyone had accidents, injuries, sickness, at one time or another. Her family and friends weren't any different.

But she, Libbie, was different. Grandmother had known it when her son and his wife had died. Uncle Phil had known it, too. He hadn't wanted her, a mere child, to live with his wife and daughter because he was afraid his wife was right, that Libbie would bring bad luck with her into his happy home.

She stopped and leaned back against the foyer wall. Max flopped onto his side on the living room rug. She pressed her hands to the sides of her head.

"It's nonsense, Max. All nonsense. Grandmother was sick in her head and heart. She was wretched and would've been the same with or without me. Aunt Margaret kept Uncle Phil from taking me in. None of it was my fault, including my parent's death."

Max's eyes, dark and adoring, supported her.

"You're a dog, Max." She chuckled at the idea of Max understanding and her anxiety abated. But almost as quickly, it ramped back up. The foyer light, though burning brightly, wasn't enough to lighten the corners and the reach of the hallway.

It was going to be one of those nights. She's had many. She'd weather it out. It usually passed with the morning light. Knowing that had kept her from total despair many times.

She'd hoped she was finished with these crazy loops of fear, regret and shame. She pressed her hands over her ears, but it did no good because the voices were inside her head. Grandmother's voice, Aunt Margaret's. Now, Liz's voice, too, saying, "You'll never see my children again. I'm sorry, but I have to protect them."

A weight fell across her feet. Max.

Libbie had one insight. Given her family history, it wasn't surprising she freaked over the idea of gaining new family by marriage, especially women. Jim might love her but if the women in the family didn't, then it would be one long drama, as it had been with Grandmother.

She wasn't a child now. She didn't have to be anyone's victim, not the fall guy or the villain in anyone's story. It was her choice to try, to succeed or fail, or to hide.

Besides, they might not like or love her, but they loved Jim and they'd want him to be happy.

She returned to the sofa. Max climbed up beside her, his paws digging into her side and back as he settled. She let him stay. He put his muzzle on her arm as she cried. She'd never cried much. Mostly she tended to hide in dark corners when she was overwhelmed, or she climbed into bed and pulled the covers over her head.

Daylight would help. She just had to wait for the sunrise. And, in the end, there was truth— what was real and what wasn't. No matter how much you cared about someone, they couldn't fix what was wrong inside of you. Only you could do that, if you could. Barry Raymond had seen that in her, hadn't he? Joyce, too. Libbie hadn't fooled anyone, except maybe Jim and his eyes were fooled because he thought he loved her and he saw what he wanted to see. What he wanted her to be. What, in a million years, she'd never be, because she was beyond flawed. She was....

****

Morning was welcome. The sun reached through the windows and filled Libbie's bedroom, chasing out the shadows and cleansing the dark places. Max rested his chin on the bed near her arm and whined. She stretched and untangled herself from the covers.

She'd made it up the stairs and into bed last night. That was a positive sign.

First, Max. Then coffee.

It amazed Libbie that after these anxiety storms she could wake whole and sane. In the living room, on the mantle, was Gladys's candle, the one she'd given to Libbie after...well, after Tommy was hurt and it seemed like the whole world, including Libbie herself, judged her as guilty.

A light on the other side. She hadn't noticed the candle last night, maybe because it was hard to see anything hopeful when the world turned dark. Next time, maybe she'd remember to look.

Yesterday had been crazy busy for her first full day home. Throw in jet lag, Max, Joyce, Jim, even Barry and Dan hovering off-stage, and it was no wonder she'd had the attack last night. Today would be a lazy day, a day to transition back to being home and on Virginia time. She took her coffee and toast out to the terrace and settled at the wrought iron table.

Libbie loved the silence—the silence that wasn't silent. A bird chirped, a squirrel scampered up the side of a pine tree. The peace stilled the noise in her head. A breeze kicked up and a handful of dry leaves skittered across the terrace. The leaves caught on the legs of the wrought iron table and chairs. Most of the trees were still green. These were the large golden leaves from the tulip poplars. These poplars aimed high and their crowns were framed by the sky which, today, was a deep, vibrant blue.

She rested her head back against the chair.

Nature, flora and fauna, allowed her to stay as a temporary visitor in their world, welcome so long as she wasn't disruptive.

Jim had called her that. Disruptive. He'd said that was why her family and she were often at odds. Libbie was okay with the word. It was like being called eccentric instead of looney.

She brushed the crumbs from her lap, confident that ants or some critter would recycle them. Just doing her bit for nature, thank you. This morning, all good things seemed possible. She could imagine picking up the phone and giving Nina Mitchell a call. She could say, "Hi, there. Wondered if you'd like to get together? Maybe do lunch? I know we're both missing Jim and...." It was Liz's voice she was hearing in her head, not her own. Liz's breezy, social style. Libbie could do it though. She'd done harder things in her life.

But not today. Today was the lazy day.

Or maybe Nina had word on Matthew's surgery? A quick call to let Jim's mother know she cared about her grandson would be a nice thing to do. Of course, Jim's mother might think

Libbie was trying to ingratiate herself. Maybe after she heard from Jim and knew how Matthew was doing….

One more sip of coffee.

The blackened remains of the garage, the layer that hadn't been scraped off and hauled away, had been subjected to a few rain showers followed by sun, and had almost fused with the concrete. Within those ashes were the unhappy memories of Tommy. At the time, Libbie had been appalled by his hideaway, but people found comfort where they could. She could shed a tear for Tommy and wonder if she might have handled it better, but in the end, she'd done her best with a situation she'd had no hand in creating, had mostly been ignorant of. She no longer blamed herself. Tommy's story was his own. She was pretty sure she was one of few who still thought of him at all.

She showered and dressed, and then drove into Mineral to buy groceries. She kept her phone close at hand in case Jim called, but no ringing yet. With the bags stowed in the back seat, she drove across the street to the little strip mall to grab some of her favorite barbecue to take home for lunch. After eating, she'd do some house cleaning, like dusting and brushing the cobwebs away and, while she was at it, it was time to take out the mental trash, including the echo of Aunt Margaret's voice in her head, and the memory of Liz's final words. Even Barry could consider himself swept away with the litter.

It was time to do some internal housekeeping because she was going to need the room. Jim and she had more memories to make as soon as he returned home. Those memories might include Jim's family. Today, the future looked promising.

Max was napping on the porch when she pulled up the driveway. As she exited the car and he smelled the barbecue, his head popped up.

"None for you, boy," she said.

He followed her inside with his tail wagging because hope was hope, but she would be firm this time.

Within minutes, the doorbell rang, followed by a double-knock. Max barked and trotted to the door.

Libbie saw the delivery car through the window and opened the door.

"Ma'am?" The man was elderly, tall and thin.

He was holding a vase of flowers. She cast a quick look at the coffee table. Flowers yesterday. Flowers today.

"Thank you," she said and accepted the vase. "Let me get you a tip. I owe you one for the flowers you brought yesterday, too. I'll be right back."

Libbie set the vase on the table and grabbed her wallet. Tip in hand, he ambled off, down the stairs and to his van.

The flowers were beautiful. Chrysanthemums and roses with tall purple-somethings for accents.

She breathed in the scents thinking of Jim and his kindness and thoughtfulness, and his apparent, perhaps excessive, fondness for sending flowers. She carried them into the kitchen and placed the vase on the table. She found the card and opened the envelope.

"Dearest Libbie – It was such a pleasure to see you in Sicily. A great and unexpected pleasure. Regards, Barry."

It hit her like a brick. Her knees felt weak. She sat. He'd broken the rules.

She left him behind in Sicily. Why hadn't he stayed there?

Whoa. Wait. Calm down.

These were nothing more than flowers from an old acquaintance. The man, himself, wasn't here. She pressed her hands to her face, then dropped them to her lap as she steadied her breathing and her heart rate.

He hadn't done anything wrong. Not really.

The flowers were thoughtful, regardless of who they came from, right? It didn't mean more than that. She read the card again. He had enjoyed seeing her, had sent the flowers, and now it was done.

Then Libbie understood why it felt so very wrong. How had he gotten her address? She hadn't given it to him. It wasn't a state secret, but it also wasn't handy. Why would he go to the effort of finding out where she lived to send totally unnecessary flowers?

She reached for her cell phone to call…someone. Who? She could call Jim and tell him she'd received flowers from Barry Raymond.

He'd ask, Who, Libbie?

An old friend. Someone I used to know.

Why now?

Well, we spent time together in Sicily.

I don't recall meeting him.

It was after you left, Jim. Just by chance.

He'd ask why she hadn't mentioned Barry sooner. She didn't have a good answer, except one that sounded like a whining complaint about being left there alone, so she wouldn't call Jim.

There was no one else. Not Liz. Not Dan. She stood and went to the kitchen door. She opened it wide and yelled, "Max!"

He came running, all excited, like it was a bonus meal time complete with an invite to lounge on the sofa. She started to tell him about Barry Raymond and the flowers and realized how stupid she sounded, so instead she knelt beside him and scratched his neck. He licked her cheek.

"Okay, Max. A snack won't hurt."

She filled his dish, but not with barbecue. He cast a second look up at her before accepting his usual dry food.

There was no return address with the note, so Libbie couldn't send a thank you note, or even a 'leave me alone' message. Hopefully, he was done, but somehow, she was pretty sure he wasn't because that would be too easy. She had to tell Jim about Barry, one way or the other. It wouldn't have been remarkable if she'd told Jim right away. But she hadn't because first he'd been in route to his injured son and then at the hospital, both times worried and exhausted. Yet now, not having told him, it felt odd. As if she'd done something wrong and been caught trying to hide it.

It was late in the evening when Jim called, and the conversation was brief, with not a moment to spare for thoughts about what or what not to say.

"Sorry to be so short. Surgery went well. They aren't totally satisfied, but we'll have to wait and see."

"Get some rest, Jim."

"I called you first, but I have to call everyone else now. Talk to you soon."

Not much, but the news was good and that

was enough for gratitude.

****

In the morning, she showered and dressed. As she was fixing a cup of coffee, Max barked. The tennis ball was on the kitchen floor between his front paws and his eyes were bright with excitement.

The view from the kitchen window was sunny. A light breeze stirred the tree branches along the edge of the woods. Libbie accepted his invitation. She grabbed the tennis ball from beneath his nose, pushed the door open, threw the ball into the yard and followed Max outside. She tossed, Max fetched.

The distraction was good for her, and it wouldn't hurt Max to work off the extra food. Every so often he dashed toward Libbie as if he were going to drop the ball at her feet, but instead he'd shift and dodge with great drama before taking off and making a fleet circuit around the house or racing into the woods and out again. This time, when he ran into the woods, Libbie followed like a well-trained doggy mom, making noises and saying silly things because it gave him such joy. It lifted her out of her own worries. When Max ran through the remains of Adam's abandoned tree fort, she felt a little sad, but it was a fact that nothing stayed the same. Not even the good stuff. Especially not the good stuff.

"Max, come here. Where'd you go?" Libbie teased him. She could see him behind a spindly bush. She turned away pretending she'd lost him and started jogging along the path, back toward the clearing and home. She was thinking of the terrace and a sit-down, or maybe the swing in the screened porch. Suddenly he shot past her.

As she came out of the woods, she saw Max drop the ball to bark his welcome. He left Libbie in his dust as he raced toward the end of the house. She stopped and waited.

Dan came around the corner. He wore his tan khakis and deputy hat. Max doggy-danced around him. The last time Dan had walked into her back yard looking for her it hadn't been a chummy visit. She doubted he was here now to welcome her home.

He looked right in his uniform. In uniform, the cop nature wasn't disguised by a soft cotton shirt and worn jeans, which was a relief. On the other hand, he'd managed the garage issue for her—at least she was pretty sure he had—and which, of course, she couldn't thank him for doing, but she owed him.

All those thoughts flew through her brain in a quick second. Dan was still nodding hello and looking uncertain as she said, "Thanks for taking care of the garage. I mean, for getting the worst of the fire debris hauled away. You did that, right?"

He nodded. "No problem."

"Would you like to sit?" She motioned toward the empty chairs at the wrought iron table.

Dan had a package tucked under his arm, something wrapped in a green plastic bag. He put the bag on the table and pulled out a wrought iron chair.

He sat stiffly upright, as befitted a deputy in uniform. Libbie took the chair opposite.

"Been a while since I saw you, Dan. Are you well?" Keep it calm and civil, she told herself. No need to relive unpleasant history.

"I'm good. You? Good trip?"

"Very. Unfortunately, Jim had to leave early."

"Because of Matthew." He nodded. "He had surgery on his leg, I hear. Rehab is next."

"Jim called late last night. Said it went well."

They were being so civil, it almost made her angry. They'd been close, boyfriend-girlfriend close, and it hadn't been long ago. Just before Jim, in fact. Dan's cousin.

He nodded, still a man of few words, but a man of decision and direct action. A little uncomfortable, too, no doubt, and with darned good reason.

Dan said, "I came to warn you."

Chapter Three

Thoughts of Aunt Margaret and Grandmother, and all the other threats Libbie had ever faced, whirled in her head.

Warning. Warning.

"Calm down." Dan leaned toward her. He touched her fingers lightly, but it was enough. It brought her back and she yanked her hand away.

She set her jaw, determined to face the worst head-on. "Warn me about what?"

He frowned again. She watched, almost spellbound, as his face changed from frown to nod to frown as he considered her question. His eyes were the dark brown of forest shadows and an unwary gal could get lost in them. She almost had. But that was before. This was now.

"Libbie, calm down," he repeated. "This is about hunting."

"Hunting?"

He nodded.

"I don't hunt."

"Exactly my point. You aren't familiar with how it works in the country."

"I was scared by coyotes before. They were stalking me."

"Well, okay, probably so, but this is more about deer. Bow hunting season opens soon and then firearms. Some hunters are careful, some aren't. Sometimes they don't control their dogs and let them run wherever. They shoot when and where they shouldn't."

Libbie was alarmed. She rose halfway to her feet. She bumped her fists against the iron table. "I won't allow hunting. I'll put up signs. I'll call the police."

Dan raised his hand. "Calm down. There's law and then there's reality. For instance, hunters can't legally bring their guns onto private property. Law requires them to leave their guns secured, then come to your house and get written permission."

"Come to my house? Strangers? Wanting a permission note to hunt in my woods?" Her voice rose.

"Didn't think you'd care for that, but it's good to know your rights. I'm all for commonsense hunting and enforcing the laws, but being "right" is small comfort if you get shot. For you, I mean."

Libbie frowned.

"I brought you a gift." He picked up the bag and pulled out a couple of bright orange items and laid them on the table. He pushed them closer to her.

She picked them up. "A hat and a vest? Not exactly trendy."

"This is serious, Libbie. You should always wear these when you walk in the woods during hunting season. Not a bad idea even if you're just out in the yard." He pointed at the thick trees on the sides and back. "Easy for a stray shot to cross here."

"When is hunting season?"

He shrugged. "Pretty much year-round for one animal or another, but you don't need to worry too much about it except for deer season. Bow hunting starts soon, and you should be in the habit of wearing these by then."

"Why should I inconvenience myself for something I don't allow on my property?"

"Because it's reality and it's your life."

She looked at the orange vest, still not touching it. "For bows and arrows…. Humph."

"Crossbows."

"Like medieval? Like the guy uses in the show about zombies?"

"Exactly."

"Wow." She didn't know what else to say, so she settled for "Thank you."

Dan fixed his eyes on her face. "Are you saying, 'thank you' the way you do when you mean, 'sure, now go away because I'll do whatever I want anyway', or are you saying you understand the seriousness of the situation and will use the brains God gave you to keep yourself safe and whole?"

Libbie didn't answer.

"I thought so." Dan leaned forward and spoke slowly. "Hunting dogs can't see property lines and every season a few idiots come from the city and shoot across the roads without thinking of where the arrows or bullets will end up." He opened the bag again and handed her another orange item.

"Please. What's this?" It was a longer and had buckles.

"For Max."

She looked at Dan and then down at Max who was sitting at his feet.

Dan read her face again. He said, "He'll wear it if you insist. He's your responsibility, Libbie. Not some stray dog who's just wandering through."

Before she could respond in anger, he stood.

"Be smart, Libbie. Death is rarely convenient and being maimed can impact your ability to live as you want. Be smart, and keep an eye on Max, too. With his size and color he could be mistaken for quarry." He tipped his hat, picked up the empty bag, squashed it in his fist, and left.

Libbie raised her hand in farewell, but his

back was turned and he didn't see.

She sat back and smiled. Dan still looked good in his khakis.

****

She should be content, but she was lonely. It was Jim's fault. She'd never minded being alone before, but being alone and feeling alone were different states. Now, she felt alone, and she didn't care for it.

Libbie straightened the stack of photo books on her coffee table. She assembled them online using the best of her road and rail photos, and then had them printed as glossy picture books. She'd planned to create a book with her niece and nephew photos, too. She'd visualized it, making it almost real to her screwy brain, and she could still see the pages laid out, as if suspended in front of her, but untouchable.

Those pages would never exist, never be assembled in the real world. The activity would be too painful after Liz's rejection. Libbie missed the kids so much, both their sweetness and the annoyances that came with ten-year-olds. She refused to believe she'd never see them again, but at their age they changed so fast and made so many new connections and memories, it wouldn't take long for their relationship to fade. It would never be the same.

But Libbie had a new project. Sicily. She could choose the print-worthy photographs and get the book started. She'd surprise Jim.

Projects always made her feel better. Goals. Purpose.

But projects didn't last.

Maybe she should find another day job?

Or not. Those jobs never worked out well for her and she didn't need the money. So, photos of Sicily and picture books were next on her agenda. And after that? Well, Jim would be back.

She stood in the wide opening between the study and the dining room. With all the renovating and painting she'd done, she'd never quite finished the dining room. The blue painters tape marking the painting lines on the ceiling had been pulled down and, in her opinion, the ceiling looked pretty grand. The rest of the room still needed touching up.

She unzipped the camera bag. The camera was in the center with the lenses on either side. The filters were in the pockets, as were the memory cards.

It appeared that the damage done to the camera had been confined to the threads where the lens attached to the camera body, but she'd send it off and let the experts have a go at assessing it. She had to have a conversation with her homeowners' insurance company about the damaged camera. The memory card seemed okay. Of course, the card could fail on its own. That was always a risk with memory cards. If you used cards with lots of memory, you risked losing everything if the card malfunctioned, that's why Libbie had a bunch.

She dug them out of the pockets of the bag. Each was in a plastic case marked with their order. Number 1, number 2, and so on. Digital leads to excess. She had over three thousand photos from Sicily. Snap, snap, snap.

She arranged her laptop on the coffee table, inserted the first card and the photographs started downloading.

Jim was supposed to be here beside her, watching the slideshow and sharing memories and a bowl of popcorn. Instead, after the download was done, she'd be watching the show alone. The upside was she'd have the chance to delete the lousy shots before he saw them. Libbie fetched a cup of tea and some cookies.

As soon as the plate of oatmeal raisin cookies hit the coffee table, Max joined her. He curled up close to her, his chin on her thigh.

"No cookies for you, Max." She gave him a scratch around the ears as a consolation prize.

The first photo was of her home here, from the vantage point of the road—an old, but charming white house situated atop the sloping lawn of green. Trees framed the yard on both sides and the trees behind the house were old and towered above the house. In her backyard was the terrace. Jim had built it. Or, rather, his landscaping company. And on it, her wrought iron table and chairs.

She'd taken these pictures before leaving on the trip. These pictures were sharp, yet still soft with the southern pines and spreading oaks overshadowing the green of the grass. A soft light. Very different from the light of the Mediterranean.

Next were photos of the Richmond airport. Steel and granite. All hard surfaces, except the rows of black vinyl seats.

She would use a few of the airport photos for context and contrast. There was Jim at the ticket counter checking their bags, and then again, Jim in his seat in the airplane.

Had she thought this would be easy? Jim and Jim and Jim. Libbie leaned her head back against the sofa seat cushion and smiled at the screen as if Jim could sense it from the far side of the country.

Then the airport in Rome.

Huge. Crowded. The air had gotten thick and hard to breathe. It was the manifestation of her worst fears of traveling—a nightmare of a building crowded with people present and past and with every emotion imaginable swirling through the air.

When had she finally relaxed? It was the boat ride. The trip across the water to Sicily. A sea of unbelievable color sparkled all around them. The wind blew through her hair and brushed her face, bringing the scents of the Mediterranean with it. And here were those photos. Water and wind. And the light. That was when Libbie truly appreciated the quality of the light and the beauty of the Mediterranean.

Centuries of artists had sought the light in southern France and Spain. It must also be true of Sicily. The light left her breathless, but it didn't stop her finger from snapping and snapping the button on the camera.

She'd closed her eyes and imagined the colorful, vivid blooms and vines and groves that the smells evoked. The colors whirled in the inner eye of her brain. It felt like her brain was absorbing them, adding to the trove it already carried.

Jim had stood behind her, an arm around her waist as she held the rail, and a nice man took their photo. Her hair was blowing into Jim's face, and they were both smiling. She remembered that farther along the railing, a group of girls were giggling and snapping photos with their cell phones and selfie sticks. It looked like fun, but on the other hand, they didn't have the bonus of Jim's arms holding them close to his chest, and his lips in their hair. Libbie believed she had the better setup.

First download was complete.

She spent hours that evening going through the photos, noting the file numbers of the ones she wanted to take a closer look at, imagining the fun Jim and she would have going through them when he returned.

Her eyelids were drooping. Her legs were cramped. When the phone rang, she jumped and groaned. She'd left the phone out of reach, but she scrambled to get it because no one but Jim was likely to call this late in the evening.

"Hi, Jim."

"Hi. Missing you."

"I miss you, too. You sound so tired. How is Matthew?"

"Recovery won't be easy. Screws in his thigh bone. He's in pain. I have to find a rehab to move him to in a week or so. He'll probably be there for a couple of weeks before we can talk about him traveling."

"Traveling? He's coming back with you? How's his mom? I never did ask about her. How is she doing?"

"Her injuries were less serious. Nothing broken. Stitches. She's released already. And yes, he's coming home with me where he'll have family to help him recover. It will be easier on his mother, too. She isn't used to having a teenager around."

There was a certain implication there, of perhaps his mother not being up to the responsibility, but in the end, it was up to Jim and the mom and the rest of the family. She added a platitude, "He's young and resilient. He'll be fine, given time." She waited but Jim didn't respond. She wanted to lighten his mood. "Guess what I'm doing?"

"You weren't sleeping. I can tell that much from your voice. And it's late there, so I'm glad I didn't wake you."

"I wouldn't have minded if you had. But, no, I've been looking through our photographs."

"Oh." A pause. "It seems so long ago." Another pause. "So, what do you think? How'd they come out?"

"It's almost like being there with you again. Almost." In that warm moment, she could've said, "By the way, guess who I saw there after you left?" but she didn't. His voice sounded so tired, so disconnected, as if the idea of photographs from their trip didn't apply to the world Jim was currently inhabiting. He deserved to be uplifted. She wanted to be that person—the supportive, encouraging person— not the needy, neurotic creature she sometimes was.

"When are you coming home?"

"Soon. Only a quick trip. Some business stuff to take care of with the nursery."

"And me?"

"You are most definitely my business. I love you, Libbie."

"I love you too."

So brief. She was glad he'd taken a few minutes to give her a call. It was an especially lovely thought that they'd spoken twice yesterday and again this evening. Given all that he was dealing with, she was touched. She removed the memory card and put it back in its case. Her eyes were tired. Enough for tonight.

"Max, we're done." Libbie stood and he followed her to the back door. He stopped at his dish for a drink, and as she touched the handle of the storm door, she looked through the glass into the dark night beyond. Amber eyes stared back. Something big. Tall. On the terrace. She froze.

A product of reflection? Of the light spilling from the kitchen?

No. Those were eyes.

After the first shock, Libbie flipped the switch for the outside light. The angle wasn't great, and the bulb was weak, but she realized the creature was small because after its first shock, the animal jumped down from the wrought iron table and ran. Libbie blocked Max's exit for as long as she could. If the critter was a skunk or raccoon, she wanted to give it a head start. Finally, she had to let Max out, so he could go.

Not quite at ease after seeing those eyes, she waited on the back stoop for Max to finish his business. He was back in moments. Done.

Tonight, there was a chill. Official autumn was only days away. In a month—Halloween. By Thanksgiving she'd be approaching nine months here. Nine months. So much had happened it was almost insane to think that this time last year she hadn't known Cub Creek existed.

They were in love. Jim lived on the far side of the county where his businesses were located. How would that work if he did propose?

She tightened her grip on the railing. She wasn't afraid of the night, but the future? That was a little scary.

Did she want to leave Cub Creek so soon? Even for Jim?

Suppose she made the wrong decision? Yet again.

The more they were apart, the more likely doubts would arise. It made sense. She had to focus on what she knew to be true, and not on fear and failure.

Libbie pushed the worry away. She'd be okay when Jim returned home.

****

Days later, Libbie spent the morning running errands, including a visit to the grocery store in Mineral, and hurried home. Jim had arrived in town yesterday and had spent the day and evening attending to nursery business. She was expecting him at Cub Creek today. They'd have a few hours before he headed back to the airport. She didn't know what time Jim would arrive, but she wanted to be gorgeous and upbeat and everything he deserved, or as close to it as she could come. She was even prepared to cook if that seemed the way to go.

As she pulled into her driveway, she saw a car parked up near the house.

Jim? This early? Not his car, but maybe borrowed or a rental? Libbie parked off to the side.

He wasn't on the porch, and he didn't have a key, so he must be on the terrace. Max was whining on the other side of the front door. She opened it and he flew past her, down the steps and across the yard. He was going to greet Jim, surely. She went straight to the kitchen. She had frozen food in these bags and the drive from Mineral wasn't a short one.

Libbie paused only to shove the frozen items into the freezer, then went to the back door, flipped the deadbolt and knob lock, and yanked it open. She froze at the storm door, motionless, her fingers gripping the handle.

He was sitting at the wrought iron table, facing the woods. His hand was on the table and he was clasping something, moving it, as if worrying it with his fingers. Otherwise, he was still. He must be deep in thought since he appeared not to have heard her car in the gravel driveway or heard her opening the door.

Max? Normally social, Max was in the back yard now, but was more interested in sniffing trees than in checking out their guest, Barry Raymond.

Could she ease the door shut again? Leave without him knowing she was here?

He pulled his hand back and shoved it into his jacket pocket.

She bit her lip and tried to calm her breathing. What gave him the right to haunt her? To stalk her? As far as she knew, he hadn't tried to contact her in years, so why now? Because he'd seen her in Sicily and she'd been friendly?

With one hand on the doorknob, and the other pressed against the door frame, Libbie eased the door closed. The hinges were well-oiled, and the latch snicked home with the tiniest of sounds.

Libbie moved to stand at the kitchen window. He was still there, sitting and staring at the woods. Max was trotting around the yard, mostly ignoring him, and he was apparently ignoring Max.

She heard the sound of tires on gravel. Jim.

Through the front window, she saw Jim's truck parked behind the car that could only belong to Barry.

Libbie dashed back to the kitchen and stole another look outside. He hadn't moved. She grabbed her sweater and purse. Max would be fine as he was until returned.

She pulled the front door closed behind her. Jim was already halfway to the porch. He stopped, eyeing the purse and sweater.

"Let's go somewhere," she said. "Maybe grab a bite."

He frowned. "Okay. What's up?"

"Nothing. Not a thing, except one thing, and I'll tell you about it while we're—"

Barry came around the end of the house. "Libbie? I heard your car. I thought you'd join me out on the terrace."

Jim looked at Barry, then turned back to Libbie.

She'd gotten no further than the porch steps. She stood there clutching the rail, trying to stay calm. "I saw you on the terrace, Barry, but I don't understand why you're here."

He raised an eyebrow, silently questioning.

She turned to Jim. "Let's just go."

Still frowning, Jim focused on Barry Raymond and asked, "What's this about,

Libbie? Is there a problem?"

"I'm Dr. Raymond," Barry answered. He walked up to Jim and extended his hand.

Jim accepted his hand automatically, but released it quickly. Now he looked confused. Barry looked assured.

Libbie kept her lips pressed together, afraid anything she said would make this encounter worse.

"I should've called first," Barry said. "I thought you'd be glad to see me, Libbie."

"Who are you?" Jim asked.

"Dr. Barry Raymond." He said it slowly, clearly, with inflection.

Jim said, his voice low, his confusion gone, "I heard you the first time."

Libbie was surprised by Jim's tone. A warning tone. An escalation. Her stomach did a flip.

"Of course. My apologies. I believe I understand the issue now. You don't know about me."

"About you?"

"Libbie and I are old friends."

Barry kept that careful, professional look on his face. Jim's face, she could no longer read.

Her hands were suddenly moist against the railing. She eased her grip and moved down a step. "I wasn't expecting you, Barry. Jim and I are on our way out."

He shrugged. "I understand. I don't want to inconvenience anyone." He looked down at the ground, then up again. "After that time we spent together in Sicily…well, it reminded me of when we used to see each other regularly." He looked at Jim. "We became friends years ago." He looked back at Libbie. "Those were tough times for you."

She would've done anything to shut him up, but she couldn't think how. Her hands clenched and unclenched on the railing and her cheeks burned.

"I don't know why you're here," Jim said. "Unless Libbie wants you to stay, then leave."

Barry looked at her. Jim didn't. She had no words.

"I see," Barry said. "Jim, looks like I'm blocked in by your vehicle. Shall I follow you two out?"

"I'll move my truck," Jim said.

Jim refused to look her way, but he returned to his truck and re-parked it so Barry could back his car out, which he did. He left with a wave.

Jim stayed in his truck. Libbie went to the passenger side and opened the door. She put her purse on the seat and slid her arms into the sleeves of her sweater, but when she climbed into the truck and fastened her seat belt, Jim didn't put the truck in gear.

His hands rested on the steering wheel as

he stared straight ahead. Libbie watched his jaw muscles tensing as he worked silently through the words he wanted to say, but held back.

She stayed silent, giving him the chance to sort it out. After a minute or so, she couldn't take the waiting. "Jim? Would you like to come inside? We can stay here now that...now he's gone."

"Libbie."

"What?" She touched his sleeve. "Jim, you have to talk to me."

He nodded. "You're right. We have to talk." He looked at her. "You didn't mention seeing him in Sicily. Your friend, Barry?"

"Dr. Barry Raymond. I don't recall whether I told you about him."

"You didn't."

"I mean about knowing him years ago. He's a psychiatrist. Liz brought him to me, to Grandmother's house after she died, to help me. And he did. It was a long time ago. You already know most of that."

"When did you see him in Sicily?"

"He showed up after you left. I was at the café, the trattoria, the one we liked so much. He was suddenly there, standing beside the table."

"And?"

"And what? We had lunch." She tried to keep her cool. "You had real life problems on your mind. He wasn't important enough to mention."

"So, one unplanned lunch and he follows you across the Atlantic to Cub Creek? How would he find you out here in the woods? Did you two keep in touch? Exchange addresses, phone numbers?"

"No." Libbie felt herself shrinking. She fought the urge to move away from him.

"Is that why you wanted to go to Sicily?"

Her unease was becoming annoyance and trending toward anger. "That's stupid."

"Is it? The trip was your idea. I invited myself along. Did I spoil your plans?"

"You encouraged me to go. I would never have gone on my own. Barry and I haven't kept in touch. As for him being here, how would I know what was in his head? He gave me no indication he was planning to return to the States." She hugged her purse in her arms. "And, for your information, it wasn't only lunch. I went out to dinner with him, too."

"I see." He stared straight ahead.

"I wouldn't want you to think I was keeping something important from you." She grasped the door handle. "You weren't there, Jim. I was alone and I couldn't figure how to shake him off. If you hadn't left me there...."

"My son was seriously injured in a car crash."

"I know."

"It wouldn't have happened if he'd been at home and not with his mother."

Libbie said, "Okay. What does that mean?"

"Nothing."

"He went there because of me? Isn't that right? Matthew went to live with his mother because of us?"

Jim didn't answer, so Libbie continued. "Nothing was said about him going and then suddenly he was gone. What kid coming up on his senior year in high school does that? So, yes, I wondered, but you didn't say anything, so I didn't. You blame me, don't you? If we hadn't started seeing each other, getting close, Matthew would've been here in Louisa, at home with you, and safe?"

"That's crazy."

"Crazy. Me. You aren't the first to say so, but I thought you were different."

This time he glanced at her. "That's not what I mean. Don't twist things to get out of an uncomfortable situation. Truth is truth, Libbie, no matter how uncomfortable it is."

"That's very nice, Jim. But the reality is I'm not so sure I know what truth is. I do think it's presumptuous of you to assume you know someone else's truth." Libbie fumbled with her seatbelt. She refused to stay in this truck. It was going nowhere fast. "You didn't mention the truth of why Matthew went to California. I didn't mention the fact that Barry Raymond found me in Sicily and we shared two meals. I have no clue what the truth is around that, so I don't know how you can begin to know."

"You wouldn't have said a word about lunch or supper, or that he was sitting on your terrace, if he hadn't come around to the front, right?" He shook his head. "Libbie. I think the bottom line truth, reality, whichever way you slice it, is maybe we moved too fast."

He was waiting, but what did he want her to say? She didn't speak.

He continued, "People said…. They told me not to rush things and I didn't want to hear it. Maybe I wasn't fair to you. Back in the summer when we decided to take the trip, it wasn't long after the trauma you went through, and the blow up with Liz. You were still vulnerable."

"Jim."

He held up his hand. He nodded as if in consultation with himself, then turned to her. His hazel eyes were dull. For the first time, she noticed the shadows under his eyes and deeper creases at the corners. He looked so weary. Her heart moved.

"I told you Matthew's coming back with me, right? I was going to tell him he had to accept us being together, so this happening now may be for the best. He'll have time to adjust. You'll have time."

"And you'll have time. That's the point, isn't it?" She wanted to be kind. He was exhausted and they were both overly emotional, but heat fueled her words. "One little problem and you're ready to run. I thought you had more grit in you."

"You lied to me, Libbie. At least by omission. I wasn't available. I was tied up with Matthew, so I could maybe understand, but what I don't understand is what I just witnessed. You should never lie, Libbie. You're face shows nothing but guilt."

Guilt. Libbie didn't want to hear anymore. She closed her ears to shut off his voice. She flung open the door and slid out, then slammed it shut as hard as she could. The window rattled. She didn't look back as she walked to the house, nor when she heard his truck come alive and start backing down the driveway. She fumbled her keys and had to stoop to pick them up and saw his truck from the corner of her eye as he backed onto the road and then shot forward to disappear around the bend of Cub Creek Loop.

She put her hands to her throat. A distant voice screamed in her head as she stumbled inside.

Guilt. Guilt about what? About so many things it hardly mattered whether any particular one was applicable. It all sort of fell into one pot.

Guilt stew.

She was going to break into a million what-if pieces if she didn't get control of herself.

Libbie closed the door, beat her fists against the wall, then collapsed against it. Her forehead cooled, soothed by the paint and plaster. Alice's house. Cub Creek. The same comfort and reassurance she'd felt that first day at Cub Creek, reasserted itself in that warm beige color. The heat in her body, in her brain, diminished as if drawn from her until she could think again.

She stepped away from the wall and stumbled into the living room where she sank to the sofa. It seemed too unreal. They had barely begun their relationship and it was already over?

But it wasn't all over—the realization hit her. Their relationship had encountered a bump in the road, had suffered a misunderstanding. Patience was required, and a little time.

She pulled her legs up onto the sofa and hugged them.

A reasonable conversation would sort things out after Matthew was better. Jim was going through emotional and physical exhaustion. Her own anger and hurt aside, she respected the pressure he was under. They didn't have to throw this away. They could fix it, if that's what he wanted.

Despite his good looks, Jim wasn't a Casanova kind of guy. Libbie didn't believe he could turn love on and off like a light switch.

Max joined her at the sofa, resting his chin on her feet. She rubbed around his ears and said silly things because she wanted him to know she appreciated his sympathy. Well, not maybe true sympathy, but an awareness of her unhappiness, a caring.

When she dropped her legs down to the floor and moved to stand, he trotted to the kitchen and waited beside his empty food dish. When she didn't rush to fill it, he nosed it around the kitchen floor, making it scrape against the linoleum with a clatter.

Libbie scooped the dog food into Max's bowl, then leaned back against the counter and observed her kitchen. The old linoleum. The scarred cabinets. They'd looked better to her before. Perhaps she should've updated them when she was giving the other rooms a facelift. She had painted the walls in here, but paint hadn't helped the fixtures. And the dining room.... Was she setting up a habit, a pattern, of not finishing things?

She felt unsettled all over again.

They would work it out. She and Jim. He needed a little time to recover from everything he was dealing with.

In the living room, the walls were lined with

her photographic excesses. Her subject enthusiasms bloomed, lived their time, then passed as some other subject assumed prominence.

In The Road photos and The Train Track photos, the focus was on the vanishing point. The road to somewhere or nowhere—anywhere but here. She'd always thought of those as her "Get out of Town" collection. The representation was clear—to get away from her unhappy past, and at times, her present. Her grandmother, her anger and helplessness. Going somewhere, anywhere, because going nowhere was better than where she'd been.

She'd tried fences, too. The gleaming white fencing of the horse pastures across the street had been a big part of what first caught her attention at Cub Creek. But photographing fences, as an enthusiasm, had dwindled before it went far, because of Max. Because of Audrey and Adam. Inanimate subjects lost out to the living ones. She touched the Plexiglas covering the photo of the kids with Max and traced their faces.

Max whined and barked at the back door. He wanted out. Life went on.

Before she opened the storm door, she saw two deer in the back yard. No, a third, a youngster. And there, barely inside the edge of the woods, keeping watch, was a fourth, a large buck with impressive antlers.

"Hush, Max." Libbie shushed him. He sat, but almost bounced in his fidgeting, as his whines grew to a near howl.

She tapped on the glass of the storm door. The deer looked up, more interested than concerned. The male moved closer and the young one dashed into the trees.

"Well, Max. They've been warned, but let's go out the front door, okay?"

He followed her, practically dancing, as he cast looks her way. He thought she was crazy. The action was clearly out back. When she opened the door, he dashed to the porch, his feet skimming the steps as he aimed for the yard. He rounded the house way ahead of her. She followed.

Considering what had happened with Jim, it seemed foolish to worry over Max and some deer. But she did.

He bounded back around, meeting her halfway and gave two short barks.

"Did they get away?"

Where there were deer, there might be hunters. Not at this moment maybe, but soon. Like the coyotes, hunters were just one more uncontrollable, potential threat. She grabbed Max's collar in a sudden moment of worry.

She couldn't keep Max inside all the time. Maybe a long chain.... No, she wouldn't keep him tied either. There was life, and then there was life that sucked.

She'd already had the second kind, and she wouldn't wish that on anyone, including her dog.

Max strained away from her and she released him. He sniffed for all he was worth around the backyard before he gradually disappeared, following his nose deeper into the woods.

Libbie understood what Dan was telling her, about her responsibility. She would wear an orange vest and cap, if necessary, and so would Max, but she had to draw the line there. There were no guarantees on this earth.

Back in the house, she picked up the orange garment Dan had brought for Max. The tag read, "Canine field jacket." She turned it over and examined the buckles.

Could she get this on him? He wouldn't like it, she was sure, and she couldn't manage it without his cooperation.

Libbie had never wanted to be responsible for anyone, including pets. But here it was. She needed to step up her game. And not only for Max. For Jim, too.

She couldn't force him to be reasonable, and if she had to, then she truly didn't want to. But she could be patient and she knew how to forgive…not that he was the only one at fault.

If they failed, or their "project" didn't get finished, it wouldn't be on her.

And if Jim decided....

Her throat suddenly ached and her eyes burned.

No.

Did she have hope or not? Did she have faith in them together, or not? Time enough for regrets later, if that's how it ended up. For now, she had things to do.

****

Days passed whether or not you were ready for the future, or able to let go of the past. Libbie forced herself to think of each day's tasks. When it came to the future, she focused on the time when any questions about them being together would already have been settled and they had everything good ahead of them. In the meantime, she had things to do and she did them, like driving into Charlottesville to pick up the new camera she'd ordered, plus a couple of new lenses because one could never be sure of having the right glass when you needed it.

She turned from the main road onto Cub Creek Loop. As always, when approaching from the south, the pastures of the Pettus horse farm first caught her eye, but then, to the left, the green slope of her own lawn below the towering trees drew her eye to her house. The white clapboards glowed golden in the late afternoon sun. The scene spoke of peace. It was a haven for squirrels, birds, and nuts like her. Not a personal put-down. Just a declaration. People were welcome to take her or leave her, except for maybe Jim. She refused to let Jim go easily.

So, she was moving forward and concentrating on herself while Jim got his life in order. She could be patient.

The car in her driveway warned her, and the woman sitting on her front porch confirmed the worst, reminding Libbie that no one can control everything no matter how desperately they desired to.

She braked to a stop at the foot of the drive and considered backing out and continuing on down the road.

First, it had been Barry.

Now she had another unwanted visitor.

Aunt Margaret.

Chapter Four

Many years ago, Dr. Barry Raymond, with his knowing eyes and chin beard, had told Libbie that her problems would keep coming back until she dealt with them. It had sounded wise at the time, like a mantra to live by, but the logic was flawed. She'd been dealing with the same problems over and over, forever. They were stubborn and remorseless.

Aunt Margaret's hair was grayer, but too graceful and artful to be natural. Margaret would never have trusted to nature and honesty to yield the correct balance of age and style. Truth was what Aunt Margaret constructed to meet her own, rigid requirements.

Anyone seeing her there, and not knowing otherwise, would see an older woman, well-dressed, but not flashy. She never wore her wealth ostentatiously and had groomed her daughter, Liz, along those same lines. Anyone seeing Aunt Margaret and not knowing her heart, could be excused if they admired her style and dignity and timeless looks.

The problem wasn't about money and in no

way was it about jealousy or envy on Libbie's part. What looked good on Aunt Margaret and Liz would never have looked right on her. She would never qualify for sophisticated and urbane. She had never wanted to. Libbie suspected that had always bugged Aunt Margaret.

At the top of the driveway Libbie cut the engine. She concentrated on relaxing her fists and her jaw, and opened the door. "Fight" was her usual response to her aunt, because it disguised her instinctive response—to flee. A dark anger-fueled fear had been carved in her heart and mind as a child. Anger was far better than allowing this woman to see her weakness.

Her aunt stood as Libbie approached the porch. Margaret's hands were gracefully clasped together.

Libbie stopped short of the steps. "What do you want?"

The smile dropped. "Some things never change, I see." She looked around. "You do have a nice property out here in the country. Liz told me about it."

Libbie crossed her arms. "What do you want?"

Her aunt's purse was on the settee. Margaret picked it up and sat again. "For one thing, I wanted to see for myself how you were doing out here. Also, I have something to give you. Some items I came across when I was going through Elizabeth's old papers."

"Grandmother died ten years ago. You're only just now–" Her immediate distrust was distracted by scratching and snuffling sounds coming from inside the front door. Max.

"How did he get in the house?" She went up the steps, brushing past Margaret, and touched the front door knob. Unlocked. She opened the door and Max bolted forward, first into her legs, nearly knocking her over, then settling at her side, agitated. He gave a short bark in Margaret's direction.

Libbie said, "I left him outside. How did he get inside? What did you do to him?"

"I did nothing. Keep your dog away from me. If he bites me, I'll call the authorities and have him put down."

"He's nowhere near you, and I'm more likely to bite you than he is. Max, hush. Max." Libbie shooed him from the porch. He went down to the lawn, but didn't go far. "Why was he shut in the house? Why is my door unlocked?"

"You're asking the wrong person. I certainly did neither. I found the front door unlocked. I used your restroom. You don't begrudge me that? Then that dog was there. Not exactly a guard dog, is he?" She sniffed. "But I'm uncomfortable around untrained animals, so I left and returned to the porch to wait. There's an old woman sleeping on your sofa."

Joyce.

"What do you want?"

Margaret paled, except for her cheeks. They flushed a deep red. She clutched her purse on her lap. "You can be as rude as you wish. It confirms I'm right about you staying away from me and mine." Her expression was like stone.

Libbie put her hands on her hips and stamped her foot once, only once, again the porch planks. "I've heard we get the family we deserve. And wow, did I get some gems." The words forced their way out. "A grandmother who couldn't stand me. An aunt and uncle who didn't want me. And that aunt–" She pointed at Margaret. "That aunt did everything she could to make sure I wouldn't contaminate her daughter, and now her grandchildren. What I've never understood was why? What did I do to you, or to anyone, that was so awful?"

"Family?" Aunt Margaret deliberately changed the direction of the question. "What does family mean to you?"

She held up her hand. Libbie saw the question was rhetorical.

Margaret continued, "You asked me? I'll tell you. It was always about you. You were always the center of your own universe. If you were miserable, everyone must be miserable. If you wanted something, everyone else's wants must wait. Most children grow out of that. You never did."

"That's not true."

"It's true. If you cared about family so much, then what about your mother's family? Weren't you curious about them?"

Libbie was speechless. Her parents had died in a car accident when she was five. There was no family on her mother's side.

Margaret laughed softly and shook her head. "Your silence proves my point, doesn't it?"

"Grandmother said there was no one."

"You never questioned her veracity? You did about everything else."

"Even she wouldn't lie about something like that. I lost my parents. I was five years old, but old enough to know other family, other grandparents, if they existed." The weight of her disbelief pressed upon each word until Libbie felt like she was whispering. "Someone would've come looking for me."

"I won't debate the reliability of your memory," Margaret said. "Stay away from Liz and the children. That's all."

Libbie leaned close to her. "Why do you hate me so much?"

"I don't, but I do know who you are. Look at your track record. Some people attract tragedy by how they think, how they act. Remember, I know what you did to your grandmother. You killed her. I protected you, but the scandal still haunts our family. It's long past time for you to go your own way."

"I didn't kill her."

"Your actions killed her. You can't deny you're responsible for what happened the day she died." Margaret stood. She opened her purse and removed an envelope. She thrust it toward Libbie. "Take this. Go find your other kin. One of the papers mentions the southwestern part of the state. A place called Preston."

Her aunt shook her head slowly. "There's nothing for you here, Libbie. Not with Liz and not with my grandchildren."

Margaret left the porch, walking with regal dignity to her car. Libbie held the envelope, almost forgotten. She was stunned. So far as she knew, Aunt Margaret had never outright lied to her. The woman was cold and cruel, yes, but was her truthfulness in question? Not to Libbie. What she said about Libbie's grandmother…

Libbie realized she'd entered the house and was standing in the foyer. Max had joined her. She moved to the living room window to watch Margaret's car disappear from view.

Joyce was lying on the sofa buried under the sofa throw.

Had she heard what Margaret said about Grandmother's death? Libbie's brain was buzzing. What, exactly, had she said? It was a blur now, and probably didn't matter because Joyce was asleep, and a wall and window were between her and the ugly words Margaret had thrown at her.

Libbie stepped quietly back out to the porch. She needed to recover before Joyce woke. She sagged down upon the settee, still clutching the envelope.

Her mother's name was Claire. Her father was Scott. They died when she was five and she had always carried the blame. She knew, as an adult, that was unreasonable, but it was hard to shake habits that take root so young.

Her grandmother, Elizabeth, took her in and raised her. Other than Uncle Phil and Aunt Margaret, and their daughter, Liz, Libbie had had no one.

She tried to remember what Grandmother had said. That her mother had no family, she recalled that clearly. Libbie had accepted it. It hadn't occurred to her not to. Why? She'd questioned everything else her grandmother did or said.

Uncle Phil had never said a word about other family. She'd trusted him absolutely.

She looked at the envelope.

The outside was blank. It was a simple white

business envelope, but stuffed, lumpy and sealed.

She slipped her fingernail under the loose end.

"There you are. I took a rest on your sofa." Joyce said, already halfway out the door.

Libbie was startled. She hadn't heard the hinges squeak.

Joyce said, "You're in another world, I see. Anything interesting?"

Libbie nodded, the envelope still unopened in her hands.

Joyce stepped carefully over the threshold onto the porch, keeping a hand on the door jamb, her cane in the other. She sat in the chair. She was wearing slacks and a knit top with long sleeves, but no jacket or sweater.

"It's chilly out here, Joyce. Are you warm enough? Need a blanket?"

"Oh, I'm fine for the moment. I need to be getting back to the Home anyway. I expected you to be here. Lucky, I knew where the key was hid. I was sure you'd be back any time, but you weren't. Had myself a good nap, though."

"I'll drive you back."

"No time to look at photographs today, I guess. You getting back so late and all."

After a long pause, Libbie realized Joyce was waiting for a response.

"Sorry. I didn't mean to ignore you."

"You're still in that other world. Have anything to do with that woman?"

"That's my aunt."

"Your aunt?"

Libbie nodded. "She was married to my father's twin brother. She's Liz's mother. You remember meeting Liz at my picnic back...whenever? Only months, but it seems ages ago." She shook her head. "Anyway, my uncle died when I was a teenager."

"Well, I don't mind saying that was one scary woman." Max settled next to Joyce and she scratched his head. "I was dozing when I heard the stairs creak. Thought it was you, though you do walk softer, lighter. But it wasn't. That woman was surprised to see me."

"She went upstairs?"

"Yes. Curious I guess. Took herself a tour. I see by your look, as I could by her sneaky face, she hadn't been invited. Had her purse but it wasn't big, so I don't think she was stealing."

Libbie surprised herself by laughing. "If she'd had something valuable, something of mine, what would you have done?"

Joyce sat up straighter, though the posture only lasted a moment. "I have my cane. I ain't afraid to use it."

Libbie laughed and the envelope crinkled in her hands.

"What's that? You're holding that thing like it

might fly away. It ain't a bill, I know that because there's no writing on the front."

Libbie held it up for view. "My aunt brought it. She gave it to me. I don't know why. I don't know what she intended. I feel like I'm being tempted by a devil. I know you don't understand, but–"

"You're over-thinking it, girl."

"What?"

"Open the dang thing and see what's in it. Life's too short to study over it more than fifteen seconds. Just open it." Joyce waved her hand. "I'll do it if you want."

Max moved over to Libbie and sat on her feet again. He was a fair-sized dog. It was awkward.

"I'll open it later when I'm in a better frame of mind." She shook her head. "I'm distracted. Still angry, obviously, since I haven't asked how you got here. You didn't walk, did you?"

"I ain't a kid. When I walk I know how to take my time and rest as I want to, so no need to fuss. But no, I didn't. An aide dropped me off."

"To visit your niece?" Libbie smiled.

"Well, of course. You told 'em that yourself as I recall." She chuckled. "At least I ain't no Wicked Witch of the West."

"Wicked Witch?"

"Sure. You called her Margaret, didn't you? When you two were squabbling out on the porch?"

Momentarily breathless, Libbie sat with her mouth hanging open and closed it with a gasp. She wouldn't ask Joyce if she'd heard what her aunt had said about Grandmother. *Keep it light, Libbie.* "Margaret? Was that the name of the Wicked Witch?"

"No. Name of the actress that played her." Joyce grunted and shook her head. "But no difference."

"How can you say that? There's a world of difference between an evil character and an actress playing a character."

"That so? Hard to tell sometimes. They tend to look alike in my mind."

Enough of that. Libbie changed the subject. "Are you hungry? Thirsty? Would you like something before I drive you home?"

"Wouldn't mind a snack. Got some soda?"

"No, but I have apple juice and iced tea." Libbie shook her head. "Oh, wait. It will ruin your appetite for supper."

"Not at all. Plenty of time for a snack. It's not like I have to walk back. You'll drive me."

Joyce rose to her feet. Libbie didn't reach out to steady her, but she was prepared to jump forward if Joyce started to tilt.

"Don't watch me like that. I'm no invalid." She settled her cane against the floor. "That sounds good."

"Apple juice or iced tea?"

"Both. Iced tea with a taste of apple."

"Ugh. Really?"

"It's all sweet." Joyce grinned. "Got anything good to eat?"

"I'll see what's available."

They moved toward the kitchen. Libbie paused to put the envelope on the mantle, then joined Joyce.

Joyce said. "While we have our snack you can tell me about what you did to your grandmother."

Libbie stumbled.

Joyce laughed. "Well, I can see you're touchy about that, and I surely cannot picture you as a killer no matter what I do, so why don't you just tell me about you and her. You never did say much except that she took you in, but wasn't nice about it."

"Isn't that enough?" Libbie settled her at the table. What could she say? Something to show it wasn't a big deal, but not much because too much would make it sound like a very big deal.

Joyce didn't wait for the explanation. "My granny, now that was a woman. She had six kids and kept chickens and taught school. She didn't put up with much. Couldn't put anything over on her."

"Do you have brothers or sisters?"

"Some of both. All gone now. I'm the last."

"I'm sorry." Libbie pulled out the cookies.

"I see chips."

Libbie pulled the bag of potato chips out. She put a paper napkin in a wicker bowl and poured the chips in, then tucked some oatmeal raisin cookies in on the side.

"Wow, now that's fancy. You learn that from your grandma?"

She pushed the bowl toward Joyce. "Wicker? Not a chance. I picked it up somewhere. No, my grandmother would not have had potato chips, much less wicker, in her house." Where to start? "You know my parents died when I was young and my grandmother took me in?"

"I do."

"My father and Liz's father were twins. My grandmother's name was Elizabeth, I told you that before. Well, she had twin sons and they were everything to her. Liz's father was my Uncle Phil. He was married to Margaret, of course. He died a few years ago." Liz and she were very close in age, so it seemed natural that she would go to live with them after her parents died, but it didn't happen that way. Libbie was left in the care of her grandmother.

"So what happened to your parents?"

"They died in a car accident. I was at a birthday party and they were on the way to pick me up. They never arrived." Libbie shook her head. "I don't remember much about that. Mostly, it's a blur. Being left at the party as all the other children were picked up. I remember standing in a corner, wanting to hide and feeling forgotten. And then Uncle Phil told me there'd been an accident. I remember something about the funerals and the wake afterward, memories like still photographs, like brain snapshots, but that's it."

"I don't doubt you were confused. Didn't know what grief was yet. Your mom and dad didn't have the same funeral service?"

"Oh, sure."

"You said services."

"I know there was another funeral, but grandmother kept me away. It was for some other people who died in the accident. I heard her tell someone she was protecting me from more grief."

Libbie shook her head. "I thought they'd come home. It took a long time to understand that they weren't going to. I kept asking. It made Grandmother angry."

"You two didn't get along."

"No, ma'am. Definitely not." She laughed. It was nice to discover she could laugh about it. "She didn't want me. I annoyed her. So I did. Annoy her, I mean. Deliberately. She and I never had the chance to resolve anything."

"Would you have?"

"What do you mean?"

"It's my experience that when it goes on too long people get stubborn and they get bent on vengeance, even if the vengeance is more like cutting off their own nose."

"To spite their face?"

"True enough."

Joyce concentrated on her last sip of tea, glass upended to drain the last drop.

Rose-colored. That's the color Libbie saw in her mind's eye when she thought of Joyce. Maybe because Joyce had been wearing a pink blouse the day they met. Today her wrinkles were deep and her face was pale, especially around the eyes and mouth.

"I think it's time for you to go home."

"I want to know about that Margaret woman."

Libbie stood, picking up the glasses and napkins. "Some other time when I've recovered from all this family stuff. Family stories, family visits. Definitely too much family for one day."

She put it out of her mind long enough to drive Joyce back to the home. She needed her wits, plus Libbie expected the staff, and maybe the cops, to rush her and charge her with elder abduction. She was only half-kidding. It had happened before, and Joyce had a way of omitting pertinent, but inconvenient details. But no cops greeted them. Only an aide with a wheelchair.

****

Libbie's father and her Uncle Phil were twins. They were Grandmother Elizabeth's only children, and long deceased. Uncle Phil and Aunt Margaret had one child, Libbie's cousin Liz. Now there was Liz's husband, Josh, and the two children. Otherwise, no family. None on her mother's side that she'd ever known about.

Or was Margaret right? If she was, did it matter? No one had ever come looking for her. There was no one. Or was it that no one had cared?

The outcome was the same.

She reran what she could recall of Grandmother speaking of 'other' family through her brain. What had she said? She couldn't remember exactly, but Libbie had understood from early on that there was no one else. There was no other family.

Might grandmother have lied? Maybe. But why would she?

Whatever, Libbie had never questioned her except in arguments that followed familiar teenage themes like, "If I had anywhere else to go I wouldn't be here."

She stood at the mantle. The envelope was next to Gladys's candle. Just paper. Why did it feel dangerous?

Because Aunt Margaret would not have given it to her unless it served her purpose. And Margaret had never wished her well.

Libbie ran her fingers along the front of the envelope. No colors. Nothing. She held the paper against her cheek and closed her eyes.

Perhaps a faint hue, maybe a slight warmth against her flesh. Maybe.

She stood by the sofa staring out of the wide, front window as the afternoon light softened. The pastures across the road made a serene landscape, as beautiful as the first day she'd seen them. When Libbie turned her head to the right, her eyes were drawn to the portrait in her study. She could see it through the wide opening of the living room, through the foyer and into the study and above the fireplace.

The unknown woman. Liz had teased Libbie, had sometimes mocked her, for surrounding herself with their grandfather's huge mahogany desk, the armoire also from his study, and this portrait. No one was sure who she was. Libbie believed she was her grandfather's mother, their great-grandmother.

Libbie took the envelope into the study. These few items she'd kept from her grandmother's house—mostly furniture from her grandfather's study—were the only family keepsakes she'd chosen to keep.

She never knew her grandfather and would

never know who the woman in the portrait was, but she could learn about her mother's family. Was trusting Aunt Margaret worth the risk? Even to know a little more about her mother and father?

If there was family out there that she didn't know about, then she could make new memories, memories born after her grandmother's death which wouldn't, therefore, be tainted by her. Memories like the ones she and Jim had been making.

She wished she could discuss this with Jim. He'd see it as an adventure. He'd apply his good humor and common sense, and all would become clear. For now, she'd do the next best thing and enjoy the photos they'd taken. She put the letter back on the mantle and returned to her desk.

Libbie lifted the laptop lid and selected the folder of Sicily photos. She put them on slide show and leaned back, her head resting against the back of the desk chair, thinking of Jim and feeling sad, but far from hopeless.

Max came from the kitchen. He plopped onto the floor nearby. Libbie's focus was on the photos sliding by, entranced by them. The clarity. The sunlight. The candlelight. The meals they'd shared in the open-air restaurants, and the sore feet they suffered while trekking along the narrow and steep roads while seeking the perfect view of the Mediterranean, equaled laughter, long discussions and sharing.

Then Libbie saw the photo. In the background, behind Jim, near the corner of a blush red building, stood Barry Raymond. He was looking straight at her camera.

She leaned forward. She squinted, checking the date info attached to the photo. A day before the near accident, but two full days before he approached her in the trattoria pretending to have just discovered she was in Sicily, at that particular cafe.

Libbie pressed her hands on either side of her head. Her brain might explode. Max whined. The high sound pierced her ears. She shivered.

She didn't know what to think. She couldn't think.

He was treacherous.

After her grandmother died unexpectedly and tragically, Libbie hadn't been able to move forward. She was frozen in the space and time immediately following the event. That, plus the regrets and what-ifs, had played over and over in her head. Liz brought Dr. Raymond to help her and everything improved from there. Both of them had been Libbie's lifelines through a nightmare time.

And then Dr. Raymond had left, after an odd

sort of confession, he said he'd lost his objectivity and he was taking time away. He'd suggested Libbie might be interested in travel. She'd gotten postcards from him, sent from Italy.

Libbie hadn't been interested in travel with Barry. With Jim, she had been interested.

Why had Barry pretended? Why had he spent an afternoon and an evening with her and never mentioned that when Jim and she had brunched at the trattoria that he'd been there, too, only a few buildings down the sidewalk, watching?

She leaned back in the chair and closed her eyes, trying to reach back into that place in her brain where the memories were stored. Back in Sicily, back at the trattoria, with Jim and the morning light brushing his hair and his face.

At the sidewalk table, as they finished their croissants and coffee, Jim said, "My mother would love to get to know you better. Come by the house more often. When Matthew is back in town, get to know him. He's a good kid. Not really a kid anymore, I guess."

He added, "Spend some time with us. Maybe go out for lunch with Mom. My sister, too. They've heard a lot about you."

Libbie grimaced. "I'm sure."

"No. From me. And it's all good." He smiled. His face was bathed in that special quality of light, perhaps the glow from the sun's rays reflecting off of the colorful buildings of Taormina, as he smiled at her and tasted his coffee. He looked a little sheepish, but sincere.

Libbie had looked away, hoping he wouldn't read the reluctance on her face.

Now, seated at her desk with night falling and turning the view in her window to black, with only the screen light from her computer providing illumination, she folded her arms on the desk and rested her face against them.

At the trattoria that day, Jim had sipped his coffee and looked at her face, and asked, "You okay, Libbie?"

The waiter removed an empty plate. Jim continued to look the question at her, pushing her to answer.

She nodded. "Sure. I…well it seems rather abrupt, for your family, I mean. Kind of presumptive. Intrusive. For me to suddenly be hanging around."

"You know how I feel about you. They do too." He waved his hand at her face, but kindly. "Where did you go when you left me just now? Are you here with me or…?"

Libbie pushed her coffee aside. "Sorry. Daydreaming, I guess."

She loved him. Long time, or short time together, it made no difference to her heart. Did she love him too much? Did he love her enough? So many struggles were ahead of them. How much of her craziness could he put up with?

That snippet of conversation had tilted the day, had set it off somehow, cockeyed.

"Headache?" he'd asked.

She looked at him.

"You're rubbing your temples. Is something wrong? I pushed you too hard, didn't I?"

She reached across and took his hand. She squeezed his fingers, wanting to draw on his strength and certainty. The contact would settle her. Would stabilize her.

"Libbie?"

"I'm fine." She forced a smile. "No need to be concerned."

"Are you sure?"

"Yes." And she was. It was stress and anxiety. She hated to admit to them.

"Why don't I take you back to the hotel?"

"No, we were going to the harbor, right?" The camera gear was in the backpack. She put a hand on the bag. "I'm fine. Truly. It was a moment of....whatever it was."

Jim looked unconvinced.

"A little headache. That's all." She touched his cheek. The anxiety attack was slipping away and it reassured her because instead of derailing her, she was bouncing right back. Such relief.

Everything was good again except the light was odd. She blinked. The light was sharp. Sharp, like prickles on her flesh. She reached for her sunglasses and realized she'd left them at the hotel. They were awkward with the camera viewfinder anyway. She blinked again and tried to get her vision right.

He took her hand and she rose from the chair. He picked up the backpack. She didn't fight for it. They'd done that little dance a few times and her protests had begun to sound self-serving. Hand in hand they moved down the stone walks and stairs. Jim kept her close. She was sorry she'd worried him. Stairs everywhere here. Uphill. Downhill. They joked that the level spots were for catching one's breath, and the shadows were for resting one's eyes. The light here was amazing. Almost too much so, today, especially. Sometimes she missed the softer light of Cub Creek.

They emerged from a narrow walkway onto the side of a street, one they'd walked many times, checking out the shops and the sights. They were caught up in a group of tourists and locals.

A man cut between them and she lost her hold on Jim. He was out of reach. The shout came from behind. The crowd surged forward. She heard the car approaching, then, as Jim fell, her view was blocked by the other people.

Her palms were damp and her heart raced at both that memory and another—she remembered the photos they'd taken that morning with the waiter, and that the waiter had snapped of them together.

Libbie raced through the photos, pushing next until she finally reached them. The last morning. Breakfast. Waiter smiling. Jim smiling. Everyone smiling, until Jim began to talk about her spending time with his family.

She examined each photo carefully. In the photo she'd taken of the waiter, a man stood in the background. The background was too blurry, the figure too obscured to be sure, but in her heart, she recognized Barry Raymond.

He'd been there that day, too.

Chapter Five

Libbie moved through the days distracted while she waited for Jim to come home. She was anxious to work it out, yet fearful that it might mean a permanent breakup. But she needed him. To speak with him. To hear his voice and look into his eyes.

Barry. In Sicily. He'd known she and Jim were there. He knew it days before he approached her. It kept going through her head over and over, around and around, sparking new worries.

In Sicily, he'd been watching. Waiting. Why? For Jim to leave? He couldn't know that would happen. So, maybe he was waiting for an opportunity to catch her alone.

Barry Raymond had been in Sicily and had followed them, stalked them, and there was no one for Libbie to tell.

The dusk had a gentle feel. She drove carefully on these roads as the day waned and the deer appeared, their eyes greenish-yellow pinpricks of light in the night as they grazed at the roadside. Tonight, Jim was on her mind. He kept intruding, mostly because he'd done nothing.

No call. No note.

Not that they didn't have things to work out, but after he'd had a chance to cool down and think about it... if he truly loved her then he would've called, right? He would want to give them a chance.

But he hadn't.

She could call him. Maybe.

Libbie turned onto Cub Creek Loop and shortly after, into her driveway. It was nearly dark. The shadows were deepening, especially beneath the trees and the porch overhang, but something on the porch caught her eye. When she saw movement, her first thought was of Joyce. But no, not after dark. Jim? No, no there was no truck or car.

Had she left Max outside? She'd shut him in today. The certainty of that thought struck her as she neared the end of the driveway and the shadow stood.

She braked, stopping abruptly.

She left her purse and purchases lying on the seat of the car. She jumped out and ran up the sidewalk to the porch.

"Adam?" She raced up the steps. "Is that you? What are you doing here?" She looked in both directions. No car and not another soul in sight. "Adam," she repeated as she touched his shoulders. "What's going on?"

He shrugged. His backpack was on the settee.

"Adam?" Her thoughts were frantic. She plucked at his shirt and jacket. He flinched, annoyed, but looked whole and reasonably put together. This made no sense, except that something must have gone very wrong in his life. In her cousin's life, too, if Adam was here alone.

"Aren't you glad to see me, Aunt Libbie?"

She tried to dial back the stress level in her voice. "Of course. It's been a while. What's up?"

"I ran away from home."

Libbie frowned. "What? Where's your mom and dad? Where's Audrey?"

By this time Max was at the front door and barking. He'd probably been hanging out next to the door since Adam stepped on the porch. She stuck the key in the lock, turned the knob and jumped back as the storm door swung wide. Max dashed past her and threw himself on Adam, his paws hitting Adam's shoulders and his tongue bathing the boy's face. Adam took a step backward as the weight of doggy love slammed into him, but he was grinning.

He patted Max's shoulder. "It's okay, boy," he said.

"Tell me this. Is anyone in danger? Bleeding? Anything like that?"

"No, ma'am."

"Then come in the house. It's brisk out here. Have a seat on the sofa. I'll get my stuff from the car and then we'll have a talk."

Adam stopped at the threshold. "I'll help you."

"No," she waved toward the door. "Go ahead in and I'll be right there."

He didn't move. "You aren't going to call anyone, are you?"

Oh, really? "Just anyone in general?"

"You know what I mean."

"I do know. You're going to be in trouble, but not quite yet. I'll hear what you have to say first, and then I have to call your parents and you know that."

He nodded and went inside. As she walked toward the car, she glanced at the living room window expecting to see him there watching. He wasn't. He trusted her.

Libbie's phone was in her purse, in the car. She could've grabbed it and dialed Liz or Josh instantly. She looked at the window. A few more minutes delay wouldn't hurt.

Easy enough for her to say. Liz and Josh might say differently if they knew their son wasn't home, safe and sound.

She came through the front door, shut it firmly, and dropped her bags on the kitchen table.

Adam was sitting on the sofa. Max, opportunist that he was, was sprawled across the cushions with his head on Adam's lap. When Max saw her, he moved off the sofa, if reluctantly. Libbie sat and Max did a body plop onto the floor, pinning Adam's feet. She watched, amazed, as Adam slid his sock-clad feet out from under the dog. Max laid flat out on the floor and Adam rested his feet on Max's side. They both seemed content.

But Libbie wasn't. She stared at Adam, waiting for him to tell her a story.

"I ran away."

"So you said. You didn't do it very well, since you know I'll turn you in."

"Don't you want to know why I ran away?"

"Mostly, I want to know why you'd put your parents through this? Not only that, but one phone call could ease their agony and you don't want me to make it. Smells fishy."

"They aren't worried. They think I'm staying over at a friend's house tonight." He shrugged and tried to look tough. "You know, to buy me some time, time to get farther away."

A ten-year-old tough guy from the upscale suburbs. Could happen. But that wasn't Adam.

"Audrey?"

"She's covering for me."

"Audrey is covering for you and you think your parents don't know something is up?"

This time, Adam looked down. He scratched at his pants leg, then his cheek. "Mom wouldn't notice anyway, and Dad's at work."

A chill hit me. "What does that mean?"

"He's up in DC for a few days. Over the weekend anyway." Adam leaned forward and stared down at this feet and Max.

"You know what I meant. About your mom not noticing?"

Without looking at her, he said, "She's not... Dad said she's not herself these days, but she told him she was, that she was fine, so he went. But she's not fine."

"What does that mean, Adam? Not fine?"

"She doesn't do much. Mostly, she sits and stares. When someone walks in the room, she jumps up and tries to look busy, but she isn't, not really. If you catch her when she thinks no one is looking, she doesn't look right. Not like she used to."

Libbie reached across the space between them and placed her hand on his back. "Maybe she doesn't know you're gone and not at your friend's house, not yet, but when she does, she'll panic. You know that. We have to call her. Tell me, Adam, how did you get here?"

"My friend's older brother has a girlfriend who lives in Louisa. He always drives over to see her on Fridays. I caught a ride with him. Paid for his gas."

"And he took you, just like that?"

"I told him my Aunt Libbie was expecting me for the weekend. He didn't ask anything else."

She reached for the phone.

"You can't call her. You're right, she'll freak."

"Your dad, then."

Adam rubbed his face. "No, if you do that we'll all be in trouble, and it'll be even worse for Mom."

"Then what did you have in mind?"

He shrugged and looked sullen.

Libbie knew what he had in mind. Help and rescue. Not only for himself, but for his loved ones.

"Okay. I have an idea. I'll call your mom. I'll say I'm calling to say hello. Been a long time since we talked and all that stuff. I'll see how she sounds."

"If she sounds okay, then what?"

"I don't know yet. A step at a time? Deal?"

"Deal."

"You hungry?"

He nodded.

"Go check in the fridge and grab yourself something. I'll call your mom."

He stood, and Max followed him into the kitchen.

Libbie stared at the phone. She hadn't spoken to Liz since that last awful day, the day when Tommy threatened the children...or she believed he was a threat. The result was the same—a dreadful and bloody day.

She dialed Liz's number.

What would she do if Liz didn't answer at all? She might not. She might choose not to answer if she saw Libbie's number on the Caller ID. Or maybe she was out with the cops and the canine units searching the woods and the neighborhood for her son.

"Hello?"

A small voice. A child's voice.

"Audrey?"

"Yes, ma'am?"

"It's Aunt Libbie."

Silence.

"Adam's here. He says you know about his…trip."

Silence.

"Audrey, if you're nodding your head, I can't hear that. Is your mom there?"

There was a quiet shakiness in her voice. "Mommy is tired. She went to bed." Then in a stage whisper that anyone nearby could've heard clearly, she added, "He's okay? I was worried he might get lost or hurt or something."

If eagle-eyed and sharp-eared mommy Liz hadn't heard Audrey's version of a whisper, then she really was upstairs and probably out cold.

"Audrey. Is mommy just tired? Did anything

else happen?"

"She's sad, Aunt Libbie." No pretense of a whisper this time.

"I'm coming over, Audrey."

"No, I don't want to get in trouble."

"Why would you be in trouble? I'm allowed to visit or call my cousin. No law against that. No need for you to tell her we spoke if you'd rather not. I'm bringing Adam home before his lie blows up and causes no end of chaos." Libbie said those words staring straight at him as he stood in the kitchen doorway with a half-eaten bologna sandwich. "Then we'll see what we see. Okay?"

Silence.

"Audrey? You still there?"

"Oh, yes, ma'am. Should I tell her?"

"If you want to. Say I called and that I'm coming to visit this evening."

"Okay." The relief in her voice was obvious.

"I'll see you in a little while."

"Bye."

Libbie looked at Adam. "Why didn't you just ask me?"

He didn't answer. He chewed.

"If I'd known there was trouble, I would've come."

He offered, "I could stay here while you go."

"Stay here without your parents' permission? I think that's called kidnapping. I love you but not enough to volunteer for jail time."

He smiled. "You kinda did though, before. Right? You could've gone to jail when Tommy got hurt, and that was for us, to protect us."

Libbie didn't like being reminded about it, but at least he remembered why it had happened. "Wipe your face and hands and grab your bag. Do you need to go to the bathroom? Go, anyway. It's a long ride."

"Yes, ma'am."

She knew she'd been played, but sometimes maybe that was okay. It wasn't easy to face scary stuff and give it a voice by asking straight out, not when it concerned something so close and vital as one's mother and family. And for a child to feel like it was up to him to handle it? Her stomach twisted and her face burned. She hadn't been a stranger to that herself. No matter how long ago, such things stayed with a person.

"Can Max go?"

"No, he may not." She filled his bowl with food and water. "Max stays here. You button your coat and let's go."

Doubt assailed her as she drove. Adam was nervous, too. She thought he was apprehensive, but also relieved. Aunt Libbie to the rescue? It scared her that someone could think of her that way. Her nephew...rather, her cousin's child, but Liz and she were almost as close as sisters a long time ago. Nephew felt more right than first cousin once-removed.

Libbie hated to let him down, for him to find out she wasn't up to that kind of trust.

"You know you'll have to tell your mom the truth? I won't go along with lying."

"She's going to be really angry." Then, in a matter-of-fact voice he added, "But she'll be so surprised to see you, she won't get that mad at me."

She wasn't so sure. "I won't take part in embarrassing her."

"Oh, no ma'am. I mean that I think she needs someone to talk to. Like a grownup."

"She has lots of friends."

"I guess that's true…but they aren't that kind of friends."

"What about your grandmother?"

"I don't know." He shrugged. "I didn't think about calling her."

Libbie was glad he hadn't seen his grandmother, being the person she was, as a refuge preferable to her. She felt a warm little glow.

It was a thirty to forty-minute drive to Liz's house in the daylight, longer at night when the snaking, narrow roads seemed less familiar, a different sort of landscape, until they reached Charlottesville and then suddenly they were back in civilization. Libbie liked the woods better.

The lights were on in the house, including the outside light. Audrey was at the window, so she must be standing on the sofa. Liz didn't allow that and Audrey was a rule-keeper.

"Humph."

"What, Aunt Libbie?"

"Nothing. Just thinking." She patted his arm and gave his hand a quick squeeze. "Got your stuff?"

"Yes, ma'am."

They exited the car in silence. Adam might be wondering how much trouble he was in, but Libbie was more concerned about the trouble they were about to stir up.

****

Liz opened the door, saying, "Why are you here?" She saw Adam standing behind Libbie and her jaw dropped.

"I brought Adam home. Let's talk."

Liz ignored her and reached around Libbie to grab Adam's coat sleeve. "Why aren't you at Billy's house?" She shook her head. "If you needed to come home, why didn't you call me?"

Libbie realized Liz really didn't get it. Now was the time to speak, but Adam beat her to it.

"I wasn't at Billy's house. I went to visit Aunt Libbie."

"You....what?" Liz stepped back. She looked at Libbie as if re-orienting herself.

Her hand fell away from Adam's coat. She put it to her forehead before turning away and walking down the hall and into the kitchen.

Libbie started to follow, but Audrey was there suddenly, with her arms around her hips, her head pressed against Libbie's abdomen, but Audrey didn't speak. Audrey, for whom the wealth of words available in the whole wide world could never be enough, who couldn't say the simplest thing in less than a verbal fountain and with a follow-up postscript, hugged her Aunt Libbie silently.

Libbie knelt. "Go with Adam upstairs, okay?"

She whispered, "Will you say goodnight before you leave?"

"I promise."

Audrey went up the stairs, following Adam, and Libbie walked straight back to the kitchen.

A house could look so normal with its lights on and everything neat as a pin with not a speck of dust or litter. The lights kept the shadows at bay in Liz's house. At least it did for Libbie, and as far as she knew, she was the only person in this family who saw such things.

Liz was turned with her back toward Libbie, facing the tea maker on the counter in front of her. She wasn't moving. Her hands were fists and they were pressed hard against the granite.

"Liz."

"Who told you? Did someone tell you?"

Libbie didn't know what to say. Since Adam had arrived with her, she thought the answer was obvious.

She spun around to face Libbie, then her shoulders sagged and she turned back toward the counter. The fists were gone. In a different voice, she said, "Go away, Libbie. I thought I made myself clear last time."

"You did. Now you need to make this clear to me—what's going on here? Why are your children so scared? Why are they so worried about you that they thought they had to manufacture a reason to bring me here to see you?"

Liz crossed her arms and hunched her shoulders. She seemed to shake herself, then turned to face Libbie.

"They are wrong. I am fine. My children are fine. We are all fine and we are no concern of yours."

"Say that again and make me believe it."

"I don't care what you believe."

"Well, you'd better because if I'm not certain that you are truly okay, then I can't feel confident about the kids' wellbeing. If I don't feel confident, then I will call Josh. I'll call him tonight. I don't care where he is or what he's doing."

She stared.

"Tell me. Now."

Her eyes started leaking. Not really crying. The wetness gathered around her lashes and traces slid along the contour of her cheeks. She pulled in a rough breath. She looked away and wouldn't meet Libbie's eyes.

What could it be, Libbie asked herself? Josh cheating? A drug problem? What on earth could possibly put such a dent in Liz's belief in herself?

Liz shook her head, still keeping her eyes averted. "I've been feeling a little sad, that's all. Nothing really. No reason. It happens."

Libbie stepped forward, wanting to offer comfort, but Liz flinched and Libbie held herself held back.

"How long has this been going on?"

Liz shrugged, still hugging her arms.

This time Libbie moved forward and grasped her arms firmly. "Stop it. Stop the excuses and hiding. Tell me what's going on. I won't leave until you do or until I call Josh."

She yanked free, shaking Libbie off, then collapsed forward, her head hitting Libbie's shoulder. Libbie expected her to cry in earnest, but she didn't. When Liz pushed away, she stepped back and pressed her hands to her forehead.

"I don't know, Libbie. I've had times

before…everyone does…but this time it won't let up. It gets deeper and harder. I want to shake it for the kids, for Josh, for myself."

"I never knew. Truly. I thought it was just me. You have those times, too?"

Her cousin gave a rough, short laugh. "Not like you. You own that wretched territory all on your own. I'm sad from time to time and I don't always know why, but it's no more than that."

Liz still had to show everyone, declare to the world that she was better than her poor, flawed cousin Libbie. Liz was still loved and still popular and envied by everyone. Anything less than perfect was no more than a momentary stumble in her blessed life.

Rude words rose in Libbie's mouth, but she strangled them. This wasn't about Liz and Libbie and their history. This was about the present, and Audrey and Adam's welfare.

Libbie didn't want to be unkind, but she needed to keep a little reality happening here, and she knew how best to get Liz's attention. She chose her words and attitude carefully.

"Oh, really? Well, I'm not the one who has children depending on her. Children who aren't feeling so good about things right now."

Liz covered her face with her hands. When she removed them, she said, "Josh is coming home tomorrow. I'll have a serious talk with him. Maybe I do need to get some help."

"You are suffering needlessly. And you have responsibilities. You have to be open with Josh."

She stared at Libbie. "I meant what I said, you know. I appreciate your concern, and I know this seems harsh, and I feel bad about it, but I haven't changed my mind about having you in the children's lives."

"Of course not." Libbie tossed her head to show she didn't care. "Never thought otherwise. Well, dear cousin Liz, don't you worry about me. I'll be perfectly fine on the sofa."

"On the sofa?"

"Sure. No trouble at all." Libbie peeled off her jacket and threw it onto the chair. "What time are you expecting Josh? I'll take off when he gets here tomorrow so you two can have a chat."

"There's no need for you to stay over."

Libbie ignored her and moved the sofa pillows to one end of the couch. "Do you have a blanket?"

Liz's voice was firm. "Thanks for bringing Adam home, but you should never have taken him in the first place. You need to leave now."

Libbie sank onto the sofa. Her resolve had weakened with each verbal assault. She would've gladly shown Liz her backside right then and there and slammed the door behind her, if not for Adam and Audrey.

"You need to listen closely. I'm not playing games here." Libbie waited a moment, allowing the pause to emphasize her words. "I didn't take Adam anywhere, except to bring him home. What you have to ask yourself, Liz— what you have to ask your son—is how he got out to Cub Creek and to my house. And while you're at it, why don't you ask yourself what would drive a wonderful boy like Adam to take matters into his own hands?"

Libbie stood and turned her back on Liz. She ignored her as she kicked off her shoes and plopped down on the sofa because, right at that moment, Libbie wanted nothing more than to hide her own face and shut Liz's out.

The stair treads creaked, then above Libbie's head, the sound of footfalls traveled from room to room. Low, undulating noises filtered down. They were unmistakably voices but the words were unintelligible. Libbie tried to gauge the tenor. Anger? Despair? Consoling? There was nothing alarming in the tone. She imagined Liz sitting at her son or daughter's bedside, smoothing the blankets as she did the final tucking-in. They were ten, of course, but tonight they needed extra soothing, as did their mother. At some point, listening to the even murmur of their voices, Libbie drifted off.

She woke during the night. The corner of the

sofa cushion was poking in her back. All was silent and the feeling was that of peace. Someone had placed a blanket over her.

Libbie closed her eyes against the dark and waited, opening her mind for whatever might be circulating in the air, and was reassured. She rose to get a drink of water and go to the bathroom. Before she settled back on the sofa, she decided to make a trip upstairs. There'd been a time when she was welcome in Liz's house, and she knew the layout well. She crept up the stairs, peeked in at each of the kids and they were sweetly sleeping. She stood in each doorway listening to the gentle breathing and the slight rise and fall of their chests, before she moved on.

Liz's door was closed and Libbie let it be. She went back down to resume her own rest.

****

Liz scrambled eggs (free-range) and turkey bacon and gluten free toast for breakfast. Libbie sat at the kitchen table with the children while Liz served them. To all appearances, everyone was okay, including Liz.

Libbie knew it wouldn't last because no one was ever totally free of negative yuck, and apparently, she and Liz were more alike in how they dealt with it than Libbie had known. Libbie could see Liz's equilibrium had reasserted itself. It was the same for her after her own, wilder, mood swings. Been there, done that, Libbie told herself. She'd already forgiven Liz for her mean words even though Liz hadn't asked for forgiveness and wouldn't thank her for it, if she knew. Libbie looked at the sparkle in Audrey's eyes and the flush of color on Adam's face, and didn't regret the awkwardness the night before with Liz, nor the rough night on the couch.

"When's Josh getting back?"

Liz shot her a hard look. "Today."

Adam asked, "Today?"

His expression raised Libbie's suspicions.

"That's right." Liz frowned in a mocking sort of way and looked at Adam. "In fact, I called him last night and told him we missed him and needed him home." She turned to Libbie. "Thanks for bringing my son home."

"My pleasure."

Liz looked at her. "I know you're in a hurry to get home."

Libbie was tempted to deny that, to suggest she could stay and visit all day just to annoy Liz, but then she remembered Max. Inside. He was good but when it came to temptation in general, or the call of nature specifically, but his capacity for good manners and self-restraint was limited.

"Max. Yes, I should be leaving." Libbie tried to measure what the kids were really feeling.

When Liz spoke to them, when she came near or touched them, Libbie saw no masking of expression on their faces, no turning away, nothing of concern. Nothing that reminded her of her own childhood interactions with her grandmother.

She gave them all kisses and hugs—no packing needed—and said goodbye.

Sensing no imminent issues and actually trusting there were none, were two different things. As much as she cared about Liz, she didn't necessarily trust her, especially in this current state. When Libbie was out of sight of the house, she dialed Josh. No answer, but she left a voicemail.

"Josh. It's Libbie. I was at the house and Liz says you're due home any moment, so I'm on my way back to Cub Creek and sorry to have missed you. I'm concerned about Liz. I think you know what I'm talking about. I want to touch base with you. Give me a call."

Before Libbie reached home her phone rang. The call picked up on the dashboard and she hit the answer button. "Hello?"

"Libbie. Josh, here. I got your message."

"Josh? Why is it you never call from the same number? I thought you were a telemarketer. Almost didn't answer."

"You don't sound like anything is wrong."

"You tell me. What's up with Liz?"

"She hasn't been herself lately. Did she call you?"

"No."

"Oh, well I'm sorry about that. I encouraged her to talk to you. This all started after the...the event at your house. She hasn't been right since. Nothing serious, but you know how she is. Anything less than perfection worries her."

"Okay. Not sure what to say about that. Liz likes to project perfection, but she's as flawed as anyone else."

"Thank Margaret for that. Liz holds herself to impossible standards. I think this time it all fell apart for her."

Libbie softened her tone. "She has you and the kids. If I know anything about being sad or depressed, and I do, she'll be fine, but make her get help. Make her talk to a professional. You all have too much to lose if she doesn't."

Josh's voice dropped, and his tone also softened. "She's not as strong as you. Never has been." After a moment, he added, "As for being depressed, I've never thought of you that way." He laughed. "Volatile, yes, but not depressed."

"Seriously, Josh, it can happen to anyone. You might be shocked if you knew how...well, how bad it can get. We all need help from time to time."

"You've been through a lot this year." His

tone had changed. "And you're still here and still helping. Shows how strong you are. Thanks for watching out for our family."

"Keep me informed this time. Okay?"

"I will."

"And, Josh, my recommendation?"

"Yes, ma'am?"

"Don't mention this conversation to Liz. Do insist she get professional help."

As they disconnected, the irony hit her. Liz had brought Dr. Barry Raymond to the house to help Libbie after their grandmother died. Libbie had needed someone to talk to. It occurred to Libbie now that when she told Josh Liz should talk to someone, she should've made clear that Liz should NOT talk to Barry Raymond.

Libbie turned into her driveway. She parked, gathered her purse and jacket, and climbed out. As she walked up the porch steps, she saw a small square of white peeking from between the front door and the door jamb. She slid it out, then opened the door for Max. He ran straight past her and down the steps to the nearest tree trunk.

She unfolded the piece of paper. The note read, "Sorry I missed you."

Jim. Here, while she was occupied with Liz's troubles.

She turned it over, examining both sides. There was nothing more.

What did it mean? Was he home again? He'd said he expected Matthew to spend a couple of weeks in rehab, so she'd guessed he'd be home closer to Halloween.

She examined the note again for any clue of intent.

Another quick trip home for business? He'd come by without calling first. Why?

Maybe he wanted to do that final breakup in person.

He was that kind of man. Honorable.

She dropped her purse on the settee and sat beside it. Max joined her on the porch, but wouldn't settle. He seemed anxious. He was probably worried about his food dish being empty.

"In a minute, Max."

Being with Jim was like having a window thrown wide open onto a beautiful spring day with the air fresh on her face and birdsong all around. Closing that window would break her heart.

Max whined. She looked down, but he wasn't looking at her. He was staring toward the woods.

Great. Trespassers? Hunters? Coyotes? Probably nothing more than deer. Beyond those woods and around the curve of the road was an abandoned house. The closest thing she had to neighbors was the Pettus family across the road and their home was situated on the far side of the horse pastures.

Feeling a chill, whether from the morning air or something else, had an easy fix. She stood, picked up her purse and went inside. Max ran off, not into that area of the woods, but rather around the house to the back.

She went inside and locked the door behind her.

Through the kitchen window, she saw Max sniffing the terrace, mostly around the wrought iron table and chairs.

As quick as the locked was flipped, Max was on the back stoop and at the kitchen door, probably remembering that empty dish. After she filled the dish, Libbie went out to the terrace herself. She stood near the table, she touched it, and considered whether Jim had been here, maybe waiting for her before he gave up and left the note. Something glittered on the terrace stone from under the edge of a poplar leaf. She pushed the leaf aside with her shoe.

A coin.

She picked it up.

From Italy. 100 lire.

Shock shot up her arm like a burning nerve ending.

She closed her eyes. Dark blue swirled in her vision and words flashed into her head. "Jim was in Sicily, too." But that meant nothing. This color, this feeling, would never be connected to Jim. Instead, she saw the table at the trattoria. Barry had held something in his hand. It had come from his pocket with his wallet....

This coin was pre-Euro. Not something Jim would carry around. Adrenaline burned her flesh. She went into the middle of the yard and turned, trying to see through the forest, into what might be hiding there.

"Barry Raymond? Are you here?" She shook the fist in which she held the coin. "Is this yours? Come out, you coward. I have questions for you."

Nothing. No one. No answer. Finally, the sound of whining penetrated. Max was stuck inside. He was unhappy, probably at missing out on the show. She was still angry, but she was also glad that there was no one here to see or hear her.

Barry. He'd been out here that day when she and Jim had had the awful fight. But she'd been out here a dozen times since and there'd been no coin on the stones.

The note. It had been from Jim, right? There hadn't been a name on it. She was in the kitchen before the thought finished. She grabbed the note from the counter and examined it. Yes, Jim. She knew his handwriting.

The note hadn't been there last night, so Jim

must've come by this morning.

Barry could've come by anytime, even yesterday. She hadn't been on the terrace late yesterday because she'd been with Adam.

Now she did truly need to speak with Jim. She needed someone with cool intellect, someone who would listen and didn't always assume she was wrong. Maybe she could catch Jim at a stop between his flights back. Or maybe he was already back in California. The lovely thing about cell phones, she thought as the swiped it to turn it on, was that they ring wherever the person is. Wherever the phone is.

Jim's sweater was on the chair. As the phone rang she held the sweater close to her cheek, like a talisman or good luck charm. Maybe not too different from Barry's coin, and who, strangely enough, could be credited with prompting this call to Jim.

"Hello?" a woman said.

Libbie's heart paused. "Is Jim there?"

"Who's this?"

"If it's not a good time.... Is he there?"

"Are you a telemarketer? Because if you are—"

"No."

"Do you want to leave a message?"

"No." Libbie hit the disconnect button.

Jim's ex. Matthew's mother. Had to be.

She should've said, "I'm Libbie. Tell Jim I'm

on the line." She might have asked the woman how she was doing after the accident. That would've been adult and reasonable and sensible.

Libbie didn't feel reasonable or sensible. She wanted to know what that woman was doing with Jim's phone. And where?

The hospital? No, not the hospital. He couldn't be back in California already. But maybe he'd left his phone back there...at the hospital or the hotel.

Jim hadn't specifically said he was staying at a hotel, had he?

Maybe he's busy with more than Matthew...or maybe he and the ex are flying together. Maybe he left his phone at her....

"Shut up," Libbie yelled out loud to shout down the poisonous words filling her head.

"Where are you, Jim?" She threw his sweater across the room. It caught on the edge of the coffee table, then fell onto the floor. She wanted to throw her phone, too, so badly that she gripped it tightly lest it fly off on its own.

She closed her eyes and fought for calm.

Chapter Six

The next morning, Libbie came out of the house, keys in hand, and found paw prints on the hood of her car. Little roundish prints, small pads, slightly dirty and stenciled in the morning dew. They continued delicately up the windshield to the roof.

Definitely not a squirrel or raccoon. A cat? She'd never seen a cat around here.

Libbie carried a box of candy for Joyce. Dark chocolate. As thin as Joyce was, the calories wouldn't hurt and dark chocolate was good for the heart. Health food. Libbie put the box into the car and went back inside for a soft, clean rag.

The dew was still wet and the marks wiped off easily. She tossed the cloth onto the back floorboard.

Joyce was half-napping, her head nodding forward, then jerking back up. She'd picked a hard, wooden bench in the narrow hallway to sit on. She had that stubborn look on her face despite being more than half-asleep. Her head eased forward again. A soft snore erupted.

Libbie sat next to her and touched her shoulder. "Joyce?"

Her eyes opened, but were slow to focus. Libbie waited until she saw recognition dawn.

"How are you?" She put her arm on the top of the bench, lightly across Joyce's shoulders. "This is an awkward spot to nap."

"Nap? I wasn't sleeping."

"And you aren't in a cranky mood either, I guess?"

Joyce wagged a thin, crooked finger at Libbie. "You are a rude girl."

"I don't think I qualify for 'girl' anymore and I do recognize cranky. Takes one to know one, right?"

"Not my fault. They're always telling me what to do. Go here. Sit there. Today I said no." She stabbed her finger into the seat beside her hip. But the bench was hard, and she said, "Ouch."

"Could we find somewhere more comfortable to sit and visit?"

"I'll stay right here, thank you very much."

"Okay. Suit yourself, but I don't know who it benefits to be miserable on this bench."

An aide, working at a rolling medicine cart a short distance down the hallway, looked at Libbie and grimaced. Her face expressed a lot.

"Well then," Joyce grumbled, "take me somewhere better."

Libbie stood and with a hand on Joyce's arm, she helped her rise.

"Here's your cane."

"I can stand by—" Her words broke off. Her gaze was fixed on the box of chocolates. "How about the sunroom?"

Nothing like chocolate to smooth out mood rumples.

Joyce settled in her corner chair. Libbie sat and worked the cellophane from the box as she asked, "Did Alice have a cat?"

"Cat?" Joyce looked blank, then shook her head. "No, only Max."

"I haven't seen cats around the property before, not until this morning."

"Maybe feral. Likely, it was dropped off. City people. Maybe suburb people, too, get cats and dogs and then don't want 'em. Ain't got sense to know better, or maybe can't find 'em a new home, so they drive them out to the country and drop 'em off."

"How awful."

She shrugged and shook her head. "Oh well, I guess so. Most of 'em end up run over or small pets, like cats, go feral or get eaten by coyotes."

"Eaten," Libbie repeated. "The coyotes eat them?"

"If they're small and not smart or fast enough. House cats, you know. They get sick or hurt and can't get away so good, especially if they don't have their claws." She held one of the chocolates in her hand. "Or tires get 'em, like I said." She bit into the chocolate.

"Terrible."

"True to a point. But if they ain't fixed and start breeding unabated, well, that's a whole other problem. They go after poultry and such. Dogs go after bigger stock, like goats. And then there's rabies." She popped the rest of the chocolate tidbit into her mouth and chewed slowly, her expression easing into pleased.

"Rabies." Libbie shook her head. "Honestly, Joyce. I thought living in the country would be peaceful, but all I'm hearing about these days are hunters and guns and bears and packs of wild dogs and cats with rabies going after goats."

"I reckon you're being funny, huh?" Joyce dabbed at a speck of chocolate at the corner of her mouth. "Nobody ever said country life was boring. Leastways, no one living in the country ever said it." She held out her hand.

"One more? Lunch is soon, I think." Libbie held the box closer to her. "You can put the box in your room and save some for a snack or dessert." Libbie placed the box on the small table next to her chair.

"You gonna mention Jim or what?"

Libbie shrugged and spread her hands.

"Jim? I miss him."

Joyce tilted her head and eyed Libbie. "You two made it up yet?"

"We weren't at odds. At least, not until…we had a disagreement." Libbie shook her head. "It was over nothing and got messy fast." She tried to keep her voice even. "It's not just the two of us and we aren't kids. We bring history and family with us."

"Like I said."

Libbie nodded. "Maybe we did move too fast."

"Maybe. I've known some, though, who moved too slowly and missed their chance at happiness. Some get scared when stuff if going good. Don't trust it, you know. They expect unhappiness."

"Human nature?" Libbie shrugged. "Jim and I will work it out, or we won't."

"Sounds like you don't care."

"I do care and I'm rooting for us. But I also want what's best for Jim." She shook her head. "Maybe I am crazy. My grandmother said I was, and ungrateful, too. She said I never appreciated what people, meaning herself, did for me."

"Sounds like she wanted credit for stuff she didn't earn. No, that ain't you, and no, you're not crazy, but your heart has failed you."

"My heart?"

"Not the first time I've seen it. Not my first go round, you know."

"Never thought so."

"If it's a guy, they call it cold feet. For a woman...." She scanned the bright room as if the words were hanging from the ceiling corners.

"Cold feet for women, too?"

"A guy thinks about what he's losing, all that running around town with his buddies, and girlfriends and such that he's already bored with, and he gets cold feet, but a woman thinks about what she's taking on." Joyce tapped her temple with a bony finger.

"I admit I've always been more comfortable doing things my way. When I wasn't happy, at least I was unhappy by my own actions or responses. It's scary to give that up. Maybe that's true for Jim, too."

"What? Hard to give up being scared and unhappy and alone?"

"Not exactly what I said, but commitment is always scary." She sighed. "I miss him. Ultimately, having him with me is worth the risk. The risk to me, anyway. I'm not at all sure about the risk to him."

"Risk of a broken heart, you mean?"

"Sure," Libbie said. "For both of us. Maybe more."

"Like what? You got something else on your

mind?"

She'd heard Libbie's equivocation. Libbie searched for something reasonable to fill the gap—something not involving Aunt Margaret and her belief that it was dangerous to care about Libbie. She said, "Liz has some sort of problem."

"Husband or kid? Sweet kids. I remember that little red-headed girl."

"The children are fine. It's Liz. She's a little down. It happens. I should know, right?"

"Well, you'll talk to her. Straighten her out."

"I tried." Libbie shook her head and shrugged. "I don't think I helped any. I told Josh she should get therapy."

"Why sure. 'Course it depends on whether she's upset about something specific or just generally glum." She picked up the chocolate box and held it, as if speculating. "If it's specific she might be able to fix it once she can see past it."

"Sounds like it's been going on for a while. I got the feeling that it's been worse since the day Tommy got hurt and Liz was so angry with me."

"I heard all about that. Quite the sensation around here."

Libbie pulled back. It felt like her muscles were drawing in. She wanted to make a sharp, clever remark about how some people got a kick out of the misery of others, but she pressed her lips together instead.

"Don't think I cain't see that look, missy. Might as well call it out. Talking about stuff takes away its power."

Libbie frowned.

"That's right. Power." Joyce waved her hand. "You want something to own the power to hurt you? Keep it hidden. You didn't do anything wrong there and no sense in acting tragic. Even his mama has moved on. So what business is it of your cousin's anyway?"

"Her children...."

"Yeah? Well, you kept 'em safe. If she has a problem with you over that, then... Well, hey, I got it. Guilt."

Libbie shook her head. "You said I didn't do anything wrong."

"Her guilt. Guilt ain't usually about what's done wrong."

She refused to follow Joyce down that rabbit trail. "Do you mean she feels guilty for being mean to me?"

"Maybe," she said. "I cain't read her mind. A lot like her mama, that one, I'll bet."

"No. Well, maybe in some ways, but mostly, no. Liz has always been my friend. Like a sister." Libbie leaned forward, her elbow resting on the arm of the chair. She was suddenly out of conversation. She stared out the nearby window at the changing leaves.

"That's a beautiful red tree."

"Sweet Gum. Pretty enough in the fall."

Libbie prepared to stand. "I'd better move on. I have an errand to run. When I get back home, maybe I'll call Liz."

Joyce grabbed Libbie's hand. It was unexpected. Her hands were cold, but the joints were hard and hot.

"Have a care for yourself, Libbie. Things like sadness can be catching, especially if you're prone to it." She released Libbie's hand. "I've had my sorrows, you know. But you have to keep it in perspective."

"Thank you, Joyce, and don't worry. I'll remember what you said."

"There's the other thing, too. Some people suck the life out of you. That's what they do. Oh, they might feel bad about it, make excuses for it, and always have some kind of sad story or emergency, but it's really just to support their drama." She raised her hand and waved Libbie into silence. "I am not saying that's your cousin. Everybody's got some kind of drama. But it's up to you to figure out who's who and what you're willing to support."

Joyce gazed past her with an expression that seemed to promise more words of wisdom were on their way, so Libbie waited.

"I had a cat once. Only a barn cat, but he

was special to me. Not much of a dog person, myself."

Okay. Change of topic. That was probably as well.

"Never thought I was either. Not for dog or cat. But no Max? I don't know what I'd do without him."

Libbie stood and bent over to hug Joyce, mindful of her thin, fragile bones. "Shall I walk you back to your room? Or back to the bench in the hallway?"

"No. Think I'll sit here and soak up the sun a while, but before you leave, I want to point out that you didn't finish answering my question and I did notice."

"What question?"

"About Jim. I hear he called you, but you don't. Communication goes both ways, don't it? Not like the old days where a gal had to sit around and wait."

"What?" She gasped. She muttered, "I have tried." She shivered at the memory.

"You okay?"

"Who told you that Joyce? Who's talking about my personal affairs?"

"Dan. He stopped by to give me an update on Jim's boy."

"Dan should mind his own business."

"Libbie?"

She twisted around. There he stood. For

how long?

Libbie looked back at Joyce who didn't seem at all surprised. She turned back to Dan. He was holding his deputy hat.

Dan nodded. "I came that day to give Joyce an update on Matthew. I apologize. Didn't intend to mess in your business."

"You are ill-informed, so allow me to correct you. Since Jim and I...had our disagreement...there's been one note from him. No calls. I tried to call and...didn't get him."

"Again, my apologies. He was home arranging physical therapy and additional rehab for Matthew. I saw him briefly. He looked tired. Hopefully things will settle down for him, for you both, soon."

Why did he make her feel like a rude bully? She looked at Joyce again and saw a tiny smile curving her lips. Joyce was stirring the pot and Libbie felt like the soup.

She stood taller. "Dan, in the future, if you have anything to say about me or my personal business, please say it directly to me and not to others." Feeling slightly more dignified, she turned back to Joyce. "I'll see you soon."

She left Joyce there with the sunshine framing her and the box of chocolates on her lap, and Dan still standing with his hat in his hands.

Joyce raised her hand in a wave. Libbie tried

to walk, not run, through the building and down the hallway to the front door.

She sat in the car outside of the Home, feeling dazed and distracted.

What Joyce had said was true. How much of her own well-being had she tied to Liz's success in life? Instead of finding her own success or happiness? Or because she had failed and was saved by the knowledge that at least one of them was happy and successful? Libbie had sometimes resented Liz's success and the way she wore it as if entitled.

She minded. She didn't mind. She wanted Liz to be happy. She wanted it for herself, too. Liz had been there for Libbie when things went disastrously wrong with Grandmother. Liz had also been there to support her when she moved into Alice's old house on Cub Creek.

Libbie had made a new life here and when Liz left her behind that last time, it had hurt, but not as dreadfully as it might have because, lucky for Libbie, life had followed her here to Cub Creek and attracted still more life. It hit Libbie like a bolt—despite the present trouble with Jim, she was as close to happy as she'd ever been in her life.

Despite her goofs. Despite the wrongs of others and her own fears. There was forgiveness. Even with Jim. Nothing in Libbie believed that they were truly over. In the meanwhile, Libbie wanted to pay some of that good stuff back. Misery might like company, but so does happiness. She was a gal in need of an opportunity to celebrate. And she wanted that to be with Jim.

No sign of Dan yet.

But his cruiser was parked near her car, so he knew she was here.

She started the engine and drove away.

****

Libbie checked her phone again for missed calls or texts, just in case. She saw a couple of missed calls, but none since their argument.

She took her early supper, a sandwich, out to the terrace. She brushed the stray dry leaves from the wrought iron chair and table and settled there.

Jim wasn't here, but she had her house and property—her special place here at Cub Creek. She had Max. Not many neighbors, but they were friendly. And Joyce, of course. It was a far cry from her life before Cub Creek.

While she was in this sort of relationship hiatus—this waiting time—she toyed with the idea of tracking Barry Raymond down. She'd like to tell him a thing or two and get rid of him for good. Knowing he'd been here twice, uninvited and unwanted, was creepy. She couldn't go to the local police because of

Dan…and, really, what could she complain about anyway? It was legal for people to come by the house and knock on her door, and petty to complain about someone waiting on the terrace, especially someone she knew.

Checking up on Barry might be a better mission for her attorney. He had resources and options that she didn't. She'd have to give it some thought. Hopefully Barry wouldn't be back.

Jim was gone from her life. Jim wasn't gone. Gone. Not gone. Another leaf, a large one from a tall tulip poplar, floated down practically landing in her plate. She picked it up to examine the perfection of the veins, the softly rounded shapes within the leaf, still perfect. Not perfect. A crack had appeared in the fragile, brittle remains. She pulled at it and a portion of the leaf broke off along the veins.

"He loves me." Libbie pulled away another section of leaf. "He loves me not."

It wasn't a question of love, but more of expectations and needs, and the framework of human nature itself. She tried to smile, to lighten her mood, but gloom was here to stay for a while. Not for long, she hoped. It was sad to acknowledge, but almost everything passed with time. Love, trust, even shame. That she knew, for sure. Guilt, though. For her, that was her personal noose.

****

It was a few days before she got up her nerve again. She held his sweater again and went out to the porch where the sun touched her face and the sounds, scents and hues of Cub Creek were all around her. She dialed his number.

"Hello?"

A woman again. Not the same one.

"Is Jim there?"

"Uh. No. This is Nina, Jim's mother. Libbie, is that you?"

Confusion hit her. Was his mother now in California?

"Is Matthew...? I hope Matthew is recovering well?"

"Well, that's real sweet of you to ask. He's still in some pain, but working hard at his physical therapy and coming along."

"You're in California, too?"

"Oh, my, no. He's home now. Both of them, I mean."

Embarrassment. Awkwardness.

Nina picked the conversation back up. "Yes. Jim's over at the nursery. He forgot his phone. I heard it ringing, so... I recognized the ring. The one he has for you."

She felt sixteen, like she was making prank calls and been found out. "I wanted to let Jim know I found his sweater." Into the silent pause, she added, "He might be missing it."

After a short delay, Nina Mitchell, said, "Sure. Of course. Very thoughtful of you. Shall I tell him to call you back?"

"Um. No, that's fine. Let him know about the sweater, okay?"

"Certainly. I hope you're doing well, Libbie?"

"I'm fine. Just fine. Thanks." Libbie hung up. Maybe not even sixteen. Maybe more like an embarrassed thirteen-year-old.

Jim was back. Apparently to stay.

Where did that leave her? Well, she was in the dark and it was time for her to get a clue. Jim had done his thinking. It appeared Jim had decided. And she was the one left out in the cold.

He loved her not.

Chapter Seven

Libbie had her music turned up while she cleaned the kitchen. It wasn't something she generally admitted, but she liked to wash the floor. The clean smell, the pristine look as it dried...it felt whole. Neat.

She turned to dump the pail into the sink and saw a man standing on the terrace.

No, not Barry.

Dan. He was in uniform.

She hadn't heard anyone knocking. Maybe the music....

Was he intending to resume the short, awkward exchange at the Home? Seriously? More likely, he was annoyed that she was making Jim unhappy.

Who would ever have guessed that she, Libbie Havens, would be a femme fatale carelessly breaking hearts across Louisa County?

Libbie stopped at the storm door. Dan was standing in the yard between the terrace and the soot-streaked concrete pad of the used-to-be garage. Standing and staring. She was wearing her house-cleaning jeans and a t-shirt. Her hair was all over the place. It didn't matter. It was Dan. And he wouldn't be staying long.

She stepped out onto the back stoop and said, "Hey."

He turned to face her. "Hey yourself."

"Something wrong?"

"Not with me," he answered.

She stiffened. "What's that supposed to mean?"

He took off his hat. "I wanted to check on you. See if you're doing okay. You were pretty angry the other day."

"Do you blame me?"

"Can't say I do."

He was so very polite, not acting like anything was amiss.

Libbie wanted to stay angry, but instead, the memory rose that, not so long ago, she'd touched his arm and had admired the blue cotton shirt he liked to wear when off-duty, and she remembered how the fabric had felt beneath her fingers. At the time, she'd thought they were falling in love.

"Can I get you something to drink? Iced tea or water?"

"No, thanks. I can't stay."

She stepped down onto the terrace. "What can I do for you?"

He nodded, but didn't move closer. Instead,

he pointed at the concrete pad.

"Are you going to do something with that?"

She answered carefully, unsure of his question. "It's rained a couple of times. It'll probably take more than that to rinse the soot off all the way." She was grateful the garage was gone, but it seemed wrong to thank him out loud for something he'd done that she was pretty sure was illegal, her property or not, favor or not. Besides, she could be wrong. That conversation with Jim seemed distant now. She might have misunderstood his meaning.

"Why do you ask?" She walked past him, pulled a chair out, and sat. "You have any ideas?"

Dan joined her at the table, after all. He sat, but leaned forward, his elbows on his thighs, his hands looked ready for action. He nodded toward the concrete pad.

"Ever wonder why they put it there? In that location, I mean."

"Why not? It's a clear path from the driveway."

"But not near the house. For all the cover it provides to the driver, you might as well leave your car in the driveway."

"Why are you worrying over it?" Libbie asked, puzzled.

Dan ignored her question. "He probably put it out there for a place to tinker. Alice's husband, Roy, I mean. Maybe to work on his car or build something. Away from the house. By himself."

"To get away from his wife?" she joked.

He shrugged. "Women. They're inexplicable sometimes."

Now Libbie was seriously annoyed. "If you have a point to make, please do so. I repeat, why are you worrying over it?"

"No reason. I was standing there, thinking. You could break it up or build another garage or storage shed over it. It's good-sized. You could use it as a dance floor if you gave a party or something."

A party? He appeared to be totally serious. Curiosity at his odd behavior kept her focused on him.

"I was thinking it might be over top of an old well or septic field, and placed in that spot to cover it up."

Libbie leaned forward to better see his face. "The septic field is over on the far side of the house. Are you feeling okay, Dan?"

"Well, it is now." Dan ignored her question, and waved his hand toward the concrete pad. "Could be an old tank under there. Thing is, if you break it up and haul it out, you might find yourself with a bigger headache to handle."

"Dan. Look at me."

He did.

"What's this about? You aren't here to speculate about what might be under my concrete."

"No, I guess it comes down to whether it's better to build on the old, or start fresh. He leaned back in the seat, smiling for the first time. His brown eyes were dark, yet warm when he smiled that way, and they promised mischief.

She tried to keep her own lips from curling up in response. She was annoyed at him. She needed to remember that. She said, "No worries, Dan. You've convinced me. The concrete pad will stay right where it is. We'll keep it for the party."

Max came jogging out of the woods and joined them on the terrace. He glanced at Libbie and went straight to Dan, leaning against his leg. Dan scratched around his ears.

"What party?" Dan asked.

"No party. You're the one who mentioned a party."

"You two ran off to Italy so quickly that no one had a chance to…to say anything. Or offer good wishes. Pretty selfish, if you ask me."

"Selfish? You know Joyce lied to the reporter, don't you? Jim and I aren't engaged." Clearly, he did know. "It started out as a simple trip and now–" She stopped. She'd gotten off track. "What's gotten into you, Dan Wheeler?"

"Well, I'm thinking…and it's none of my business, of course."

"Of course."

"I was thinking that if you had an official engagement party, then people would have the chance to congratulate you, support you two, because face it, it's not so easy for people your age to jump into marriage."

"My age? What age?" Now she was angry. "I'm younger than you are. You talk like I'm Joyce's age."

Maybe it was the tension between them, but Max walked off and sprawled on the steps to the backdoor.

Dan watched him walk away. He shrugged. "Set in your ways, and all that. Jim, too. So, another thing about a party and being so public, it might make it harder for you to back out when you get scared."

His expression had changed, had become directed and somber. And targeted at her.

Plunk. Her anger, her curiosity…all of it hit the pit of her stomach with a solid, sour splat. She rose to her feet. "We're done here."

Dan reached over and put his hand on hers. "Something to think about."

She shook his hand away. "You should talk to Jim."

He picked up his hat. "I wasn't thinking about Jim necessarily." He stood. "Though I suggest you do speak with him. The problem is that he isn't talking since he got home with Matthew. Anyone tries to talk to him, they're lucky if all they get is a cold shoulder."

"And you figure it's my fault?"

"Fault?" He shook his head. "Not about fault. Aunt Nina called to ask if I knew what was up. Remember, she lives with him. Not much fun. I didn't know, but I could speculate. Not to her, of course. Decided to ride out here and see for myself." He looked at the inside of his hat. "I remember that time when I tried to ask about your history, your grandmother. The cold shoulder that came my way was like an instant ice age."

"I was sorry we didn't make it, Libbie." He paused. "So I was thinking about Jim. He has a better opinion of human nature, in general, than me. Maybe more than most of us. Be a shame to see him persuaded otherwise."

She gripped the edge of the table. Wrought iron. He was fortunate it was too heavy for her to pick up and throw at him.

"Are you seriously suggesting that I'm bad for Jim? That I'll...I'll disillusion him about humanity?" That last bit ended on a high note.

Dan smiled. He twirled his hat on his index finger and then placed it on his head. "No, ma'am. Just suggesting you throw a party. Nothing like friends and family to help get things back on track." He nodded at the concrete base. "You know, you could build a whole new garage. Do it better this time."

He walked a few feet past her, then stopped and looked back, but without the smile. "Unless you really don't love him. If you don't, then for everyone's sanity, be blunt with him. Do the right thing and call it off."

"For your information, Dan Wheeler—not that it's any of your business—Jim is the one who called us off. If he did. If that's what he meant to do. And if he truly is unhappy about it, then he's the one who needs to make up his mind and declare it."

Her harsh words made no dent in Dan's composure.

"One last thing, Libbie. Someone's been talking to Jim. I don't know who, but I'm pretty sure it's not the right person. Not someone who's your friend. Speculation on my part. Jim shuts me down when I ask. That's really your business anyway, as you mentioned at the Home, so I'll keep out of it and let you get on with handling it."

She was speechless. In that silence, Dan turned back toward her and said, "Hope you're taking my advice."

Her temper nearly did her in. Before it could erupt, Dan added, "Make sure you and Max wear the orange garments. I see neither of you have them on right now. No time like the present, Libbie, to take care of business."

****

Dan left. She didn't know what craziness was churning in his brain, but her own was spinning wildly and her body was joining in. Her palms were perspiring. Her face felt flushed. Max joined her at the kitchen door as she opened it and beat her across the threshold. He went straight to his food and water.

She was so angry, so agitated, she paced through the rooms, along the entire circuit of kitchen to dining room to study to foyer to living room to kitchen and over again. What did he mean? Who'd been talking to Jim? His son? His mother? His ex?

Libbie couldn't settle to anything. Even the approaching sunset couldn't draw her in. She paced right out the front door and stood at the top of the steps, her fist against the nearest column. She was ready to fight something or someone. Adrenalin roared through her. She blamed Dan for what would come because when the adrenalin rush was done, the subsequent gully would try to suck her back in. She was always at risk of falling back into those dark times when everything seemed too hard, and nothing was worth the effort. Hopelessness.

But maybe not this time. Maybe this time she wouldn't break down. Maybe.

She'd left the front door open and Max had followed her out to the porch, making it past the storm door before it closed. He sat at her feet, perhaps sensing her panic, or maybe wondering why the heck she was standing out here staring across her front yard, and beyond the pastures opposite, when he was here and available for attention.

Libbie sat on the top step. Dan thought women were inexplicable? Well, men certainly were. What was all that crap about the concrete pad? Tear it up and risk finding a worse mess, a septic tank or well, beneath it. Build it better? A dance floor? Oh, that was for the party—for support and encouragement since she and Jim were so elderly and brought so much baggage. What had he said? Declare it to everyone and move forward?

Or let Jim off the hook.

The shame of it was that she, Libbie, was securely on the hook. She needed Jim to let her off definitively, because nothing less seemed able to convince her heart that it was truly over.

She'd never had trouble walking away before.

It was chilly outside and finally, her anger having burned itself down, she stood to go back in the house. The storm door was hanging open an inch or so. The pressure mechanism needed adjusting and it hadn't closed all the way. She pulled the storm door closed securely, making sure it latched, then shut and locked the front door.

****

For the rest of the afternoon, and into the evening, Max whined and cast accusing looks her way. It began to unnerve her until she realized he was probably picking up on her own leftover irritation with Dan. She vowed to relax—relax without crashing. She turned the television on and found an oldie but goodie movie. Turning up the volume, she went into the kitchen to make a roast beef sandwich.

When she sat on the sofa with her plate, Max leaned against her leg, his chin on her knee. He wanted to be invited up, but she couldn't always be a marshmallow. He'd taken a few steps backward in behavior recently. She blamed herself. He deserved consistency. Which, considering that she was the polar opposite of consistent, was a problem.

Max glanced toward the kitchen, then back at her.

"You already had your supper." She patted his head. "Settle down. We'll watch the movie and call it an early night. It's been a crazy day, hasn't it?"

Max huffed.

A tiny noise came from the kitchen. If not for Max's hyper-alertness this evening, Libbie probably wouldn't have given it a second thought.

Max looked up. Libbie looked down. Their eyes met. Max gave that little chuffing bark again.

She set her half-eaten sandwich on the coffee table. She rose and tiptoed across the living room to the kitchen door, reached inside and flipped on the switch.

Everything was fine. One chunk of Max's food was on the floor. Otherwise, all was as it should be.

Libbie stared at it, assessing. Max hadn't been in here since she left with her sandwich. The floor had been clear at that time. In fact, his dish was almost always empty.

Nothing else was out of place. She tossed the chunk of food into the dish and went back to the living room.

On the coffee table, her plate was empty. The sandwich was gone. Max hung his head in shame.

Great.

So, all was well, except for the sandwich. But suppose there had been a problem?

Loneliness hit her. Aloneness. She sat on the sofa again. If something had been wrong, there was no one to call for sympathy or help, for anything short of fire or robbers.

She turned the TV volume louder. The movie was stupid. Making it louder didn't improve it.

Max's nerves were getting on her nerves. She switched off the TV and said, "Let's go to bed."

Gladys's candle caught her eye. She stopped to breathe in the vanilla scent. It was fainter now than when it was new.

She felt restless, but nowhere near despair. "I think I'm going to be okay this time," she whispered.

Aunt Margaret's envelope was tucked beside the candle. No decision had to be made yet. Beside it was Barry's coin. That had yet to be addressed.

She stopped to let Max out. In the cold night air, she thought she heard coyotes calling. Their voices were high and thin and distant. She stepped out onto the porch. "Hurry along, Max." So far there hadn't been a problem with them, but there were no guarantees.

Max followed her upstairs and settled on his pallet. Throughout the back and forth of brushing her teeth and getting ready for bed. Max stayed edgy. He kept his eyes pinned on her.

She scratched his head and told him everything was okay and he settled down. She fell into bed. The pillows received her aching head. The silky pillow cases, and the plush, top-of-the-line feather quilt soothed her. Tomorrow would be better. The last sound she heard was in her own head—Jim's voice telling her everyone had down times, that it was normal. She pulled a pillow into her arms and curled around it. Through her closed eyelids, she saw a tiny, faraway light—Gladys's candle. Always a light on the far side. Tomorrow would be a better day. Everything always looked better in the morning light.

But morning was still many hours away when she woke.

She was lying awake in the dark. Why?

Libbie listened so hard her ears hurt. Max was asleep on the floor. He whimpered. He was dreaming. She dismissed it, and listened again.

There it was. A different sound. So soft that only her subconscious could have heard it and responded by waking her. She moved her head slightly, looking to one side and then the other.

From the foot her bed, two bright orange eyes burned through the dark.

Libbie screamed.

The quilt held her down. She fought it and Max was up and barking. He had gone into full-blown wolf howls by the time she escaped the feathers and cotton. Libbie fell to the hard floor, banging her knee.

Those eyes again, but now staring from the dark below the bed. She scooted away, scrambling to her feet, and jumped back onto the bed. She switched the bedside lamp on.

Max had ceased howling but was so agitated, Libbie was worried he'd start again. "Max. Here, fella. Come here."

He jumped onto the bed with a crazy mixture of fear and joy on his face. He'd never been invited up here before. He turned this way and that, until she pushed him down.

"It's okay, Max. Okay. Stay."

But it wasn't okay because something was beneath her bed.

What was she supposed to do?

The bed was a large, luxurious life raft, but it harbored a creature below it, one who'd actually been on top with her while she innocently slept. The light had gone a long way to calming Max, but he was now back to whining. He moved suddenly as, without warning, the creature from under the bed jumped up, digging in its claws into the quilt to pull itself back up onto the bed. It then stretched and gave a long meow.

It was mostly white with gray and tan thrown in on its head, body and paws. A cat.

Max stuck his nose perilously close to those claws, then, casting Libbie a look of accusation, he jumped down from the bed, and returned to his pallet. He kept his gaze on her.

"I don't have a cat." Libbie said to Max.

She said it again to the cat, who obviously believed Libbie was incorrect because it lay down on the quilt cover and stretched until it was nearly twice its normal length. The cat peeked at Libbie through half-closed lids.

A cat. The cat who'd left paw prints on her car a few days before.

He, she, it. The pronouns were annoying.

"For now, you're a she." Libbie left the bed and moved around to the foot.

There was no telling where this cat had been. She didn't belong on the bed, that was for sure, and Libbie wasn't done sleeping. The cat had to go.

Max perked up when she opened the door. Libbie came back to the bed to grab the cat. She would settle for shooing it out of the bedroom, if that was the best she could do.

Libbie reached for her and in a shot, the cat was up and moving. Quiet and quick. Back under the bed.

Now what? She considered trying to lure the cat out of the room with food, but with Max in the mix, that was pointless. He'd gobble anything remotely edible before it could work its magic on the cat.

Suddenly, it seemed too complicated. She was standing here in the middle of her bedroom in the wee hours of the night. Because of a stray cat. Which probably had fleas.

The bedding could be washed.

She climbed into bed, pulled the covers up, and reached over to switch off the light.

Max stood. With a disgusted chuff, he walked out of the room. She listened, but didn't hear him on the stairs. He'd gone to the guest room, the room he slept in when Adam was visiting.

Libbie was exhausted, but to tell the truth, she was also mildly amused. It would be fun to call someone in the morning and tell them her ridiculous story.

Yeah. Who? Well, she could tell Joyce. Joyce would appreciate the story. After all, Libbie was her entertainment, wasn't she?

Sometimes being alone sucked.

At some point during the night Libbie became aware of a weight near her feet, but that was it. Max woke her in the morning with his wet nose on her arm.

Images of a dream stayed with her as she reassured Max and slipped out from beneath the covers. Of the dining room. But finished. And furnished. Of warm light spilling across the wood and the faces of people sitting around it. She hugged it to her, at least mentally. It was almost a balm of healing, or maybe a promise of such, for the rest of the mess in her life.

Max barked.

"I'm coming." She pulled on her robe and looked back over at the bed.

The covers were disturbed, but there was no sign of the cat she didn't own, only the quilted wallow where she'd slept.

****

Libbie let Max out the back door and filled his food and water dish. The gloom of having no one with whom to share bad news or good news, lingered. When she opened the door to allow Max back in, the cat meowed and scurried outside, brushing Libbie's legs with her furry coat.

Was that goodbye?

She wandered into the living room and stood in front of the mantle.

Aunt Margaret's envelope.

She slipped the envelope from behind the candle and held it in her hands, feeling the fullness, the crackling of paper when she pressed on it. Was there really family out there? Her family? Other cousins? Aunts and uncles? It was hard to believe and almost impossible to embrace the idea. It would've been easy for her mother's family to have tracked her down if anyone had cared enough to try.

So. An opportunity perhaps? Have her attorney make discreet inquiries? He could check on Barry and on possible relatives. If she didn't like what he discovered, she could... or was following this path just another way of avoiding her present?

Alice, her predecessor here at Cub Creek, had intended to move to an assisted living in Charlottesville, but she never made it. Did Alice run out of time? Libbie could see the effect of time on Joyce. They all had expiration dates. Did she, Libbie, want to run out of time, too? She supposed it came down to the reason for the delay, plus the delaying reasons of the other party. For that, she had no answer.

****

The cat Libbie didn't own showed up for lunch. She meowed from the back porch loudly enough to be heard through the storm door and into the living room.

Libbie stood at the door and looked down. The cat wasn't shy at all with the door between them.

"I don't have cat food."

Did cats eat dog food? Probably not if they had a choice. Libbie scanned the pantry shelf. No tuna. A can of chunk chicken?

When she set the dish of food on the porch, the cat backed off. Libbie stepped down to the terrace and sat in a chair to put on her sneakers. Her new camera was on the table next to her. She had plans for fun. She needed some fun.

She looked back to check on the cat who was hunched over the dish and gobbling the chicken, all the while casting wild looks this way and that. Max had been out since early morning. Libbie hoped the cat would have a few minutes of peace in which to enjoy her food.

"Libbie."

She jumped to her feet. "Jim."

She wanted to fly forward, to throw herself into his arms. With the least encouragement, she would've. But the expression on his face—those eyes she loved, the lips which knew exactly the right way to kiss her, even his complexion, seemed off. Wary. He was wearing a jacket and he put his hands in the pockets.

"Sorry to drop by like this."

Her tongue seemed stuck against the roof of her mouth, her jaw felt rigid. She shook her head, needing the blood to flow, the muscles to move.

"I wanted to see how you were. See for myself. The last time, well, it was…was…."

"It was…not good." She tried to keep her tone calm. "You had a lot to deal with."

"Yes." He nodded. "The thing is, right now, it's still…things are still up in the air."

"I see."

"Matthew's wound got infected. He had to have additional surgery. Seems like it's all I do these days. Matthew. Work."

"I'm sorry about that." She'd shoved her own hands in her pockets. What was his purpose here? His demeanor, his voice, didn't have a happily-ever-after tone.

"I haven't forgotten about you, about us. When things are back on track...."

"When things are back on track?" She shrugged roughly, shaking her head. "What does that mean? Do you really expect things to get back on track? Does that happen in real life?" She bit her lip and held it.

"When things are back to relative normal, and we can talk and think things through."

"If you wanted to know how I was, you could've called." The sentence got louder with each word. Again, she tried to pull back the tension.

"I wanted to speak with you face-to-face."

"Haven't seen much of that either."

He frowned and shook his head. "Libbie, this may surprise you but it's not all about you. I missed you. I missed us. I came home and the first thing you did was try to hide an old...old acquaintance from me. I'm not a kid. This whole thing with my son has been exhausting. And, in the end, he needs me. It's that simple. My son needs me. When he's better...."

"Fine. Great. We'll talk then, I guess." The snarkiness in her voice silenced her. She looked down at her sneakers, then tried again. "Okay, Jim. Do what you have to do." She sighed. "You really have a lousy opinion of me. You think I'm too needy myself to help you take care of your son?" She took a deep breath. "I guess you're right, Jim. You do have some thinking to do."

"And you, Libbie. You need to decide what you want, too. And who."

He left. She stood, rooted, stunned by the image of him turning his back and disappearing around the corner of the house. She was so caught up in frustration, hurt, and disappointment, the air surrounding her looked all smeary and blackened.

Libbie set off at a run across the back yard. In her head, the words chased her, running with her.

You could've been kinder. You're running the wrong way. You're messing up your chance to work it out.

She followed the path through the woods, slowing to a walk as the low hanging branches and exposed roots, demanded her attention. Finally, she stopped to breathe and listen.

She hadn't seen or heard anything that warned of hunters in the area. She reached up. The orange cap was on her head. But she'd left the camera behind.

Max joined her. She heard him coming through the thickets and kicking up leaves in his wake.

She greeted him. "Next time I let you out, you have to wear your field jacket, Max."

Together they walked to the creek, Max broke away at different points, dashing off into the woods, then racing back again, scaring all the bunnies and squirrels for miles around. The leaves were multi-colored, many were already down and scattered on the path. They were crisp and colorful in an early autumn kind of way.

Libbie crossed the boards carefully. Not too fast, not too slow, or disaster—a cold, wet disaster—might result. The path up the slope through the Lady's Slipper clearing was seldom used. But something looked different.

At the top of the slope, the leaves were disturbed, the earth gouged. Tire tracks? Maybe a three or four-wheeler up here? It looked like they'd been braking and turning.

She scanned the area. The damage was less noticeable along the path beyond, but still visible. She returned to the clearing. They'd encroached here, too, but less so.

Hunters? Did that make sense? ATVs were noisy. The noise would scare the game away, wouldn't it?

Dan had said some of the hunters weren't too smart, especially the weekenders who came out from the city.

There were dark stains on the leaves. She knelt for a closer look. They were no longer wet, but might have been blood. Someone's boots had scuffed the earth, leaving tracks. She looked back down the slope toward Cub Creek.

They must have carried the kill to this point and used the ATV to haul it the rest of the way out of the woods.

Had they crossed her bridge? Trespassed on her property?

Suddenly she didn't care what or why, only that strangers had used her property without her permission. The earth had been marked and spoiled along her beautiful path. It wouldn't take much more than a few more boards to get that ATV across the creek, too.

Libbie didn't know who owned this side of the creek. Probably no one gave a thought to who owned any of this. It would all look like one big forest to strangers.

No matter what Dan said, she'd post signs. She'd buy a ton of them and nail one to each tree on her property line all the way around her fifteen acres.

The beat of anger started in her heart, quickened in her chest, and thrummed through her veins into her arms and her hands. In a matter of steps, she was back across the bridge to her side of Cub Creek.

She dug her fingers into the mud around the end of the board, the widest board, the one that Jim had helped her carry. She scrabbled her fingers deep into the mud and found the wood. She tightened her grip and pulled. The end came up with a sucking sound. Libbie's foot slipped in the mud and one leg went into the water, but with adrenalin fueling her, she recovered her balance in a heartbeat and backed away, tugging the board. When she had it mostly out of the creek, she leveraged it up. Heedless of filth and splinters, she grabbed it and with strength that rage alone could give her, she heaved the board away. It went up, then forward, and fell into the stickers and brush only a few yards away.

All the effort, the frustration.... She dropped to her knees. Her hands hurt, as did her arms. She hugged them to her. This wasn't about hunters or pristine paths. This was about hurt and emotion and control. Control of her life.

Margaret. Liz. Barry. Even Jim. Forget them. All of them. She was sending them all packing, back into that long ago, faded place where unwanted memories resided, with Grandmother and the other ghosts of her past.

The mud soaked into her jeans, chilling her knees.

Max licked her cheek. She put her arm around his neck.

"Okay, Max. I know. I do know. How many times, right?" She shivered, truly cold in contrast to Max's warmth. "As many times as necessary until I get it right."

After one last sniffle and sigh, Libbie rose to her feet.

"Let's go home, Max. Back to where we belong."

Chapter Eight

Libbie drove to Louisa to do some essential shopping. Among the items she purchased was a pink plastic cat carrier. The cat was NOT going to be happy with her. But some things weren't negotiable. The appointment with the vet was for tomorrow, assuming the cat was still hanging around.

When she returned home, she took care of a few quick tasks and settled at her desk to resume going through the photos of Sicily—the seemingly endless photos.

She heard a noise outside and looked up.

A familiar, shiny, expensive dark car pulled over to the far side of her driveway and parked almost out of sight.

Not Jim's truck.

Jim had disappointed her. Liz was no better. Libbie stepped out to the porch to greet her.

Her cousin looked reasonably well put-together in slacks and a silk top with a sweater. Libbie was glad to see it.

Had Josh told Liz about their conversation?

"What a surprise," Libbie said.

"Maybe I'm returning your surprise visit to me." Her voice was soft, almost too low to hear.

"I don't see the kids? Where are Adam and Audrey?"

"At school."

Liz's eyes were clouded with slight bags beneath them. Her hands were tucked into the folds of her sweater. That first impression of Liz's appearance didn't hold up on closer inspection. Her slacks were wrinkled with a stain on the thigh. Her makeup looked a day past fresh.

"Well, come on in. Let's sit down and have some coffee. Or tea. Whatever. Isn't school already out for the day?"

As Liz climbed the steps, she met Libbie's eyes for the first time. "My children are fine. You don't need to worry about them."

Libbie remembered their last encounter here, when everything had blown up. And more recently, at Liz's home, where nothing had really been discussed. Would Liz tiptoe around it all again? Maybe this time one of them would have something worthwhile to say.

Liz kept her arms and hands close to her body. There was no offer of a hug. No touching. Libbie stepped back and allowed her to proceed into the house, but once in the foyer Liz paused and shivered.

"Are you cold? Shall I turn the heat up?"

She shook her head, but ran her hands up and down her arms. Her shoulder bag strap slipped, caught on her forearm and bumped awkwardly against her legs. Her expression didn't change.

Libbie forced herself to move. She touched Liz's arm tentatively, as if her cousin might blow up or shatter.

"Talk to me, Liz."

She guided her toward the sofa. It was cushiony and brightly-flowered. For all her lack of sociability, Libbie was a comfort-creature person. She pulled the rose-colored throw aside and after Liz sat, she removed Liz's purse strap from her arm and put the purse on the coffee table. Libbie arranged the throw across Liz's legs. When she rested her hand on Liz's, for the first time ever, she perceived a color from her. Not around Liz like she'd heard people say of auras, but rather she saw it in her head. Like when she touched inanimate objects. With Liz, the color she perceived was a murky brown-gray. Like mud.

"Liz, why don't you lie down? Put your head on the pillow and your feet up on the sofa. Rest while I fix us something."

Liz moved as she was told. Libbie was alarmed to think she'd driven in this condition.

Her cousin Liz had always enjoyed the best of life. She had everything. Always perfect, always the girl, then the woman, that every other girl/woman envied. Watching Liz lie there on her side with her eyes closed…Libbie almost didn't recognize her.

Hot chocolate was the way to go. Chocolate could be considered medicinal and if it didn't cure you, at least, it tasted good. She pulled the canister of mini-marshmallows out.

They needed more than chocolate and marshmallows. Grilled cheese, maybe. She peeked around the doorframe. Liz was totally out.

Libbie seized the opportunity. She stepped out onto the back stoop and called Josh.

He answered with the first ring. "Libbie. Hi." His voice was low and brisk.

"Did you know Liz was coming here?"

"She left a note. I've been encouraging her to speak with you, like we talked about. I was with the kids at an after-school event. We got home and I saw the note. I guess I could've called to let you know… I was…all I could think about was what to tell Audrey and Adam."

"They're okay?"

"Sure. It's just that knowing their mom hasn't been herself…and this must be the first time she hasn't attended a school event with them. Ever. You know how children are. They always think that when something goes wrong with mom or dad, it's their fault." Josh paused, then asked, "What about you? Are you okay?" Josh asked. "With her being there, I mean? What did she tell you?"

"She didn't tell me anything. She lay down on the sofa and went to sleep."

"She hasn't been sleeping well. Maybe this will help."

"Josh, you're scaring me."

"Don't be, Libbie. I'm glad she went to you. It's been going downhill for her since that day when she told you to stay away. She was already edgy before that, but that seems to have been.... The last thing she needs is Margaret. That's the last person any of us needs." There was a long pause. "But we need Liz, back the way she was."

"Josh."

"If you two can work stuff out—"

"Are you kidding? Really? She needs to—"

He interrupted. "She's been to the doctor. Family physician. She said she didn't need more specialized help and that he agreed."

"Lovely. I guess the question is which Liz did he talk to? Not likely the one who's racked out on my sofa."

"Maybe. But he's the expert. I'll keep trying, if necessary, but sometimes they do more harm than good. Like with over-prescribing medications and such. Isn't this worth trying first?" After a long moment of silence, he added, "I can't manage without her."

Libbie felt like she'd run out of words. She searched her brain and came up with a platitude. "Everyone has down times. Maybe that's all this is."

"Let her rest, okay? Then talk. She has something on her mind. Guilt. Regret."

"Guilt?"

"Trust me, Libbie. She finally confided in me, at least in part. Please get her to talk."

She reassured him. "I'll try, but Liz has never been one to confess her shortcomings, not to anyone. Certainly not to me."

"I hope she will. If she doesn't, I'll tell you myself. But that won't help her, she needs to…clear her conscience."

This made no sense. The water came to a boil and Libbie moved the kettle off the burner before the whistle screamed.

"Josh, I can't make Liz do anything, but I'll try. Give the kids my love."

"Will do."

Libbie stood in the kitchen doorway. Liz was still sleeping.

Her hand dangled over the edge of the sofa. Her lips were parted, and her breathing seemed easy. Libbie went to the sofa, lifted her hand and tucked it under the blanket. Liz never stirred.

Max wanted out. He was sitting quietly at the

front door but staring at her. She opened the door and followed him out, closing the door softly behind them. Suddenly exhausted, Libbie sat on the wicker settee. The cat appeared from nowhere and jumped up. She meowed, almost like a warning, and then lay down, her tail slapping Libbie's thigh.

Well. Okay, then.

Max dashed down the slope toward the road, and stopped short to sniff around some bushes.

No one seemed in a hurry to go back inside.

Here at Cub Creek, sunset began beyond the far pastures. Soon, it would reach around to the sides of the sky. Libbie watched the colorful streamers of pink and lavender being born. Night would soon begin to creep out of the forest and across the rolling landscape.

A white pickup came around the curve. Libbie leaned forward. It slowed in the roadway but didn't stop. She forced herself to breathe.

Max was back, waiting to go inside. She opened the door and he went in. The cat, too.

Libbie watched, a bit mystified. Cats were very different from dogs. Dogs were much easier to keep track of and easy to please. As for the cat, Libbie had a feeling they'd struck some sort of bargain. But she had no idea what the terms of the deal might be.

She locked the door and stopped by the

sofa. Liz hadn't moved.

Libbie fixed two bowls, one for each, and set them down several feet apart.

Too close? No. Max set to eating immediately, and with gusto. The cat was a little slower to accept it, but finally tried a few delicate nibbles. Libbie had expected more uneasiness between them. There was distance, yes, and perhaps a wariness, but no sense of threat. That was it. No fear. For all she knew, they'd been running into each other outside and had their own little truce. Satisfied, Libbie went into the laundry room and came out with a white plastic pan filled with pine-scented litter.

She held it out toward the cat. "This is yours."

The cat watched, offered no expression that Libbie could read, but she did see it.

Libbie nodded toward the laundry room. "It's in here. For when you need it. Don't make me regret this."

The one-sided conversation with the cat felt light-hearted, a relief compared to the atmosphere that was creeping into the kitchen from the living room and making its way throughout the house.

The air was heavy. It seemed to drain the color, the clarity, the light, from the rooms, beyond what nightfall could do on its own.

She left the kitchen light on, but didn't turn on the light in the living room, lest it disturb Liz.

Libbie sat in the corner chair. The photo collections surrounded her. Roads, train tracks, a few fence rails, and then the precious ones of the kids. Soon the Sicily photos would join them.

There was a certain symmetry in this situation. Libbie had fallen asleep on that same couch more than once, wracked with self-doubt and despair. Something had changed inside her, first when she moved to Cub Creek, and then, weeks before that trip to Sicily when Jim reached across the wrought iron table, clasped her hand, and talked common sense. From a sad world to one that, regardless of geography, was colorful and full of life.

She wanted to speak with him now. She felt the aching need in her chest and hugged her arms close to her body.

Max joined her after a while. She didn't know where the cat went. Thinking of that, Libbie went quietly up the stairs and pulled the quilt from the bed in the guest room and carried it back down. When she tucked it around Liz, she stirred, and buried her face deeper in the pillow. Libbie didn't think she woke at all.

Her heart ached for her cousin and her family.

What had she, Libbie, gotten herself into?

How could she help Liz? She didn't even know what the problem was.

It didn't matter. Some things you signed up for on purpose. Some things signed you up without consulting you, and there it was. You just had to do the best you could.

****

Pain in her neck forced Libbie awake. She groaned as she pushed up to a sitting position. She'd fallen asleep in this chair and dawn was peeking through the draperies. The sofa was a dark jumbled mound of quilt and pillow. Somewhere in there, Liz was buried.

Libbie stared in the feeble light of morning, at the chaos where her cousin lay sleeping, and she almost panicked. What folly had allowed her to think she could help Liz fix her problem?

She crossed the room and stood over the sofa. She squinted, straining her eyes to pick out Liz's form. She knew before she touched the quilt that Liz was gone.

Libbie stood without moving, her hands over her heart, listening with her eyes closed.

The house was silent. Liz was gone. The house spoke resoundingly of being empty.

She looked out the front window. The back end of Liz's car was barely visible, but definitely there.

Libbie turned slowly, calling out, "Liz?" She

listened.

Nothing. Nothing, but there was a thin fragrance in the air. Cocoa from the night before? Libbie followed it into the kitchen.

Sunset happened at the front of her house. Sunrise happened in the back yard, but the thick forest blocked the horizon. The first hint of morning would come as the sun twinkled between the leaves and branches where the forest allowed, and then the sky would begin to lighten above the dark banks of trees.

This early in the sunrise, the sky assumed a deep shade of indigo, and among the trees the shadows were a dense deep green and black. Through the kitchen window, she had a clear view of the terrace and the wrought iron table. Morning mist hung above the ground. The scene was almost ghost-like. But no Liz was in sight.

Did she run away? Perhaps up the winding narrow road of Cub Creek Loop to be lost in the deep forest, or fall into the cold, rough current of Cub Creek?

Libbie stopped herself there. She was thinking of Liz as past tense and working herself into a spin over nothing. This wasn't some dark gothic novel, this was real life. Libbie tested the kitchen door. It was locked from the inside.

The dining room was next to the kitchen,

with only a short hallway in-between for the bathroom and laundry room. As she entered the dining room with its French doors and many windows, she saw Liz on the screened porch beyond, sitting on the swing. Not moving. She was sitting and staring at the dark woods. The rose throw was around her shoulders like a shawl. Her feet were bare. Her toes brushed the green painted floor planks.

Cub Creek wasn't far from the mountains and this was mid-October. The frosty feel would evaporate as the sun rose because autumn was still early in its season. Even so, at this hour, it was more than chilly.

Libbie retrieved the quilt from the sofa and returned to the French doors. She joined Liz on the porch.

Liz knew Libbie was there. She had to. Yet she gave no sign. Libbie wrapped the quilt partway around herself. When she sat on the swing next to Liz, she placed some of the quilt across her cousin's legs.

Liz shuddered. "I'm sorry." Her voice was hoarse.

"About what?" Libbie kept her tone light.

"A number of things. If you don't mind, I won't list them right at this moment."

"Okay."

"Don't misunderstand me. I'm not asking for forgiveness."

What did that mean? Libbie pushed stray hairs back behind her ear. Despite Liz's present trouble, Libbie noticed her hair was perfectly shaped. Liz had often said that a good cut could get a gal through a lot. She said it because Libbie didn't spend much time getting her own hair cut and styled.

Liz continued looking away.

Libbie said, "I don't understand any of this, but you can explain it if, or when, you want."

Her cousin shook her head. She pulled the throw closer, working her fingers into the folds seeking warmth. "What I mean is, I'm not asking for forgiveness because if I had it to do over again, I'd like to think I'd behave differently, but I'm smart enough to know I probably wouldn't. Plus, it's wrong for me to expect forgiveness."

"Well, that sounds cheery. Are you talking about how you cut me out of your life this past summer when I was trying to protect your children?" It was becoming harder to be patient, to keep her voice calm and even.

Liz shrugged. "We are who we are, right?"

"I still don't understand."

"The sum of our parts. Our genetics, our environment, our culture. It's all mixed together by the people who sire us, the ones who raise us. The people in our lives who influence us the most. It shows in our choices and our choices show in our actions."

"No, I disagree."

For the first time, Liz faced her. She looked angry. "That's not something you can disagree with. It's fact."

"Bull." Libbie readjusted the quilt, wishing it was physically possible for her to pull her feet up under it, but sharing the swing made that movement impossible. "We are more than that. As thinking, learning people we are that, and so much more."

Liz didn't answer.

Libbie continued. "I refuse to live life as the person Grandmother wanted me to be. Her lifestyle never fit me, and she was twisted, Liz. Twisted, whether you want to admit it or not. Fighting her, and fighting to fit in at the same time, nearly tore me apart. It's taken a long time, but I feel like I'm finally emerging from a dark place. I'm finally becoming myself. Imperfect. But with something worth fighting for."

"What?"

"Myself. My present. My future. I wasn't created to stay in that darkness. I know that because I...we, are gifted with the ability to fight our way out."

"So, you're okay now?" Liz's fingers emerged from the blanket for a better grip.

"I'm getting there. I have setbacks." This

time she chuckled softly. "But now the good days outnumber the bad."

"Signs of progress?"

"Exactly."

Liz sighed. "I thought I knew my world, Libbie. It had rules and laws of nature and what-not. Like a landscape. I knew how to navigate it. I understood what happiness was. I knew how to achieve it. I did what I had to do to keep it. Somehow it all got tipped upside down. I lost my gravity. I can't find right-side-up again." There was a long moment. "I'm afraid."

"Of what?"

"I have responsibilities. I'm a wife, a mother, a daughter. I have a position in the community. I volunteer, I help at the kid's school, all that. People expect certain things from me and they have a right to because I made those promises. I have to live up to them, but I'm not sure I can. I can't find my bearings. Sometimes I feel like I'm suffocating."

Libbie stretched her arm across Liz's shoulders. Phrases like "nobody's perfect" or "tomorrow is a new day," were too pointless to waste breath on, but she shared a little more of the quilt with her cousin.

"You wouldn't understand that. You keep yourself free of commitments. Sometimes I envy your ability to do that."

"We all have commitments and

responsibilities, Liz."

"Of course. Some just have more."

"Some volunteer for more, and I don't believe for a minute you'd be happy without that level of engagement, so you won't get sympathy from me for what you do to yourself." Libbie lowered her voice. "What happened, Liz? What upset your landscape?"

"It's not one thing. Fixing one thing is easy. The second time it needs fixing you're still okay because you already know the fix. But somehow, over time, the accumulated weight of each mistake becomes overwhelming." Her shoulders hunched and she put her hands in front of her face. When she pulled them away, she pressed them against the blanket over her legs. "I'm cold."

"Yeah, I'm freezing, too. Go upstairs, take a warm soak or a hot shower. When I hear the water stop, I'll start cooking breakfast."

"Food?"

The word, from her lips, sounded forlorn.

"Some things, like a warm bath and hot chocolate are optional. Sleep and food are not. Not optional. Not negotiable."

Liz nodded. They both stood, untangling themselves from the quilt and throw with a few, brief giggles. Max came running through and whined at the screen door.

"Okay. That, too, isn't optional." Libbie

unhooked the door and opened it for Max. The cat whooshed out after him.

"You have a cat? I didn't know you had a cat." The dark circles were still under her eyes, but the glazed look had lessened.

Libbie felt a surge of confidence and it warmed her. Hope. Sometimes it hurt. Sometimes it felt like a hug.

"Help yourself to my closet. We still wear the same size."

While Liz was washing up, Libbie made coffee. She heard a noise at the back door. She looked out to see Max and the cat sitting side by side, staring up at the door with nearly identical expressions. She opened the door and they came in together as if they'd always been buddies.

When Liz came down for breakfast, she was still wearing her own clothing, stains and all.

Libbie waited until she was well into eating before saying, "You should call Josh. He'll be worried and wondering how you are."

She shook her head. "Not yet." She looked up at Libbie. "He knows I'm here, right?"

"Yes. He said you left a note."

"Good." She closed her eyes and rested her head against her hand, her elbow on the table. "I'm so tired, Libbie."

"Is it Josh? Did he do something?"

"What?" She shook her head. "No, not Josh.

He's…fine."

"He's worried about you."

"Mostly, he wants me home. He wants me to get this out of my system and come home again, my old self again, to pick up where we left off."

"You sound bitter. Many people would like to have a fraction of what you have."

"That's not the point and you know it." She sat up straight and began gathering the odds and ends of breakfast together. She stacked the plates, placed the forks and knives on top all facing the same way, then twisted the lid back on the jelly jar, and so on, and kept talking. "One morning—it was while you were out of the country—I was standing in front of the vanity mirror about to put on some lipstick when it hit me. I don't know what to call it. I couldn't find the right shade. The shade I always wear with my lavender sweater."

She pointed at empty air. "I looked in that mirror, at my reflection and thought…. I thought, if I can't find the right shade of lipstick, then what's the point? What's the point of anything?" She shook her head. "I know how stupid that sounds, but it felt as if my world had crumbled. And having it crumble over a missing lipstick terrified me."

"That's what started this?"

"No, that's what finished it. I thought I was

holding it all together and that took me the rest of the way down. I couldn't see how to climb out. And there you were, moving forward with your life, in love and making plans. I hope you believe I only, ever, wanted the best for you." She paused and seemed to shake herself, then she resumed. "I knew I had to talk to you. But I couldn't. I didn't know where to start. It was like I was frozen in place."

Libbie believed that. The old Liz would've have had the dirty plates and utensils washed and put away by now. This Liz sat at the table staring at the stacked dishes on the table.

"We don't have to talk about anything you don't want to talk about. It's that simple."

"I wish it was simple. It isn't." Her tone sounded like she was flirting with danger and anticipating doom.

Libbie resisted the sudden need to cross her arms. She didn't like bad news and, in fact, avoided it when possible. Did the new Libbie have a responsibility to listen if it might help?

Liz leaned toward her. "Why don't you go upstairs and get yourself together? You look like you slept in a chair all night."

"Because I did."

"Seriously, I'll do the dishes. We can talk more after."

Libbie nodded, glad to get away for a few minutes. She went up the stairs as Liz ran the water in the kitchen sink.

So Liz had fallen apart over lipstick? No, it's never the lipstick. It's all the stuff that adds up, that people stow away in the dark closets of their minds, and gets triggered over something stupid.

Not Josh, she'd said. Not the kids.

She and Liz grew up in separate households, but close households. Almost together. Almost like sisters. But their personalities and circumstances were so different that by the time they were teenagers they had less and less in common. Liz lived with her parents. Libbie lived with Grandmother. Grandmother was wealthy and greatly admired, but not loving.

Liz was only now dealing with unpleasant issues. Libbie had dealt with them for many years. She had the emotional scars to prove it. Libbie was a pro when it came to misery. If anyone could help Liz, she could.

The hot water felt wonderful. She let it rush over her face as she rinsed her hair. She took her time trying to chase all of the negativity away and tried to visualize warmth and light. You had to have it, feel it, before you could share it.

Liz was sitting at the kitchen table, her hands clasped on the table top, waiting.

"Liz, you need to talk. Let's get on with it."

She nodded. "I'm glad you and Jim are...I'm glad you and he have something special between you." She smiled at her entwined fingers. "I told him how happy I was for the two of you."

When she called him in Sicily? What that when she'd told him? Libbie opened her mouth to speak, then caught herself. She refused to invite Liz into any discussion about Sicily, and she didn't owe Liz a status update on her relationship with Jim.

Libbie said, "You have Josh and the children. So much to be happy about. Tell me why you aren't."

"When did you stop loving Dan and start loving Jim?" Liz looked at her. "It was such a short time between your relationships and so much was happening at the time. Aren't you worried about marrying Jim and leaving Cub Creek? What about Max? And now you have a cat, too."

"Don't do this, Liz. Don't change the subject."

Liz nodded. Libbie waited.

"Before I forget. Jim called while you were in the shower."

Libbie jumped up ready to put her cousin off for Jim, but Liz grabbed her wrist.

"He said he'd call you back. Sounded like he had something important going on and didn't want to be interrupted. He said he'd call back, but it might be a day or two. He was sorry."

Libbie sat down.

"I told him you would understand."

"Okay." She could hardly say thanks.

Liz sighed loudly. "So, after the thing happened with Tommy, I was upset and so overwhelmed." She rubbed her hands over her face. "All of those old memories, and how Grandmother died. Remember, I was there. I saw it. It's etched in my brain forever. But with Tommy, maybe I went too far. Maybe it seemed easier to cut ties with you than to continue to try to work things out. I'm tired, Libbie. I'm tired of being caught in the middle between you and Mother."

"Not fair." Libbie rejected her words. "She and I don't get along, but I never asked you—"

Liz cut her off. "You didn't, but you wanted to be part of our family. It put us all in a bad position." Her voice drifted off. "We were friends right from the first, weren't we?"

"I thought so. I don't remember much of anything before I was five. But from then on...we were more than friends, I thought. Like sisters."

She nodded. "That's right." She reached across and touched Libbie's hand. "You can see I didn't set out to hurt anyone. But Daddy... I was worried. Daddy wanted you to live with us. Mother was angry. She said he cared more about you than his own daughter."

Libbie's pressed her hand over her heart. What a terrible thing for a child to hear.

"I thought she was right." Liz kneaded her hands. "I could see how it might be that way."

"Liz, your parents adored you. You can't really think—"

"Shut up, Libbie. Seriously, let me say this and then you can hate me for the rest of your life, and I won't blame you. But you won't. You won't hate me and that will be even worse."

Libbie crossed her arms and kept her mouth shut, her lips pressed together.

"I lied," Liz said.

Chapter Nine

"I told Mother that you said Daddy loved you more than me." After a pause, she added, "She bought me a new coat. Exactly the one I wanted. The shoes I wanted, too. Do you remember them? The pink ones with the shiny buckles?"

Libbie had always viewed Liz and her mother as a team. She had envied them their unity. But now she caught glimpses of an unquiet relationship, manipulative and perhaps adversarial. It was like seeing a new bright swash of red where you'd always seen shades of blue. The room had taken on a greenish cast. Vague alarms were sounding a warning in the back of Libbie's head. She stood to dispel the thickening air and moved toward the stove.

"Let me get you some coffee. I need some."

No response. She turned toward Liz. Liz was staring at her.

"You really don't want to hear unpleasant news, do you? How far and how fast will you run if I force it on you?" Liz shook her head and sighed. "Well, don't panic. These are the crimes of a child. Small crimes, long ago but unconfessed."

Libbie stayed by the counter. She waited for Liz to continue.

"I told Grandmother you stole my doll."

"You gave it to me."

"That's the point. I gave it to you and then I told her you stole it. She was angry. I told her that I wanted you to have it anyway." Again, a pause. "She said I was kind and generous." She sighed. "I'll always remember that. That's who I wanted to be. Kind and generous. I was only six."

"Are you kidding me?" Libbie's face hurt. Her chest ached. The door was a few steps away. Fresh air, her woods, the creek....

Liz grabbed her hand and pulled her back to the table. "Sit down, Libbie. This isn't a case of leaving well enough alone. I have to tell you this. I can't move forward without confessing. I hope it won't throw you into one of those horrible dark moods that you're so prone to."

Was Liz smiling? Perhaps an apologetic smile? Libbie wanted to slap it off of her face. Instead, with a deep breath, Libbie slid her hand over Liz's and rested her fingers across her cousin's.

Libbie forced the words out. "Children do things. I wish you hadn't felt threatened by me. I can't imagine why you did. I had nothing going for me. Nothing."

"Well, that was a big part of it. When someone has nothing, then what do they have to lose? You wanted a father. You and my daddy, well, the two of you enjoyed making stuff up, like that time in the basement about the pirates, remember? I was afraid of everything. If you'd come to live with us...." She shook her head. "Daddy and Mother had a big fight. He told her you were coming to live with us. Then he told me. He thought I would be happy about it. I said no. I said I didn't want you to live with us. I told him you were mean to me, and I cried and cried until he stopped saying it."

Bereft. Libbie's heart, broken so many times in her life that the parts had been super-glued together, cracked again.

"There's more. Do you want me to tell you the other things I said?" She sounded eager.

Libbie stood, pulling her hand back. She was surprised her legs supported her. She walked across to the sink and fumbled with the faucet, wondered why, and then realized she needed to wash her hands. They felt dirty.

"Do you hate me?"

She shook her head, but kept lathering.

"You do. I don't blame you."

Libbie turned the water off. She spoke softly. "How can I blame a child?"

"I said worse."

"No."

"When we were older."

"I don't want to hear it."

"I told my father that you—"

"Stop it, Liz."

"You should hate me. I was a coward and jealous and I lied. I lied about you just before you were leaving for that boarding school. Do you want to know what I told people?"

"No, and if you don't stop saying these things," she clenched her fists to control them, "I may never be able to forgive you. So stop."

"You do hate me."

Libbie spun around, shouting. "No, I don't. Maybe I do, but I don't. I should. I wish—" She hit her fist against the counter top. Dishes rattled. "I don't know what I wish." She whispered, "Yes, I do know. I wish you weren't here."

"The damage I did happened long ago. All these years since, I've had to live with the knowledge of what I did to ruin your life." Liz shook her head. "Don't hate me, Libbie. And don't hate Mother. You know what hate does inside, right? I couldn't keep this ugliness inside any longer and you deserved to know. I want what's best for both of us."

"Remember, Libbie, I was there when Grandmother died. I was there for you. I've tried to be a good friend to you since. I told myself my actions were the small mistakes that children make, that they didn't matter. But they did, I guess, and when I said those things to you last June, I think part of me wanted to cut you out of my life because then I wouldn't have to think about it again. I wouldn't have to think about any of it."

Liz shrugged and looked up. Her eyes were teary. "What do we do now?"

"Do? I don't know what you're asking me." Libbie felt numb. Her lips tingled. She pressed her fingers to them.

"You've gotten the short end of things most of your life. I can't help wonder how things might have been different for you, me, too, if the truth had been known."

"Different? I guess. More so, if my mother hadn't died. That wasn't Margaret's fault. That wasn't Grandmother's fault."

Liz looked stunned. Then she leaned toward me and asked, "Do you wonder about that? About your parents' death?"

"No. Car accident. Rainy night. There were on their way to pick me up from a child's birthday party."

"Seriously?"

"What?"

"A child's birthday party? It was my birthday party," Liz said. "Our birthday party."

Libbie tried to recall.... She and Liz were

born a week apart.... "Ours? Maybe yours. There was noise and lots of colors and craziness. I remember standing in a corner watching and waiting for my parents to arrive. I wanted to leave. I remember that much, and that they didn't come for me. The other children were loud, excited, then suddenly they were leaving. You left with your mother. I remember that, and then your dad picked me up and told me about my parents. After that, my memory goes mostly dark."

"That's so sad. Or maybe it's a mercy. I don't know." Liz shrugged. "I'm impressed by how you've taken this, Libbie. I truly am. You make me feel almost silly for being so distressed about it." She drew in a breath and released it with a great sigh. "Are you really okay? Please tell me you are."

There was a loud ringing in Libbie's ears. She felt lightheaded. She couldn't process this, bring reality to it, so she settled for nodding. Anyone else, other than Liz, and she would've kicked them out the door without apology.

"I'm so glad. I can't begin to tell you. Truly, I'm glad. I hope you'll consider keeping this to yourself."

Liz must've read something in Libbie's face because she followed quickly with, "I can't see how it would do anyone any good to talk about it." Liz shrugged. "It isn't like it was criminal or anything. A child's lies. Libbie, I don't want Adam and Audrey to know. Think of how it would affect them. How they'd feel about their mother. They couldn't understand. To them it would seem...."

Was she serious?

"What about those other things, Libbie? The colors and the shadows and things. I never believed you about that. I thought you were just trying to get attention. Dr. Raymond said it was real. That synesthesia thing, at least part of it. You told me you don't see those any longer. Is that true?"

"No, that was a lie, Liz. I do still see them. I hear voices from time to time, too. Mostly my own, but there it is. Furthermore, it doesn't mean anything is wrong with me. It's how I am and how my brain works. So shut up about it."

Liz smiled. "Now you are sounding more like yourself. Rude. I mean that in the nicest possible way." She shook her head. "I never understood about all that psychic stuff anyway. It's all very popular on TV and movies and books. Now they have reality shows about it. Talking to dead people and all."

"I'm not psychic, Liz. I wish I was. Knowing the future or being able to read people's minds would be handy because then I would have realized all those years ago that you were stabbing me in the back." Libbie stared at her.

"You were my friend. You and your father were the only people I could trust. My only connection to a reasonable world. You were not only my friend, but my sister—the sister of my heart. And it was a lie. All a lie."

Liz paled. "No, we were and are friends. I loved and still love you. It wasn't you. It was…your neediness. My father liked you. He responded to you and your need in a way that he didn't worry over me."

"Why should he? You had him and a mother who'd move the world for you."

"It was my fear that stood in the way."

"Not fear. It was jealousy."

"Jealous? Of what? You?"

"Of your father's attention."

She nodded and shrugged. "Maybe. I'm sorry. So sorry."

"You said you weren't looking for forgiveness."

"I guess I lied."

The irony hit Libbie and she couldn't help herself. She laughed. Not nicely and not happily. Still it was laughter. After a moment of shock, Liz tried to join in, but she looked confused and uneasy.

Libbie wanted to say something mean and devastating, but she didn't because, in the end, it didn't matter. What was, was. Today was the thing. It was the steps today that would her away from yesterday and lead to tomorrow.

"I am so impressed by how you've taken this. I think you really are okay. Libbie, if we can put this behind us and not mention it, I think it might be good for the children to spend some time with you again. How would you feel about that?"

"I...of course." The kids were a bribe for cooperation?

"I feel so much better and I have you thank for that, Libbie. Poor Josh has tried to be patient, but it's been so hard with this weighing on me."

"Yet you told him about it."

"I told him some. I had to. He started saying things like I should see a psychiatrist. I had to tell him something. Who sees a psychiatrist for childhood lies?"

Her? Libbie? Though she hadn't been the one telling them.

Was Liz so desperate to make this thing go away that she was willing to dangle her kids like carrots, suggesting they might be included to sweeten the bargain of keeping this between the two of them? Liz knew Libbie loved Adam and Audrey. She wouldn't hurt them for anything.

Did Libbie believe Liz would allow the children to visit again, much less stay over like they had before, with their Aunt Libbie? No. Liz couldn't trust her because she, Liz, didn't have a clue about what trust, or being trustworthy, meant.

Liz looked perky again. "Well, now let's see…where did I leave my purse?"

They walked to the door.

Liz said, "I'm glad you came to visit me, and now I've returned the visit. Almost like old times." She hugged Libbie. "We have to do this again real soon."

There was something wrong with Liz's smile, her tone. Or, Libbie thought, maybe there was truth in it, a truth she hadn't been willing to see before. But more. This was about more than lipstick and childhood lies.

"Liz, listen to me. You feel better and you think you're all good now. Mostly all you did was throw darts at me to relieve your conscience. Whatever pressure you've lessened by doing that, doesn't solve the issue at its heart. Get help, Liz."

She pursed her lips and shook her head so that her shiny hair bounced and then found its shape again, perfectly. "I don't blame you, Libbie. Of course, you're hurt. Angry, too. But you forget—we are very different people." And she was down the steps and to her car in a matter of seconds.

"Liz," she called out, startling herself.

Liz stopped and turned back.

"Remember a few months ago when you suggested I take Grandmother's dining room set out of storage?"

"Sure."

Curiosity lit Liz's eyes.

Let her wonder.

"I'm going to do that. Just wanted you to know."

"Okay?"

Liz was waiting for more information, an explanation, something. Libbie herself wasn't sure why she'd said it. But it sounded right.

"Goodbye, Liz." She didn't stay on the porch. She watched at the window as Liz drove away, returning home to her life. Libbie pressed her hands to her face. Her cheeks felt hot, almost feverish. Confession might benefit the one who confessed, but not necessarily the one being asked to forgive.

Liz. Margaret. It made Libbie's head spin.

How clearly she recalled Grandmother's dark house. Elizabeth Havens was a dead-hearted woman living in a house of mirrors and dark wood. And Uncle Phil. How many times had Libbie watched from her bedroom window high above as he descended the stone steps, leaving Grandmother's house and heading to his car, his bright yellow hair glinting in the sun. He left Libbie behind, with HER, going home to his wife and daughter.

In a daze, Libbie went out the back door and down toward the creek. Where else would she go? She had nowhere else, and no one she could talk to. Not about this, or about anything that mattered.

Max, trotting along beside her, brushed against her leg.

She didn't get far. About halfway to the creek, in a grove of young pines a short distance off the main path, where the pine tags carpeted the forest floor in a thick, fresh mat, her knees weakened, and her legs folded. She was blind before she hit the ground. The tears fell in a torrent and there was no one to see so she surrendered to it.

When the worst had passed, Libbie wanted to continue lying there like an exhausted lump of flesh, but Max started licking her cheeks. She pushed him away gently and rubbed her shirt sleeve across her face. She sighed. The breath sounded ragged and felt rough as it passed through her throat. Her chest, her throat, her eyes—it all hurt. She dropped back onto the forest floor and dug her fingers into the earth. Max stretched out next to her and reached one paw forward, gently, to rest on her arm.

"I told her it didn't matter, Max. And it doesn't. Or maybe it matters more than anything. But we can't go back. I don't want to go back. Uncle Phil let me down. Shame on him, Max. Shame on Liz for lying and shame on Phil Havens for knowing better and leaving me in HER house anyway."

Libbie had always viewed Margaret as the gatekeeper. Apparently, Liz was a gatekeeper, too, and Libbie would never be allowed admittance.

Liz felt badly about how it made her, Liz, feel. It made no difference to Liz otherwise. And that was probably what hurt the most.

There was an upside. Libbie had helped Liz, if only by letting her talk. But it was no more than a temporary improvement. Liz's cure would last only as long as her personal lie, her disguise, held up.

Everyone was flawed. Some people hid it better.

What was it that Jim had said to her in that really dark time last summer when Liz told her to stay away from her and the children? When Libbie had asked him how he knew whether or not she was guilty of her grandmother's death so many years before when she, herself, wasn't always sure? He'd said he knew she was innocent because that's just who she was.

Well, Jim was right. This was who she was. The rest didn't matter.

****

Libbie and Max trudged back to the house.

"The vet. I forgot the appointment." She was emotionally spent and dispirited. It was still early but all she wanted was to crawl into a dark place and hide. But she wouldn't. She refused to give into that defeatist, negative behavior any longer. At least, not today.

She picked up the phone on her way through the house. She dialed the vet.

"I need to reschedule."

"It's for that stray, right?"

"Yes. Unfortunately, I can't find her." True enough.

"No problem. If she shows back up, bring her on over and we'll fit her in."

"Thanks. You guys are the best."

"No problem. How's Max?"

Libbie smiled. Weakly, but still a smile. "He's fine. Max is always good."

"Yes, ma'am. Well, hope to see you soon."

She sat on the front porch, her feet on the step below, her arms crossed over her legs and her head cradled. How much time had passed? Liz had left before noon. It was some time after that.

Libbie needed someone to talk to, other than the vet's receptionist, but she had no one. No Liz. No Jim. Max nuzzled her arm and something warm nudged her foot and ankle. The cat.

The cat was dozing on the step at Libbie's

feet.

She heard an engine rumbling and looked up. Mitchell's Lawn and Landscaping was here. A huge pickup truck with a wooden flatbed trailer loaded with mowers and other yard-working equipment was pulling alongside her yard.

The driver parked the vehicle and trailer on the side of the road. The road was narrow. She held her breath.

A man climbed out of the truck and Libbie stood.

He went around to the back of the trailer and dropped the gate. Libbie sagged. Not Jim. Another man was walking up the slope to the house. Not Jim, either.

"Ms. Havens?" He called out.

"Yes."

"We're here to do some cleanup, leaf removal mostly."

"I see." Her eyes, no doubt puffy and red, gave her away. She reached for Max who was sniffing the man's shoes and pulled him away. "Sorry."

"Is there a problem, ma'am?"

She shook her head. "No problem at all. We'll be inside."

"Yes, ma'am." He took off back down to the truck where the other man had donned a large backpack-type leaf blower.

She re-gripped Max's collar wanting to get him inside before the noise started.

The cat had vanished.

Libbie stood at the study window as the blowers blew the leaves and twigs into piles and into the woods. How simple it looked. How badly she needed it for her own mind. How impossible to do.

The sign for Jim's company, Mitchell's Lawn and Landscaping—she stared at it until the tears threatened again.

Enough.

****

Josh arrived soon after the lawn care guys drove off.

Alarmed, she raced out the door to meet him. "Why are you here? Where are the kids?"

He joined her on the porch. "Everyone is fine. Liz returned home, and Margaret is there with her and the children." He sat next to Libbie. "I don't know what you did, but you made a difference. She's much better now."

Libbie made a noise that sounded almost rude, but she let it stand on its own. What more could she say?

He touched her arm and she looked at him.

He said, "What about you? You look like you've been through a lot." He dropped his hand. "Liz told me some of it, about how she resented the attention her father paid to you. She wouldn't be the first child to be jealous. But I'm sorry, Libbie. For then and now. I hope you'll be able to forgive her."

Libbie couldn't respond to any of that. It was beyond her. She had always liked Josh, but this was too much. She shifted the conversation.

"I hope the kids are okay. There's no guarantee her improved frame of mind will last. Please insist she get help. Therapy won't hurt her. It can help."

She could tell by his expression that he had no worries along that line. Only relief.

"That's why Margaret's there. Just to be sure."

She'd always had a soft spot for Josh. His blonde hair was so much like Uncle Phil's. Josh was safe leaving Liz and the kids for now, but Libbie hoped he wouldn't blind himself into thinking the calm would last.

"I have to get to work. I'm supposed to be up in DC, but I had to thank you first and make sure you were okay. Try not to worry too much."

They stood. She walked with him down the steps. He put his arms around her and hugged, and she hugged him back.

"I care about you all so much, Josh."

"I know. We feel the same about you. Liz especially. Sometimes she...." He hugged Libbie again and she planted a small kiss on his cheek.

He released her. "Enough drama for one day, right?"

"I am tired. Yes, enough for today."

As they turned toward the driveway, Libbie saw a car moving slowly along the road. As soon as she saw it, it sped away.

Libbie couldn't make out who was driving, but it looked vaguely familiar.

Jim and Josh had never met.

Whoever the driver was, it didn't matter. Everybody knew everybody around here and Jim would soon know she was making out with a blond-haired man in her front yard.

One more notch on her belt of conquests.

****

"Someone saw you embracing a man—a man who wasn't Jim."

No one had said it yet, not to Libbie's face, but it was inevitable that it was being discussed somewhere in the county. As a bonus, a new hint of scandal would spark the slightly older gossip about Dan and her.

She could wait and see what, if anything, it spurred Jim to do. Or she could embrace the action herself.

If she'd been more understanding, more open with Jim when he came to her that day.... She shook her head. Nope. They both had to want a future together.

The Mitchell family business was located on the far side of the county. It was closer to Fredericksburg and Richmond, whereas Cub Creek was close (close being a relative term) to Richmond and Charlottesville.

The nursery complex was large and attractive. The garage complex where the big equipment was stored and maintained was trim and neat and away from the nursery area.

Libbie parked in a corner of the customer parking lot out of the main foot traffic path to the building.

What next? Suppose he did walk by? What should she do?

Get out and speak with him? What a concept.

She'd reached a new low. Too bad she hadn't thought to bring toilet paper. She'd never toilet-papered a house. Wasn't that the kind of thing lovesick teens did to the house where the object of their affection lived?

She turned the car off.

Jim's truck wasn't in sight, but then, other than the earth movers, the Mitchell trucks looked mostly alike, big white pickups with magnetic signs on the side.

The house was up on the hill. Relatively old, but it looked modern. Large, too. Although that was also relative. Jim's home was smaller than

Grandmother's fancy townhouse, but larger than Libbie's modest house at Cub Creek.

Jim had told her that his mother moved in to help with Matthew a few years ago, right after her husband, Jim's father, died. It made sense for everyone at the time. It might technically be Jim's house, but with a woman already there.... Jim's sister was there a lot, too, according to Jim, but she lived a few miles away. So lots of family wandering the hallways and already comfortable and at home in that house. They wouldn't necessarily welcome one more.

She watched more intently as a man walked out of the front door of the house. Too far away to make out who, but really, the shape of the hat identified him.

Dan had been there for some purpose and was now leaving. He climbed into his vehicle.

It moved slowly down the dirt road from the house to the paved section that bordered the nursery. Would he recognize her car? She didn't think so, but she slumped down in her seat.

Talk about cowardice. Libbie might have the desire to act, but the proof was in the action, wasn't it? And clearly, she wasn't up to the job. Some part of her was apparently still in hiding.

****

She'd had some photos printed and she put

them in a small photo book with inserts in the clear plastic pages. Joyce wanted "printed" pictures. Now she'd have them. She could keep them, too, to share around with her friends. Libbie included a few photos of Jim, just because.

She swung by the barbecue place in Mineral because Joyce loved it. By the time she arrived at Ethel's Home for Adults, the car was saturated with the aroma. Joyce was sitting just inside the front doorway with her cane and tote bag, already wearing her jacket.

Cardboard pumpkins and dried gourds were arranged on the tables as decorations.

Libbie asked, "You ready?"

"Don't I look it?" Joyce said loudly.

Her volume was intended for the other ladies who were sitting around the room. They'd gathered to share in Joyce's plans. Living at the Home, or any place like it, was a group event no matter who was actually involved, or invited.

Joyce refused the wheelchair, so an aide helped her down the ramp to Libbie's car. As they drove, Joyce stared out the window, taking in the sights. It was short trip and at the house, Joyce kept a hand tight on the railing and Libbie was ready to grab her if she got shaky. Max met them at the door. As the door opened, the cat meowed. She'd been nowhere in sight that morning, probably curled up and sleeping somewhere, apparently left inside. Good thing Libbie had the litter box handy for her.

They stepped into the kitchen and Libbie guided Joyce toward the table.

Joyce pointed at the place settings. "Oh, my, now that's pretty."

"Yes, ma'am," Libbie helped Joyce off with her jacket and hung the cane over the back of the chair. "Tablecloth and real dishes today. For you."

They shared lunch and then Libbie showed Joyce the photo book. Joyce's eyelids were hanging heavy.

Libbie refilled Joyce's iced tea. "You seem especially tired today."

"I was up early this morning to get ready. Takes me a while these days. Wouldn't want to keep you waiting." She looked aside. "'Course you weren't early so I had to sit a long time."

"We'd better get you home, then."

Libbie put her own jacket on, added a long scarf, and then helped Joyce on with hers.

The trip back wasn't long enough for even a short doze. As they pulled up, an aide brought a wheelchair down the ramp. Joyce saw it and pouted.

"I can walk." She looked at Libbie.

Joyce held tight to the ramp's railing and Libbie and the aide walked close behind her, prepared to grab her. By the time they reached the top Joyce was ready for the chair. "Scoot that over here." She sat with a long sigh.

In the sunroom, she took her usual seat in the corner. Libbie chose the settee.

Joyce yawned, but said, "Pass that book over. Let me see those photos one more time."

Libbie passed it to her. Joyce flipped a few pages over to where the view from the harbor and a picture of the sidewalk trattoria faced each other and pointed her finger at the plastic page.

"So many people in these streets and restaurants," she said. "You never did tell me what happened with your cousin."

"What?" A change of subject. "Not sure I want to discuss it."

"You know you're going to. You might as well get it over with while I've got a mind left."

"Well, it's a subject that hurts me, but let's not allow that to interfere with your entertainment." Libbie rubbed her temples. "Sorry. That came out differently than intended. Let me think where to start."

She pressed her hands to her face. When she took them away, she drew in a breath and then spoke. "My cousin Liz discovered she isn't perfect and it upset her. She decided to make it my problem. My fault, too, because I was an orphan and needy. Needy. That's what she said."

Joyce snorted. Whether by choice or accident, Libbie couldn't tell.

Frustrated, Libbie said a little more than she'd intended. "She had the nerve to ask if I was psychic. Can you believe that?"

"Well, okay. You got my attention with that one. Are you?"

"No." She shook her head, then shrugged. "I see colors. Shadows, too." Libbie felt almost stunned to hear the words said out loud in a place like this where anyone could overhear. "I mean that sometimes the light changes."

Joyce looked disappointed. "I see colors. Not so good now with the cataracts, but I got a good color memory. Not much color in shadows, though."

"No." Libbie leaned forward, surprising herself again, laughing. "No, when I say shadows, it's more like how the air, the light changes, when something is about to...." She stopped, then jumped back in with a slightly different tack.

"I mean when I touch things, I see colors or hints of color in my head, but mostly, I think, it's because there are scents left behind...smells that I'm not aware of...but my brain is. Often, I see colors when I smell something or hear music. Or hear music when I see...." Libbie wanted to look away from Joyce's face, but didn't.

"Well, that sounds handy."

"No, it isn't. When people notice me putting my hands on things, or sniffing the air, they think I'm having some kind of crazy communion with the walls or nature. They think I'm nuts."

Joyce laughed. It was the loudest, deepest laugh Libbie had ever heard from her. It shook Joyce's frail body. As her laughter slowed and her chest and shoulders relaxed again, she said, "There's nothing like a good laugh, is there?" She took a slow, deep breath. "I don't see any color when I touch a wall, unless it's the actual color of the wall." She laughed again, tickled by her own wit. She shook her head and rubbed her eyes. "But you should see how folks look at me when I'm talking to Alice."

Her fine hair was white and flyaway. Her eyes were a weak, faded watery-looking blue, and her wrinkled skin had nothing between it and her sharp bones.

Libbie leaned forward and touched her hand. "Alice is gone, Joyce. You know that."

Joyce leaned forward, too, and spoke loudly. "Alice's voice is as clear in my head as it ever was during the sixty years we were friends. I always knew what she was going to say about everything and anything." Joyce tapped her temple with her finger. "Death don't change that. You, and the rest, can label me old or senile or anything you choose, but it don't change what I know. It don't change the fact that sometimes, from the corner of my eye, I see her walk past my door. One time she sat right in that seat where you're at. Just sitting and smiling."

She paused for a breath and shrugged. "Was she there? Does it matter? She's here," She tapped her chest, and here, she tapped her head again. "No one has the right to call me senile or incompetent unless I ask them to set a place for her at the dinner table."

Joyce sat back with a grunt. "And that's what I have to say about that."

A thin woman wearing an aide's outfit, filled the doorway. "I'll set that place, Ms. Inman, and I'll finish eatin' what she doesn't." She carried a glass of apple juice. "All this talking is making your throat dry. I hear that rasp in your voice."

She looked at Libbie. "Can I get you something to drink, ma'am?"

"Name's Libbie. My niece." Joyce waved her hand. "Libbie, this is Mellie."

"Nice to meet you, ma'am." The woman, Mellie, nodded with a smile. "I could hear Ms. Inman laughing clear down the hallway."

"I hope we didn't disturb anyone."

"Goodness no. Not enough laughter anywhere far as I'm concerned." Mellie lingered in the doorway. "I have a theory about this."

"Please, go ahead."

"Like when I turn on the car radio and it's playing the song I was thinking of, or when I finish my mama's sentences, or go somewhere and there, out of all the stores there are, there's the friend I was just thinking about moments before."

She took Joyce's empty glass. "You have stuff like that happen? Don't you think most do? People call it coincidence."

Mellie continued, "Some people have better eyesight. Some have better memories. Some sing like angels. It's all to do with the brain, I say. Frankly, ma'am, as a group, folks aren't that bright. No one should be surprised we don't understand everything. My mama would say leave it to God."

Libbie sighed. "But in the meantime, we have to live with the people who don't want to think about it, who want us to be the same as they are."

"True enough." With that, Mellie turned and left.

Libbie looked at Joyce. "She's smart."

Joyce said, "Being smart is having common sense and using it." She scratched her cheek. "Sounds like your cousin got you all riled up."

"What I want to know is who set the rules? Who has the right to say someone is too needy emotionally? Or shouldn't be seeing colors or hearing voices? Where'd they get the right to do that to other people?"

Joyce humphed. "You're on some kind of high horse today."

"Me? You think I'm the problem?"

"I know you aren't any more perfect than anyone else. Even the so-called normal people."

"I'm not the one pinning on labels."

Joyce coughed, then said, "Let me tell you about labels. I was a daughter, then a wife, and a widow. A divorcee once. Now they call me old. Kind of a social shorthand. An introduction of sorts so folks have some idea right off of who they're talking to. Some folks are too stupid to build it out from there, to see what's beyond the label, and we label them stupid or bigoted. Or shortsighted."

Libbie leaned forward kneading the fringe of her scarf between her fingers. "I'm different. I never fit in. Instead of letting me be different, they label me, almost like saying she's such or such and so it's okay not to treat her like one of us."

"Tell me this. Why would you want to hang out with folks like that?"

She groaned. "I don't. I want to be accepted. Maybe to be appreciated a little. Besides, it's not so easy to avoid those people when they are your family."

"Oh. Well, Family's different."

"Make up your mind."

"You're a rude girl. That's a label, too, I guess." Joyce cackled.

"I'd apologize if you weren't enjoying yourself so much at my expense."

"Nah. Can't fault you for snapping when I'm poking at you with a stick. I was having a little fun but if all you're going to be is dreary, then I won't bother."

Libbie put her hands over her face to hide the smile that was trying to find its way out. "I give up," she said.

"Quitter. 'nother label."

Libbie raised her hands. "I surrender."

"It ain't the labels. It's the ideas that get attached to them." Joyce surprised Libbie by reaching across the space between them to pat her hand. "Can't blame people. Brains can take in only so much. People try to keep their worlds small and manageable by sorting everyone out, by smacking on labels and putting them in that just-right spot on the pantry shelf. But the thing is that nobody stays on that shelf for long. It would save a lot of anguish if people could figure that out and take folks as they come. But for you? You've got to figure out how to let folks go."

Libbie looked at Joyce for a long moment. "Not Jim."

She grimaced. "No, not Jim. I mean that cousin of yours. So, you decided you want Jim? Run him down. Make him talk. A good conversation, straight and to the point, will fix it."

Libbie laughed. It wasn't a happy sound. "I've had enough rejection to last a lifetime." She examined the scarf fringe she was shredding. She smoothed the threads. "If Jim wants me then he needs to step up and say so. If he doesn't, then maybe it's for the best."

"Best how?"

She shook her head. "A trip to Sicily was one thing, but I can't imagine living on the far side of the county away from my house, from Cub Creek." She paused before adding, "I only see us at Cub Creek. I dreamed...." She cleared her throat, the tried again. "I dreamed we were sitting around the dining room table at Cub Creek. He and our friends." She whispered, "It was wonderful. It's hard to let that go."

Joyce closed her eyes. Seconds stretched into minutes and Libbie thought she'd dozed off. Having exposed her heart and soul, Libbie was annoyed, but then relieved. Maybe Joyce hadn't heard most of that mess she'd spewed and would forget the rest. She was contemplating a quiet exit when Joyce spoke.

"I reckon your business at Cub Creek ain't done yet." She nodded. "Alice didn't leave 'til her business was done."

Libbie couldn't keep the sarcasm from her voice. "Alice died. That's why she left. It's not how I plan to leave. What held Alice there? She wanted to sell and move to a retirement home in the city. She should've done it sooner."

"It was her family home for generations. She was born and raised there on Cub Creek. It was where all her memories lived."

"Did she wait too long? Did she run out of time?"

In a slow, measuring voice, Joyce answered, "If I see Alice, I'll be sure to ask her." She sniffed. "One thing I have noticed is that you don't have a dining room table."

Libbie stood. "That's true, but I'm going to."

The leftover cans of paint, the champagne shade with the different finishes for the ceiling and the slightly darker tone for the walls, were stored under the kitchen sink. It had been a few months since she used them. Next trip to Louisa, she was taking them along for a good shaking. She needed to grab some paint chips, too, because she had ideas for the trim.

The dining room furniture was coming out of storage as soon as the room was ready. Those unpleasant meals with Grandmother? Forget them. This furniture was about to have a better future than its past.

Chapter Ten

Libbie discovered that a sure-fire way to tick off a cat was to grab her and shove her in a carrier.

Another way was to put that carrier in the car so that the cat had no idea where it was going or why. Top it off by toting the carrier through a vet's waiting room with yapping dogs and meowing cats, and then setting the carrier on the cold, steel examining table—and you had trouble.

The vet tech looked at Libbie. "Does she have her claws?"

"Yes."

The vet tech was young but not new to unhappy cats and dogs. She eyed the carrier. From its depths, the cat emitted a low rumbling, yet high pitched warning.

The tech and Libbie looked at each other.

"Feral?" The tech reached for a pair of thick, long gloves, but didn't put them on. She said, "You're trying to do a nice thing here, but feral cats can't always be.... Sometimes the kindest thing is to—"

Libbie pulled the carrier closer and hugged it. The cat swiped through one of the holes and scratched her finger.

"She's not feral. She's scared."

The veterinarian walked in. "Who do we have here? I understand you have a cat now, Ms. Havens?" He leaned closer to the wire grill door. "Hello."

"Be careful. She's scared, I mean. Normally, she's calm."

"Hard to tell whether she's more scared or angry." He spoke in a dreamlike voice. A soft voice. Calm. Libbie found herself leaning forward, toward him, swaying a bit. In that same gentle voice, he said, "Make sure the room door stays closed."

He continued speaking, but low and soft. He opened the carrier and placed his hand flat on the table, his fingers resting barely inside the opening. The cat moved forward sniffing his fingers. All the while, that mellow, mesmerizing voice went on.

Libbie watched how he drew the cat's attention, then her trust, then her head emerged, and she allowed him to touch her. Libbie was spellbound. The cat seemed impressed, too.

The hand and the voice never wavered. By the time, the vet was done, and the cat was back in the carrier, Libbie was almost disappointed to leave. The vet said, "Clearly she's domesticated, but we don't have the records, so I've given her shots and all the required stuff. The vet tech will give you a card with the list for your records. We maintain a copy here, too. Keep her in the house, at least for a few days, and schedule an appointment to get her spayed."

In the car, driving home, the cat was silent. Libbie tried talking to her, hoping to reassure her. She talked all the way into the house, trying not to bump the carrier and scare her worse. Max rushed up as she placed the carrier on the floor. He began sniffing like crazy all around it. Libbie was worried that his nose might come too close to danger, but the cat stayed crouched in the far end of the carrier.

Libbie coaxed, "You're safe now." She opened the carrier door. "Come on out."

The cat hissed and streaked off, a few hairs floating in the air in her wake.

****

Halloween. Two days since she'd spied on Jim's home.

Mary Pettus from across the way, had knocked on her door and invited her to their party.

"It's mostly the kids and their friends, but a lot of adults and parents come to. I hope you'll join us."

"Thanks, but no. I've already got the candy and plans and all that. Sounds like a lot of fun, though."

She nodded. "Remember, you're welcome. Any time. If your plans change, please come on over."

Libbie waved goodbye as Mary backed her truck down the driveway.

Maybe she should've said yes. No doubt, Mary and Allen Pettus and their kids had done the decorations up right for their party, with maybe a bonfire with marshmallows or even S'mores to roast. One of the many things she'd never done that regular people did.

She was tempted. She knew these people, at least some of them. They were nice. If not for the uncertain relationship with Jim, she might've joined them. But this was a small town environment. Everyone would know something about her, or her and Jim, or her and Dan. Some might know stuff she didn't, whether true or not. Libbie wouldn't risk facing that for a bonfire at a Halloween party.

Libbie opened the bags of candy and emptied them into a bowl. She didn't expect any trick-or-treaters, but was prepared. As with the hunter thing Dan had told her about—that they might come to her door—Libbie couldn't figure out which was worse, being home alone while strange children came to her house, or sitting inside and refusing to answer the door. But, again, as with the hunter thing, perhaps this would come to nothing because no trick-or-treaters would hike all the way out here for bubble gum or a snack-size candy bar.

It was a perfect October night. Chilly but only a little. The smell of clean, crisp leaves mingled with the occasional whiff of wood smoke from across the way. It reached to where she sat on the porch with a large bowl of candy on her lap and Max dozing at her feet. No sign of the cat. She'd stayed scarce since the vet visit. There was evidence of her appetite in the litter box, but otherwise....

Max's muzzle twitched from time to time, either smelling the smoke or the candy, probably. For once, she had him on the leash with the end secured around the porch rail. Didn't want to put any kids at risk. Or Max.

The door light was burning. A car drove by and she felt on stage, exposed to view. She got up and switched off the light. If she saw someone coming, she'd switch it back on.

Then again, she looked at the unlit bulb and back at the road. She didn't want strangers driving up to her house in the dark. That seemed like potential trouble.

All this thinking. Ridiculous. She needed to get a life. A better one, this time.

Grandmother didn't participate in Halloween, but after Libbie moved into her own small townhouse in Fairfax, she'd answered the door to all trick-or-treaters. Of course, there were lots of outside lights, and lots of people knocking on doors, answering doors, and families walking past, the adults chatting as they carried the babies, the children swinging bags full of candy. She felt like she knew the rules. Everyone did. They played by the rules and everyone was happy.

The night was fairly well lit all on its own by a big fat shiny moon. A few cars passed but no one slowed down. From across the horse pastures, music drifted faintly on the breeze. She sat and listened.

Another car passed. The headlights grazed the yard, highlighting something briefly but having seen the outline and the way the eyes reflected the car lights, she knew it was a group of deer. They were munching on something in her yard.

She glanced at Max. He was sleeping.

What was planted down there? Nothing special, surely. They were welcome to it. Pretty cool, actually. She knew deer could be pests. Well, so could she. She laughed at the thought.

After all the turmoil with Jim, with Joyce and Dan acting like a Greek chorus, and never mind Liz whose behavior was simply unacceptable, it felt good to laugh a little. If you must be a pest, then be it well. Be the best pest you can be. She was enjoying her own wit until the deer suddenly moved. They moved as an irregular, but almost solid shape. Max startled her, barking. She heard the crashing of the brush as they fled into the woods. She looked in the other direction.

Nothing.

All dark and shadowy over there. Hunters wouldn't be wandering in the dark, would they? Bears? Coyotes?

Max had settled back down.

So, no danger, but now the mood was spoiled. Time to go inside.

Libbie stood. Max looked at her and barked once. She untied his leash, then unhooked it from his collar altogether.

Headlights grew brighter as a vehicle drove down the road. It turned, cutting a bright path across the trees, up the driveway, and reaching to the porch.

Libbie recognized the vehicle.

Max ran down the steps, barely getting in one bark before Dan exited the SUV. Instantly, Max's attitude changed. His stubby tail wagged, and he butted Dan's leg with his muzzle, and half-leaning against him as Dan walked.

"Dan." She came to the front of the porch,

her hands on the railing.

"Libbie." He nodded. "Everything okay?" He stopped at the foot of the steps. "Any kids come by? No trick-or-treaters?"

"Not a one."

He was driving his own vehicle and he wasn't in uniform.

"Why are you here? I mean...."

"Just checking on things."

"Did you have some reason to suspect there was a problem here?"

"Not specifically."

"So?"

"Historically."

"Don't make me pull this out word by word. You are perfectly capable of going on and on. I know that personally. In fact, I remember when we went out to lunch together and you told me my house was haunted." She stopped. "That's it, isn't it?"

"I said...and it was months ago now...that the old Carson Place was believed by many to be haunted. That's different that saying it is."

She waited.

"It's not unusual for some of the local teenagers to come by, especially on Halloween, up to mischief. The Pettus kids are having a party across the way, so I thought I'd drop by."

"Dan, is this serious? I don't want people,

teenagers or otherwise, messing around my house."

Another car passed. Dan gave it a quick look. "Don't get worked up," he said.

"Easy for you to say."

"No. You misunderstood. I'm headed over to the Pettus place. I figured I'd stop here and—"

"Oh."

"And," he said, drawing the word out for emphasis. "If you'll let me finish?"

She nodded.

"You should come over with me."

Libbie frowned.

"Listen. It's good for the area kids to see you. Harder for them to justify mischief if they know the person, and a lot of the parents will be there, too. It's a whole lot tougher for a kid to get up to mischief when the person knows not only them, but their parents, too." He paused. "Besides you might have fun."

She relaxed her grip on the railing. "Dan. That's sweet. It makes sense, too. But I can't."

"If you're shy, you don't need to be. It's not much different than a block party, but it's in the country. Lots of family and friends. A get-together."

"Dan."

He stood still, waiting. "Libbie?"

"Jim."

He scratched the back of his neck, a

mannerism she recognized. He was thinking. She let him.

"It's not that kind of party. Not like a date."

She smiled, crossed her arms and leaned against the post. "That's how it seems to you. But is that how it will look to the people who know you? Who know Jim and his family? I mean, I don't want to imply that we're celebrities, but we've caused some gossip in our time…my brief time here at Cub Creek. Do we want to feed it?"

"I see your point."

"Besides, when it got back to Jim, how would he feel about it?"

"No problem there. I checked with him first. I told him you might like to go across the street and did he mind if I encouraged you and offered you a ride. He thought it was a good idea."

Somewhere between "He" and "Idea," Libbie's smile faded.

"I see, too, I guess." She pushed away from the post. "Thanks, but no." She walked to the door. "Max? Come in."

"Libbie."

"Go away, Dan."

"I'm sorry. I must not have said it right. I didn't mean to imply that Jim was okay with you and me going out, that is, going to the party as a couple."

"Well, that's real nice of him not to try and

plan my life or anything. He breaks up with me and then gives you permission to find entertainment for me."

"No one meant it like that."

She was angry and hurt and hijacked by recklessness. She walked toward the steps and stopped at the edge. He was still standing below, and she had the advantage of looking down and she liked it.

"Okay, Dan Wheeler. You tell me this. If you had a girlfriend, someone you claimed to love, that you said you wanted to marry, and if you decided it might not work between you, but you still loved her, would you give another man permission to take her to a party, even as an escort, knowing the man had been her boyfriend, and recently, not six months ago, even if your present relationship was on some sort of hiatus?"

Libbie moved closer, taking one step down. "Would you tell him it was okay to go to a party with me, her, unless you don't plan on resuming the relationship, and don't care enough to worry about it?" She steadied herself with a hand on the railing. "Was maybe looking to get her completely off his hands?

Dan's brown eyes, dark and warm, looked at her face. She gave him credit for not looking away. His lips stayed firmly together. She could only assume he had no answer, at least not one he was eager to share.

"Goodnight, Dan."

Libbie turned, went inside and closed the door.

****

The next few days moved without her. She was there, present but numb. She wanted to stay numb. The alternative was unacceptable. Perhaps dangerous. She spent a lot of time napping on the sofa or the bed. The cat came out of hiding. Sometimes she was there purring, sometimes not. Max wanted out. Max wanted in. Cat took advantage as she saw fit, but was pretty much silent otherwise. Max wasn't. Occasionally, Libbie could hear him nearby making noises in his sleep. Dreaming. But the noises sounded fretful. It was as if she was poisoning the atmosphere of the house for every living creature.

She tried to take a walk, but when she reached the terrace, she made it no farther than the wrought iron chairs. She sat. Max arrived with his tennis ball. She ignored him. She heard shots in the distance and remembered the disturbed ground on the far side of the creek. Brittleness built inside of her. It grew to a certain level of vibration and she became afraid of what might happen if it reached the perfect pitch. She would shatter. It was all about collateral damage, right? Who else might she take with her?

Collateral damage. The cement block, all that remained of the garage, sat a few yards away. Evidence of folly, and of the efforts of good friends to help, even if it made no sense to them, as it surely hadn't. Still, they'd been there. Dan, no doubt at Jim's request. Who else?

And what had she done?

Gone back to the same old dark space.

Shaking, Libbie shoved her hands in her jacket pockets and kept the fabric between her skin and the door knob. She was careful not touch the walls, nor the stair rail. She was poison. She climbed back into bed fully dressed and pulled the covers over her head, accompanied by the fear that this time, the dark might not go away. Ever again.

****

She woke. It was late. The sun was up, and streams of light passed through the window glass and touched her face. Dust motes danced in those streams. The cat was on her chest purring so hard that it vibrated in her lungs.

Feline forgiveness?

Maybe, but it was disconcerting and incredibly uncomfortable. Plus, Max had broken all the rules by joining her on the bed.

He'd stretched his long body across her legs.

She was trapped. But she wasn't alone.

A wet cat nose touched Libbie's. Max's head popped up.

Libbie stretched out an arm and touched the sunbeams with her hand. She waved her fingers through the particle stream and the motes danced around them.

Yes, she was still here, and back.

She shoved the cat aside and wiggled her legs to dislodge her dog. He jumped up but when Libbie tried to exit the bed, she was caught up in the covers and rolled over the edge and onto the floor. This time, with a softer landing.

Max was delighted and washed her face.

The cat meowed loudly from the doorway. It was breakfast time.

Wash the water bowls and food bowls. Change the kitty litter. Refill the water and food bowls. Watch the dry pieces fall, once again, on the linoleum. Max was messy, though, to his credit, he ate it all.

Libbie had had a spell, with a basis in reason as Joyce might say, and she'd come through it on the other side. That candle on her mantelpiece, a gift from a friend, was a reminder that a valley is only a valley. It's a valley because of the amazing views from either side of it.

She wouldn't depend on any living person, not her unfortunate family, nor Jim or Dan or anyone, for her happiness.

Furthermore, she was going to postpone that book of Sicily photos. Jim was in too many of them. Instead, she'd pick some favorites, get them blown up and framed. Scenery. Lovely scenery and a lot of good memories, too, which she'd appreciate someday in the future.

Libbie forced the orange vest onto Max. He fidgeted while she was tugging it over his head and tucking the sides under him to buckle it, but he didn't mind once it was done. But then, he'd do almost anything for a walk in the woods. It was new and fresh to him every time. Libbie put on the orange vest and hat, too.

The weather had chilled significantly and many of the trees were bare, or nearly so. As they walked along the path, she kicked the clean, dry leaves in the air and Max jumped at them. She crossed the one, rickety remaining board over the creek and kept going. Max ignore the board and with one, great, running leap he crossed a narrower spot and raced up to join her. They went beyond the Lady's Slipper clearing and along the path. She'd never gone the whole way before.

They heard small sounds in the brush but didn't see another soul. It was a long, winding walk and in parts the path was almost nonexistent, but with the leaves down the view was good and the sun reached through and dispelled most of the shadows until they reached the main road. Ethel's Home for Adults across the road and a ways up. This was a main route. A car whooshed by. Max barked and started forward.

Libbie grabbed his collar as another car shot past. She had to dig in her heels and lean backward to hold him.

"Stay with me, Max."

She needed a leash. Max, his eyes flashing and his tongue panting, looked at her like she was crazy. She kept her hand tight on his collar until they were well back along the path, then she fell to her knees and hugged him. He waited patiently. When she released him, he ran off, dashed back, and ran off again. His orange vest flashed in and out among the tree trunks and thickets.

Libbie loved him like that. Realizing it, she felt the potential loss.

What had she thought the other day? That there was life, and then there was living a life that sucked? And loss? That was part of life, too.

No matter how much she wanted that safety for him at this moment. In the end, fate was fate, and if either of them had a date with it, then at least they wouldn't regret the time spent while on the journey to meet it.

****

Almost two weeks later, Libbie was in the grocery store. It was packed and humming with shoppers. The woman ahead of her, paying for her groceries, said to the cashier, "It's too early for snow."

"Not so. We get an inch or two in November every few years," said the man in line behind her.

An older man at the next register chimed in. "We got a decent one back in 1980-something. About a foot?"

The woman in front of Libbie responded, "A foot? Not hardly. I remember. 1987. That's when my Billy was born. About half that, but it was enough, let me tell you. Thought he was going to be born at home."

"I'll bet you were scared," the young cashier said.

"Not half as scared as my husband."

Everyone laughed.

In Libbie's brain, she heard the silent, repeated protest, 'but it's only November.' Then it hit her. She said aloud, "November 11th. Veterans Day snowstorm."

The old man nodded. "That's right. You are correct, ma'am."

"I lived near DC. We got almost a foot and a

half. That's what I heard anyway." Did she really remember the feel of the snow? She'd been hardly more than a baby. The flakes had been cold on her face. Someone had held her and laughed. A woman. A woman with dark hair who'd hugged her and laughed, wiping the snow from the infant's cheeks.

Was it a real memory?

Her heart rate increased, but in anticipation, not in fear. Then, happily succumbing to the same instinct that drove everyone else, she gave up her place in line and went back to grab a container of milk and a loaf of bread. Toilet paper, too.

Herd mentality? Maybe, but it was comforting in its own way and unexpectedly fun to be a part of the group chaos. Not really chaos, as the people and carts moved in an orderly flow through the aisles, but they were all sharing an experience, and she didn't mind the crowd at all.

****

The snow fell. First the flakes were tentative, lightweight, and flyaway. A tease. It never occurred to her to worry.

Down it came. Libbie stood at the window as the snowfall thickened and sometimes swirled and the visibility went to nil, but that didn't last and each time the flakes resumed their well-mannered descent.

She went to the front door and called Max. She yelled his name again and finally he came loping across the yard. Apparently in joyful appreciation, he jumped and rolled in the now snow-covered grass. As he bounded back to his feet and raced up the steps, she yelled 'Max' again, attempting to stop him. Water, flakes and ice flew from his coat and his paws as he shook the wet loose. She ran to the laundry room for towels.

Libbie had seen snow before, of course. City snow. She'd shoveled her short walk when she lived in the townhouse in Fairfax. When it was too deep she stayed home until the plows came through and the townhouse association cleared the rest.

She made sure the storm door latched securely and then flipped the thumb lock, but she left the front door open. She wanted to view the falling flakes. They looked like music to her, something in the rhythm and pattern of their descent. She began mopping up the melting snow from the floor. Max assisted by rolling his body in the remaining icy lumps of white, and then lapping at the small pools of water. The cat watched from the arm of the stuffed chair in the living room. She didn't appreciate snow.

When had Libbie last seen the snow shovel? Last winter when she was still living in the townhouse? Or maybe the year before?

So, she'd stood in that grocery store line with bread, milk and toilet paper on her mind, but had forgotten about a snow shovel.

Shopping list time. Snow shovel went at the top. Maybe a little rock salt, too. After all, it wasn't officially winter yet, so this could be a hint, or a warning, of what might yet come. She'd always been self-sufficient, but out here on her own it was her job to pay attention.

Libbie pulled on her boots, then grabbed the broom and used it to sweep a walkway across the porch and down to the sidewalk, then with her boots off, she crossed the foyer and went through the hall to the kitchen where she put them back on. She swept the back stoop and the steps. She wasn't expecting anyone, but it seemed the responsible citizen thing to do, plus the snowstorm infused her with energy and she needed to be doing something.

After only about four inches, it stopped. The sky overhead was still heavy-looking, but the air was quiet. The snow hung in the tree branches, thicker in the pines, but in high, narrow ridges on the limbs of the leafless deciduous trees. A fluffy, decorative snow.

Libbie stood on her front porch and snapped a few photos, letting the lens capture the treeless, and, thus far unspoiled, snow-covered pastures of the Pettus farm. Dissatisfied, she set her camera on the kitchen counter and fixed a grilled cheese sandwich for lunch. As she ate, she stared out through the kitchen window. The heavy gray sky hung low over the trees, but in the nearer view, where the back yard met the woods and the path became visible, that area had a pinkish cast. The snow, the path as it stretched toward its vanishing point, even a small area of the clouds overhead, were pinkish. It didn't change. Some sort of weird reflection.

She picked up the camera. On the back stoop, once again wearing her boots, but otherwise shivering, she snapped some photos.

Back in the kitchen, she pressed the button to view the photos on the LCD screen on the back of the camera.

No pink. Not the slightest pinkish tone.

So, what did that mean? Anything?

Libbie left her mind blank to see if a thought would come. None did.

Could be the settings on the camera. Maybe.

Max saw Libbie donning her coat and fidgeted and whined.

"Not yet, Max. I'd like to get some pictures before you spoil the snow. I promise, when I come back...." No way she could say she'd let him out later, because 'out' was a magic word for Max.

She wrapped the wool scarf around her head and neck, picked up her camera and made use of those swept steps.

Snow in the city was pretty, at least while it was falling. If you could stay home and had supplies, the snow was mostly someone else's responsibility. Snow in the country had a life of its own. Its own rules. The landscape changed. The features became smoothed over and everything, innocent or guilty, ugly and dangerous or alluring and pleasing, was covered. As Libbie paused in her back yard, even the sounds were absent as if they'd been soaked up by the white blanket.

Beyond her, the pink cast, fainter now, still drew her.

Chapter Eleven

Libbie could still see the pink cast, but as she approached the woods, the trees dominated her view, and the pink faded as did most of her view of the sky. She entered the woods, shielding the camera with her scarf to protect it from any snow bombs falling from the tree branches overhead. She tried a few snapshots of the woods here and there, then turned back to face the house. There were some interesting angles where the white of the snow contrasted with the tree branches or the wrought iron table, but none of the scenes in the viewfinder grabbed her. She snapped them anyway because she was out here, and though the pink color was gone, her curiosity wasn't.

The path through the woods was an untouched sheet of snow except here and there, where tiny feet had poked through. Twiggy bird feet. A couple of trails looked lightly brushed in addition to the footprints. Squirrels.

In this silent, snowy world, the music of Cub Creek was clearly audible though it was still distant. She closed her eyes and listened as the water spilled around and over the rocks in rivulets of color.

When she opened her eyes, she stared up at the branches. They were laden with snow and interspersed with views of the clouds. Shades of gray and white. She wished the sky was blue. The eerie, moody atmosphere of the woods under snow was too hard to capture. With the sun, the moodiness would vanish and the photos would be much sharper.

She stood feeling encased in the clarity of the pure air and undisturbed snow, feeling it in her head, but not in words, her mind silent, until her feet turned cold. The curiosity was gone now about the pink sky. Whatever. She could no longer see it anyway. This experience was sufficient unto itself. Well, except for her cold toes.

A squirrel scampered overhead shaking snow loose and disturbing her peace. Suddenly, a male Cardinal, flagrantly red, passed by in a short flight, to alight on a nearby branch. Seeing her, he took off again, flying down the path toward the creek. Libbie tucked her camera back under her scarf and followed him.

At the creek, the board she'd moved was half in the brush and partly covered in snow. It gave her a bit of satisfaction in an embarrassed way. Temper tantrums always seemed reasonable in the moment of heat. That seeming reasonableness paled when rationality resumed. Yet this was her land and her board, and they'd been trespassers.

The end of the board, not shielded by the bushes, was covered with snow. The snow filled in the flaws and it appeared almost too perfect in its shape and form. She knelt to snap the shot, then moved closer to the creek. She took a few more photographs where the dark water met the rocks. The snow was sculpted by water and gravity into a small ledge, thin and fragile, over the edges of the rocks.

Libbie stood upright, nearly slipped, but got her footing back. She congratulated herself on not falling into the cold water, and gave an appreciative shiver.

She tried again, but it was slippery near the creek. After one more slip, she stepped away. It was far too cold for a swim today, and too much risk for the camera.

Something caught her eye on the far side. It lay at an angle, on the slope, different from the trees standing starkly upright. Everything else on the ground was covered.

Then the flakes began again, touching Libbie's nose and cheek and catching in her lashes. She unfastened a couple of buttons and shoved the camera inside her coat. With her arm tightly against it on the outside, the camera was secure and protected. Another burst filled the air like the earlier snow swirls, and then the wind picked up abruptly, shaking the branches overhead. It was hard to tell what snow was falling from the sky and what was falling from the trees.

Libbie ducked to dodge a chunk of snow and in that moment, she saw movement on the far side, something running swift, low and dark from the clearing and into the brush. Then another. Coyotes?

A sharp moment of fear. She wished Max was here. No, she didn't. He wouldn't scare them off, he'd chase them. Then she'd be really worried.

She heard a small sound. She couldn't pick it out. She stared across the creek at the dark form that was quickly being covered, and she knew what—no, she knew who it was.

Frantic, Libbie grabbed the board from the underbrush, dragged it, hoisted it, tried to balance it and swing it across the creek. The adrenalin surge made it possible, and the board landed in the right spot. There was nothing in her brain except to get across the creek.

Two steps maybe. No more. No slipping, More like flying, and she was across. She did slip as she scrambled up the slope but hardly noticed, then she was there, on the ground beside Joyce.

She touched her cheeks and called her name. "Joyce? Joyce!"

No response. Joyce's eyes were closed. Her wispy hair was dotted with snow. Her cheeks were pale. Libbie put her arm under her friend. The old woman wore a coat and shoes, but it wasn't enough against the cold and ice. Her flesh was cold. Libbie pressed her hand to her chest. She felt the beat, faint, but there.

They couldn't stay out here.

"Okay, Joyce. Let's get you up and moving."

Joyce needed help. Libbie needed help. But Libbie couldn't leave her to get help and she hadn't brought her phone. Only her camera. The camera was gone. She didn't remember when or where, or care.

Joyce wasn't much more than skin over bones, but even so, Libbie couldn't properly carry her. She half-carried, half-dragged her down the short slope to the creek and across the boards. If she slipped, both of them would go into that freezing water.

Later, she didn't remember much about crossing the boards with Joyce, except for the desperate prayers. Only the words of her prayers remained solidly in her memory, and she was grateful.

On the far side, she lowered Joyce back onto the ground. She let her down gently, but she'd roused a tiny bit. Her lips moved. Her eyelids fluttered.

"Hang in here with me, Joyce. I'm going to try to make you warmer, then I'll get you back to the house."

As quickly as she could, Libbie stripped Joyce's coat from her and replaced it with her own, still warm from her body. She put Joyce's cold coat over it hoping it would help insulate the warmth inside. Libbie yanked Joyce's shoes off and pushed her boots onto Joyce's feet. And that was about all she could do.

Libbie stood and tried to lift her. She'd carry her if she could, for as far as she could. Either way, Libbie would get her to the house, because not doing so wasn't an option.

She prayed she wouldn't drop her, or fall, and land on top of her and her frail bones. Libbie muttered, "Alice, while you were talking to her why didn't you tell her to stay put at the Home?"

Then there was no spare breath for muttering. Those first few steps felt almost easy, then her arms and back burned with the strain. Her feet, bare except for socks, grew colder than she thought possible, burning in a new way. Libbie reached the edge of the woods and thought about taking a short break, even a moment to adjust the load, but was afraid that if she did she wouldn't be able to lift her again. She would have no choice but to drag her.

Her chest ached. Her knees felt wobbly. The falling snow caught in her lashes, blinding her, and she couldn't brush them away. Joyce's limp form began a slow slide from Libbie's arms and Libbie couldn't stop her. She fell to the ground beside Joyce, gasping.

Libbie stayed in the snow, her back, her lungs, her feet burning from the strain and cold. She kept her arms around Joyce and tried to think of good things, of sun and strength and joy, but it was too cold and reality was too stark. She remembered the story of a child who'd carried a larger child to safety on her back. She couldn't remember the novel, but she tried to do the same. She didn't succeed, but in the effort, she was able lift her and stand. Libbie walked backward with her arms under Joyce's and her boots digging through Libbie's own footprints as they backed out of the woods and toward the house.

Out of the relative shelter of the woods, the snow fell in nearly blinding gusts. The back steps were covered again and Libbie didn't dare try to climb them with Joyce. She sat. With Joyce on her lap and her arm around Joyce's mid-section, Libbie pushed up with her legs to reach the next step. Joyce slipped to the side. Sit-push-sit, repeat. Once more she told herself she'd deal with Joyce's condition after they made it inside. She'd think about that then.

Right now, she must sit, push up and sit again, until she could stretch around and up and touch the knob. When she could, she pushed the door open and they both fell backward across the threshold and onto the kitchen floor.

She pulled Joyce clear of the door and closed it.

Her pallor frightened Libbie, not into paralysis, but into motion. Joyce was conscious and peeking at her, but with no sign of recognition.

"I'll get some blankets." Libbie grabbed the rose throw from the sofa. She pulled the boots off of Joyce's feet and rubbed her feet and hands with the towels. Her limbs were so fragile, the skin so thin, Libbie was afraid she would rub too hard and damage her.

Words. Joyce's lips moved and Libbie put her ear close to her face, but couldn't understand.

What to do? They needed warmth. Soup? Hot water. Her thoughts were frantic. First things first. She had to get Joyce off the cold, now wet, floor.

She could do this. She lifted Joyce once more and put her on the sofa. She didn't feel as heavy this time, perhaps less of a dead weight. Joyce's hand touched her as Libbie slid her arms out from under her.

"Gone. Tried to...."

"Hush, now. Don't try to talk yet." Libbie pushed Joyce's hair out of her face and patted her cheeks gently. "I'm heating water. I'll drop a couple of bouillon cubes in it and we'll get you warmed up inside, too."

Max was suddenly underfoot. He woofed softly, then pressed his nose against Joyce's arm. The cat climbed up the back of the sofa, her claws plucking the upholstery. Libbie grabbed her and put her furry body on Joyce's feet. To her amazement, the cat stayed.

"...cross. Couldn't."

Libbie grabbed her cell phone on the way to the kitchen and called 9-1-1.

In that moment, for whatever reason, she remembered her camera. Out in the snow, probably buried in a drift. Oh, well. She'd lost the camera in Sicily when it was smashed by the car. It had taken the brunt of the force that hit Jim and had, thus, served her well. Now she'd lost another camera, but this time to the elements of nature.

Joyce had something to thank a camera for, as Jim did.

Libbie held Joyce's hand as the water heated. She looked at Joyce, stared at her face, and tried to send her warm feelings and images of sun and sand and summer flowers. But she didn't feel the connection and knew it didn't help. So, they waited.

****

A tree was down at one end of Cub Creek Loop and someone had had a minor accident at the other end. The driver was uninjured. The end result was that the EMS techs arrived sooner than expected, but on foot.

The kettle shrieked and Libbie ran to turn it off while they checked Joyce out.

Joyce made a noise. Her eyelids fluttered again and Libbie said, "Hi, there."

She shivered. "Cold. Very cold in my bones."

They wrapped her gently. "We'll get her to the hospital. They should have the road cleared and the vehicle up here soon."

Within minutes, they heard the noise of the ambulance easing down the snowy, crunchy road. Carefully, but without difficulty, the vehicle rolled up her driveway.

"Finally got the road cleared, ma'am."

"Where are you taking her?" Suddenly Libbie realized she wasn't invited to go along with the EMTs, plus if she did go with them, she'd be stranded there without a car after the roads were cleared.

If she couldn't go with them, she'd drive herself there, snow or not.

"Where? I'll follow."

"Charlottesville, ma'am. I don't recommend driving. Wait until everything's clear. Lots of accidents out there."

The keys felt heavy in Libbie's hand. Now that the first urgency was past, and decisions could be given conscious thought, she was indecisive and was suddenly sure that if she stayed behind, it would be because she was a coward and a bad friend.

She picked up her coat. "I'll be fine."

They carried the stretcher out to the vehicle. Libbie was trying to force her feet into the wet, cold boots when Dan arrived.

"I was down the road at the accident scene. Got word about Joyce being missing about the same time your call came in."

"Oh, Dan." The pent-up emotion, the adrenalin, all whooshed out of her. She threw her hands up to her face almost giving herself a black eye with the keys, crying out, "Suppose... suppose...."

Dan stepped toward her as she stumbled with a foot half in the wet boot. She grabbed him, and he grabbed her back and kept her from falling. He was the closest thing to a friend she had, especially with Jim gone from her life, and they both loved Joyce.

A man's voice floated over to them. "Dan?"

He released her and called back, "I've got this. Keep me posted."

"Will do."

Max barked, and Dan, with a hard, firm

voice, called him inside. He shut the door. Libbie went to the window and watched the lights come alive on the ambulance. She started to shake.

Dan asked, "Got any coffee? I'm half-frozen."

Coffee? "I have instant."

"That'll do."

"But Joyce...."

"She's in good hands. For now, your part is done. They'll call with an update as soon as they know anything."

"Are you sure?"

He nodded.

"Okay. Coffee." It was good to have something to do. A purpose, even if it was only coffee. She glanced over at Dan. Had that been his intent?

Joyce's coat, wet and limp, lay on the floor. Libbie stopped to pick it up. Joyce's shoes were somewhere out there by the creek, with Libbie's camera. But Dan needed coffee and she was glad.

"Where was she?"

She looked up, coat in hand. Dan was standing at the kitchen door.

He continued, "The Home didn't know what happened. Only that she wasn't there. Don't tell me she took a walk?"

Libbie nodded. "I went for a walk myself

294

when the snow stopped." She shrugged, deciding not to mention the pink light. "I took my camera." Libbie looked toward the woods. "It's out there now, somewhere out by the creek with Joyce's shoes."

He looked down at her feet still clad in wet socks.

"She lost her shoes?"

"I took them off of her. They were wet. I gave her my boots. She wasn't conscious most of the time."

"Probably sleeping deeply. The cold can do that."

The kettle whistled. Libbie poured water into the cup of coffee for Dan and the hot chocolate for herself.

Dan said, "Everyone was distracted with the snow, so they didn't miss her for a while."

Libbie looked at the window and stirred the chocolate to cool it. The last light was fading. Dan's hands were wrapped around his mug. The steam rose.

"Don't you need to go?" she asked.

He pointed at this radio. "They'll call."

"I feel like it was my fault. Not really my fault, but still...."

His voice came back harshly, almost suspiciously. "Why?"

"I moved the board. The big one. She wouldn't have been able to cross on the skinny one."

He frowned.

"I'm talking about the boards for crossing the creek. The bridge. I moved one. She must've intended to cross the creek, but couldn't because the board had been moved. Only the skinny, crooked board was left. She must've tried to go back home, but didn't make it all the way up the slope."

Dan shook his head. "Moving the board probably saved her life. A snowy board? She'd have fallen. In that creek, in this cold, she wouldn't last more than a few minutes."

Libbie hadn't thought of that. She sat at the table. Suddenly, she was grateful to the hunter who'd pissed her off. She was truly, deeply grateful to Dan for pointing out that her board-tossing tantrum hadn't nearly cost Joyce her life.

She reached across the table and touched his hand, briefly and lightly. "Thank you."

His phone rang. He slipped it from his pocket. "Wheeler." He listened, then said. "Hold." He looked at Libbie. "She's good. They made it to the interstate. They'll be at the hospital shortly." He stood and walked into the other room, talking softly.

Libbie tried to enjoy her hot chocolate, but as she sat she felt her energy draining. She sagged, leaning forward, her arms on the table.

Dan returned. He put his hand on her shoulder, warm, yet gentle.

She turned to look at him. "You're not in uniform. You drove up in your truck, right? Are you off duty?"

"I heard the call come through. In this kind of weather, no one's off-duty. With the road conditions, I'd rather be driving my SUV than my cruiser, anyway."

"Dan, does she have family? Not someone like me, but a real niece? We need to let them know. Joyce can't be at the hospital all by herself." She stood. "I can call the Home. They should know about her family. Do you think they'll tell me? They already think I'm her niece."

"Calm down. Steady. I know she doesn't have family." He rubbed the back of his neck. "I understand what you're saying, but you're better off here."

"Think about how she feels, all alone at the hospital after nearly dying." Libbie shook her head. "It's not right, Dan."

"Okay, I'll get you there." He leveled his gaze, firmly at hers. "But the snow is still coming down and you'll be stuck there awhile. I can't come back for you until tomorrow. Maybe not even then if I'm on duty. Give me your spare car key. If the opportunity arises, I'll have someone bring your car over tomorrow, if I can't."

"Thanks so much. Let me grab a dry coat."

He called after her, "Dry socks, too. You're gonna have a long night."

****

Dan backed down the driveway. The tire marks left by the ambulance were nearly filled in. The flakes were big, highlighted by the bright headlamps as they splatted against the windshield. The windshield wipers raced across and swept the bits away. Clearly, Dan's vehicle meant business and wasn't prepared to be sentimental about a pretty snowfall, and that's exactly the attitude Libbie needed.

She warned, "Watch out for the ditches."

"No."

"No, what?"

"Don't do that."

He said the words calmly, as if assuming cooperation.

She sat back and tried not to offer more assistance. He was doing her a big favor, after all.

"I'm taking you as far as the service station just this side of the interstate."

"What?"

"They have volunteer drivers who drive the nurses and docs into the hospital in bad weather. One of them is doing a run right now.

We'll meet him there and he'll take you the rest of the way."

"I thought you were...."

He nodded. "I'm needed here. This snow is forecast to keep going through the night." He spared her a quick look. "Sometimes the forecasters get it right. We'll see."

The driver would be a stranger, but a ride was a ride and, for Joyce's sake, she needed one.

"Thank you, Dan. I appreciate you going to all this trouble for me. And for Joyce, of course."

He nodded, but kept his attention on the road.

The halogen lamps, like islands of fuzzy light high overhead, lit the adjacent area. There was also a light on in the service station, but the parking lot was empty, its snowy covering nearly unmarred. The tail end of a parked car was visible beyond the corner of the building.

Dan checked his watch. "Any time now."

Without Dan's driving for Libbie to focus on, suddenly the silence felt awkward, as if Jim was sitting in that car with them and it felt crowded.

"How's he doing?" she asked.

Dan didn't ask who. He said, "Ask him yourself."

"He doesn't want to talk to me right now. Not until life is normal again. Whatever that is."

Dan's arm straddled the steering wheel. He

tapped his fingers on the hard vinyl.

"When he changes his mind, he knows where I am and how to reach me."

He turned toward her and stared. "Do you want him to? Someone's been talking to him." He stopped suddenly, looked angry and turned his face away.

She frowned. "What do you mean? Of course, I–"

The words were slammed out of her mouth from behind. The SUV jumped forward, stopped suddenly, and then spun, pivoting. Ice, maybe. Something had hit them and she caught a brief glimpse of it as the world revolved. The other vehicle, an old, low-slung sedan, continued past and, in what seemed a slow, lazy crazy-eight spin, it slid across the lot. By the time their next revolution was complete, the other car was gone.

So fast. It happened so very fast. Both Dan and Libbie were wearing seatbelts. The airbags didn't even deploy. Dan worked to gain control of the vehicle. As soon as he did, he called out to Libbie, "You okay? Get out of the car." and he was out of the vehicle, rounding the front and opening her door. He pulled her out. "Stay out of the car. Go inside."

With an arm around her to steady her on the slick parking lot, he propelled her across to the lit convenience store and pushed her inside.

The clerk was staring in excited shock and holding a phone. Dan left her there. Back outside, talking into his phone, he crossed the lot carefully, but quickly to the side of the building where the ground sloped away. Beyond that, Libbie could see the thick trees beyond, but knew the interstate was on the other side. Between here and the trees was a big, dark gully.

Dan paused for a moment at the top of the slope. How could he see through the dark and the snow? But he must've been able to see something because he went over. He vanished from sight.

She clutched her purse. She hadn't consciously grabbed it. Habit. She searched in the side pocket for her phone—not there—then realized the clerk and Dan had already called for help. The clerk was saying something but Libbie ignored him as she opened the door and stepped out. Damp or not, her boots had rough rubber soles and gripped well. She had to see where Dan had gone and if he was okay.

It was dark down there, especially near the trees, but she could see more than she expected because the snow seemed to fluoresce. It coated everything with a gleaming whiteness, probably enhanced by the reflections from the tall light poles. The car was half-buried nose-deep in a snow drift.

Headlights behind her projected her shadow forward, as if she was reaching down that slope, extending freakishly elongated arms toward the car. Another SUV had arrived. Must be the hospital ride. Had to be. She stepped toward it, waving it away from Dan's vehicle. Waving a warning was probably unnecessary given the angle of Dan's parked SUV, not to mention the story told by the churned up snow and the wheelie tracks crisscrossing the lot and others marking the grass.

The falling snow had slacked off again. Libbie hardly noticed the few flakes now hitting her face, but her nose and feet were cold. She'd had as much snow as she could stand, first earlier today and now this, and it wasn't yet officially winter.

The driver rolled down his window.

"What's up?" he asked, as his eyes moved past her to the tracks beyond.

"A car hit us while we were parked here. It spun around and went over the slope there." She pointed, then turned back. "Dan Wheeler went down after it."

The man rolled up the window, opened the door and came out. He grabbed a heavy coat from the seat and put it on.

"You should stay inside the station."

"I will."

As he walked away, she moved around to

the passenger side. The passenger was already stepping out.

"Come on," the woman said.

They went into the station, but Libbie was anxious and impatient.

"Coffee?"

She looked around. The woman was standing at a coffee counter putting the plastic lid on a heavy paper cup.

"No, thanks."

"You're worried about your friend?"

"Dan. He's a deputy, but it's dark down there. It's...."

"It's what he does. Don't waste your worry."

"Pardon?"

"I was married to a man like that. Deputies. Firefighters. Soldiers. They go places where they can reasonably expect to be injured or worse. Still, they go. It's what they do." She sipped her coffee. "Ouch. That's hot."

Maybe the woman might be right. It might be easier to be the doer than the one who waits. Action, like trying to carry Joyce to her house, was scary and difficult, but all forward motion. No waffling. No time for vanity or self-torture or what-ifs, focusing only on the task.

"Tea, I think." She walked over to see what was available and tried to be sociable. "You're a nurse?"

"I am. You? John said we had to pick

someone else up."

"Me, but I'm not a nurse."

"Well, take it from me. Try not to worry over him too much. It's tough when you love someone like that, but you have to let them do what they must."

Libbie fumbled the cup. "Oh, no. We're not a couple or anything. I have a friend who was injured earlier this afternoon and was taken to the hospital. She's alone. I was trying to get there to be with her and Dan helped me." She added, "She's old."

"Well, as soon as the driver gets back up here, we'll be on our way."

Libbie stood nose-close to the large plate-glass windows. The cold radiated for several inches into the room, a tease of what it must be like down that hill. Lights, like flashlights, shown above the crest of the hill from time to time. Then she felt the rumble of a powerful engine and the plate glass reflected the lights of an emergency vehicle.

She turned to look. A large tow truck.

The woman said, "Not much longer, is my guess."

Chapter Twelve

The nurse at the hospital said, "She's been admitted." She gave Libbie the room number.

Libbie sat in the plastic-covered chair, pulled up next to the bed. Joyce appeared to be sleeping peacefully with no additional apparatus attached to her, other than an IV. It was clear liquid. Probably saline. Libbie leaned her head back.

"She's here for the night, at least," the nurse had said.

Joyce's color looked better. Better, in fact, than she'd looked recently, even before today's adventure. Her face looked plumper. The wrinkles were diminished.

"Dehydration is a big problem for the elderly," the nurse had added.

Libbie sat in the chair near the bed and let it all slip away. Jim. Dan. Liz. Margaret. And Barry, of course. She was suddenly exhausted, and it was sufficient for her to be in this moment only. She pushed every other thought aside. The past and future could take care of themselves for now.

****

"Libbie."

A whisper, slightly hoarse, woke her.

"Joyce." She leaned forward scooting to the edge of her seat so that she could touch her arm. "How are you feeling?"

"It is you. I saw you and couldn't think where I was."

"Do you remember what happened?"

Joyce made a sound almost like humming. Her eyes had closed again.

"Rest. We can talk later."

"Juice," she said without opening her eyes.

"There's water here by the bedside." Libbie reached for the pitcher.

"Juice."

"I'll check with the nurse. Be right back." When she returned, she told her, "Apple juice is all they have."

No movement. Asleep again. Libbie sat the small bottle on the bedside table.

Joyce stirred. One hand fluttered atop the white coverlet. "I was always an early riser."

Libbie handed her the juice with a straw. She steadied Joyce's hand as she held it and sipped.

"It's three a.m. That's not early. That's the middle of the night."

"I could've gone home. Seems like false

pretenses, me still being here and taking up a bed." Another sip. "But I was cold. So cold. Couldn't get warmed up. I was willing to stay. They warm up the blankets. Toasty." She took another sip, then held it out. When Libbie had it in hand, Joyce laid her head back against the pillow.

"Are you warm enough now?"

"Oh, yes. I'm good." She looked at Libbie with tired eyes as if seeing her here for the first time all over again. "What about you?"

"Fine. I went for a walk in the woods to see the snow, and found you."

She stared at the ceiling, then the wall opposite. "Is it still snowing?"

"I don't know." Libbie pushed the curtains aside. "Hard to tell. Maybe lightly."

"Did you bring me here?"

"No. I got you as far as my house. The EMTs came and they brought you here."

"Oh, my. Well, I've caused quite a lot of fuss. I don't suppose I'll hear the end of it from the matron."

"As it should be. You can hardly blame her."

Joyce shrugged. "I recall I was thinking about Alice. Thought I'd go visit her." She went silent for a few seconds, then added, "Well, not exactly visit, but you know what I mean."

"Revisit memories?"

"Something like that. Felt almost young

again, starting out down the path." She chuckled. "I remember once, back when Alice's husband was travelling and my first husband, Johnny, had spent a year's salary on a new car. Men and flashy cars, you know. I was so angry. I grew up poor and had no patience with foolish vanity and a waste of good money. I stomped over to Alice's house to vent. Alice always had a way of evenin' it out for me."

"I wish I'd known her."

"Humph. Likely she would've seemed like one more old woman to you. But maybe not. Now I think of it, she probably could have helped you sort your head out. She had that way."

"Sort my head out?"

"You got a lot going on in there."

Libbie stopped herself from replying and changed direction. "Don't you think you should get some rest?"

Joyce dozed and Libbie settled back into the chair. She may have nodded off, too, because when Joyce spoke again, her voice was dreamlike in the dim room.

"I always heard about that tunnel and the light. Thought I was ascending, going up to meet my maker. I was surprised. I expected it to be gentle-like. Sort of like flying, like with wings, but without having to work for it." The dreamy quality gave way to her usual, sharper tone. "Instead I was manhandled like a sack of potatoes. I bet I got bruises all over me."

Libbie stayed relaxed in the chair. She was reassured to hear Joyce sounding more like herself. "Good thing you don't weigh more than you do or I would've had to drag you the whole way. That surely would've been unpleasant."

In a voice, no longer dreamy or complaining, but almost in a whisper, Joyce added, "They were sniffing around me. One of them…I felt his breath on my cheek before he ran off."

Coyotes. "Scary, but it was his movement that caught my attention, so it worked out."

"When you get so cold, you sort of don't care much about anything. Like going to sleep. I've heard that said. It's true. It hurts at first, but not for long."

"Then I'm glad I disturbed you."

She chuckled. "Me, too." She sighed. "Well, I'm stuck here, but you should go home. Get some rest and do it where you really can."

"I'm content." Libbie propped her legs up on the heater. "Besides, with the snow, the roads are a mess. I got a ride in. Dan, or someone, will pick me up in the morning."

"Get some sleep, girl."

"Oh, I've been up at three and four a.m. many times. I'm a pro at it."

"Restless nights? Insomnia?"

"You could say that. Though, it hasn't

happened in a while."

"Dan, did you say?" Joyce lifted her head an inch off the pillow and eyed her. "I must be getting slow. Why Dan? What happened to Jim?"

"Dan? Dan was in the area. He showed up as they were taking you to the hospital. I wanted to ride along, but they wouldn't allow it. Dan arranged a ride to the hospital for me." She skipped over the drama of that ride.

"And Jim? Have you sent him packing? So to speak, I mean."

"No. We broke it off. I think."

"Did you move on since you're spending time with Dan again?"

"No. Remember, I said Dan came to my house because of you? As for Jim, it's over but it doesn't feel over. Not in here." She touched her chest over her heart.

Joyce put her head back onto the pillow. "No surprise you can't sleep. Got men on your mind."

"No. In fact I just said that I've been sleeping unusually well despite the mess with Jim."

"No conscience, I guess."

"Too much conscience, if anything. Too loud. But it's been so much better since.... The longer I've been at Cub Creek, the better...some things have been." She was thinking more about what she wasn't saying.

She wouldn't say aloud to Joyce that she'd messed up. She'd had her chance with Jim and had thought, at one time, that it would all work out. True love should work out. If there was such a thing.

Joyce's eyes had closed. Silence. She'd dozed off again. Libbie rested her head back against the chair and tried to do the same.

"You think too much."

Her voice was so soft, the words so feathery, that they drifted around Libbie's head for a few seconds before her brain pulled them all together and she realized Joyce was speaking again.

Libbie opened her eyes. Joyce's were still closed. Her breathing was low and regular. Libbie settled back again in the chair.

Had she said those words? Or had Libbie dreamed them? Either way, it was too true.

****

The doctor came early in the morning to check on Joyce. He suggested she might want to stay another night, but she was adamant, both surly and charming at the same time, so he agreed. Dan arrived after breakfast. The orderly insisted on a wheelchair for the bon voyage and Joyce didn't argue. She was exhausted by the time she was settled in the SUV.

There was a slight dent on his back bumper.
"This is it?" Libbie asked.

He nodded as he stepped back from belting Joyce into the back seat. Libbie sat in the back seat next to her.

"Are you sure you're okay?"

She sighed deeply, then said, "I might as well be a baby the way you treat me."

Dan laughed. "On our way."

Joyce sniffed. "Well, then." She waved her hand. "No place like home, I guess."

It was enough of a distance that Joyce got in a decent cat nap. Libbie started waking her while they were still a few miles shy.

They stopped at the Home first. An aide came down the ramp with a wheelchair as Libbie undid Joyce's seat belt and Dan helped her out.

"I don't need a chair."

The aide said, "You do, whether you do or not. Let us get you inside where it's warm."

She sat. Dan pushed. Libbie and the aide followed behind. Someone had swept and treated the ramp, so the walking was good. As the wheelchair was rolled over the threshold, Dan stepped aside and stopped Libbie with a hand on her arm.

"We'll see you later," he said. He touched Libbie's arm. "Let's go."

Libbie gave Joyce a quick hug and followed

Dan out.

"Will she be in trouble?"

Dan shrugged. "Some."

He turned her back toward the car and escorted her down the ramp.

"But Dan, shouldn't we talk to Ms. Hughes? Make sure she isn't too rough on her? After all, it's really the Home's fault for not keeping track of her…negligence and all that."

Dan opened the car door for Libbie and she climbed in.

She persisted. "Seriously. They might be angry. Harsh."

"She'll be fine. They won't be too hard on the woman who pays their salaries."

"Pays their…. Oh, you mean like Medicare or Medicaid or something like that?"

He laughed. "I guess you wouldn't know. Joyce owns the place. Used to be her house and she added on when she decided to prepare for her own retirement. Brought the old folks home to her instead of having to go out and find a place."

No, Libbie thought, too stunned to say it aloud.

He laughed again. "You don't believe me?"

"I do…I don't, but I guess I do. I mean, why would you make it up? How would you think to make it up?"

"I have no imagination? Is that it?"

"Stop acting hurt. You know what I mean."

In the daylight, the accident from the day before was obvious. Someone's vehicle had slid off the road and dug trenches in the ditch alongside the road.

"No one was hurt here?"

"No. The ground was so soft it cushioned the impact. Lucky."

"Anyone I know?"

"Allan Pettus. He's driven this road for many years, but when you hit the right slippery patch, anything can happen."

"The right slippery patch...anything can happen. Sounds like a life philosophy." She nodded. "I'm glad he didn't hit the bridge or go down in a steeper spot. They're good people." She smiled at Dan. "You told me that once yourself. When you took me to meet them? You said I needed to meet my neighbors. Seems long ago, but it wasn't. Only months."

"Things measure differently."

Oddly expressed but Libbie knew what he meant.

"Time can be surprisingly flexible," she agreed. "I never asked about the driver you went down the hill to rescue last night."

"He's fine. Snow can be a challenge, but if you're lucky it can also give you a soft landing."

"Luck. No real substitute for it."

"Doesn't pay to depend on it." He pulled into

the driveway and parked up near the house. "By the way, I have something for you."

She got out of the car and Dan took a bag from the back of the SUV. He held it toward her.

"Yours."

She looked inside. "My camera?"

"I went out this morning and found it. Joyce's shoes, too."

Libbie was thanking him as they walked, and she stumbled on the steps. Almost dropped the camera again. Dan was right beside her, steadying her. Max was already barking. Poor Max. Another night alone. When Libbie opened the door, he dashed out.

"What's that?" Dan asked.

"My cat." She was sitting on the stairs. She stood, stretched, and dropped lightly to the floor and swished her tail as she went into the study.

"You have a cat?"

"She has me. Not sure I have her. Anyone missing a cat around here?"

"Not that I've heard," he said as he followed her through the living room and into the kitchen. "Sometimes they get dropped off."

"So Joyce told me."

Libbie carried the bag to the kitchen counter and sat it next to the phone, her phone. She checked it. Dead. She'd charge it later. For now, she removed the camera from the bag. It was surely ruined. The memory card, too. The camera might be fixable. Not likely true for the memory card. She set it on the kitchen table. This was becoming an unfortunate trend for her high-end electronics.

"Dan, thank you for everything. For helping me and Joyce." She waved his words away. "I know you don't need thanks, but I'm still grateful."

"Call me if you run into trouble. It's not too late for a tree to come down and take out the power. You should get a generator. Unless you're going to be moving."

There it was again. The idea of leaving Cub Creek versus the loss of Jim. It must've shown on her face.

"Don't get so wrought up over stuff, Libbie. Clear your head and relax. You'll figure it out."

She turned the burner on under the kettle. "Is there anything left to figure out?" She stopped. Had she said that aloud? "I need hot chocolate. Would you like some?"

"No, I'm good, but thanks."

The turn of his shoulders, the incline of his head, told Libbie that he was about to leave. She stopped him with a hand on his arm.

"Dan, we never discussed what happened the day Tommy was hurt and then we, you and I, stopped being friends."

He frowned. He didn't look angry, but puzzled. "Do you want to discuss it? I remember the last time I tried to discuss a tricky subject with you—your Grandmother—I was invited, in no uncertain terms, to leave your porch."

Libbie smiled in apology. "I know, and if you wanted to chat about her today, I'd probably do the same, or worse. That's in the past. My grandmother is dead and buried. The memories are stubborn, but I'm moving forward, getting better and stronger every day. That's all I have to say about that."

This time Dan smiled. "You are hardheaded. If your grandmother was as hardheaded as you, then it was probably hell for you both."

"Let's move on. I want you to know how much I appreciate your help, with everything, from garage removal to Joyce. I'm glad you've gotten past being angry with me."

"Angry? I wasn't angry."

"I think you were, but let's call it disappointed instead. I'd let you down, and then when you pushed me away...."

"I was helping Tommy, a young man with a profusely bleeding head wound."

"Of course." She felt a moment of hesitation. "Yes, but you wouldn't even look at me. I was upset and frightened and maybe in a little shock, and you told me to move back."

"Because I was attending to a young man with a profusely bleeding head wound."

317

He said it all without rancor. At the most, it was said with a degree of curiosity, but nothing more. Maybe kindness.

Libbie opened her mouth, then closed it. She didn't know what else to say.

Dan said, "I came back. Several times, in fact. I'm pretty sure you were home, but you wouldn't answer the door and you wouldn't take my calls."

True. It was true.

"After a while, I decided it would be better to stop bothering you, but, for the record, I don't think we ever stopped being friends."

"Dan."

"It's okay, Libbie. Everyone has to deal with trouble in their own way. I understood that."

"Thank you, Dan." Impulsively, she hugged him.

When his arms came around her, she was almost surprised, but not really. Dan's arms were comforting, and she put her face against his chest. His hands moved up her back with increasing pressure.

From the doorway, she heard a noise. They both did. Dan released her.

Jim laughed harshly. "I was worried about you with the weather and when you didn't answer your phone.... Guess I didn't need to worry. You've got it handled, without me. Both of you."

Dan stepped back. Libbie watched Jim turn and walk out the way he'd come in.

Well, of course.

She wanted to laugh, cry. Maybe scream.

She started forward. Dan grabbed her arm and held her there.

"I'll talk to him," he said.

"Are you kidding? You expect me to let him walk in and walk out again? Just like that?"

Dan tightened his grip slightly before he released her arm. "Cool off, Libbie. Stay here." He walked out the door.

Cool off? What did that mean? Was he insinuating she had a temper? A hot one?

She didn't. Or didn't used to. But the timing was unbelievable. She had every right to be angry.

Libbie ran to the door. Too late. Jim was already backing down the driveway almost to the road, and Dan's vehicle was right behind.

She tripped over the edge of the rug, and fumbled with the door knob. She flew down the porch steps as both cars reached the road, and sprawled flat out. She landed in the snowy grass, soft, as Dan had said of that ditch. Snowy and muddy. She pushed up from the ground and made it to her knees as Dan's vehicle vanished around the curve in Cub Creek Loop.

Chapter Thirteen

Not long ago, Libbie would've locked the doors and turned off the lights. She would've shut out the world until the world forgot her again. She'd stopped doing that and it seemed the result was a hotter, shorter temper and a tendency to cry. She didn't like the temper. It reminded her too much of that last, disastrous encounter with her grandmother.

But no matter what, she wasn't going to hide again.

She trusted Dan. She had trusted Jim and still did, though she couldn't say it made sense. She wasn't sure either man deserved her trust, but there it was despite them being related. They were cousins and lifelong best friends. When she'd first met them, each had sort of deferred to the other, more solicitous of each other's feelings, guy feelings, than of the new girl in town.

Dan had said to give him a chance to speak with Jim, and so she was doing that. She waited, pacing, as one hour ticked by and then another. Her anger dropped to a low simmer—

still hot with the potential to flare up quickly. Finally, she heard the gravel crunching in the driveway and ran to the window.

Not Jim.

She left the window and went out to the porch. As they had at Halloween, Dan stopped at the foot of the steps. She stood at the top, but then sat down, suddenly discouraged, wet planks or not.

"No Jim?"

Dan shook his head. "Give him time, Libbie. Give him some time."

"No. I've given him enough time."

Dan looked down at the puddles on the sidewalk.

"Come on, Dan. This makes no sense. He's upset about Barry. I can understand that, somewhat, but it was nothing. I handled it badly."

"Jim knows that. He knows it was bad timing for both of you. With Matthew and trying to manage things long-distance, then no sooner than he gets home, Matthew has the infection…and on and on. Then someone from the nursery saw you with a blond-haired man."

"Josh. I hugged him as he was leaving. Again, nothing." She pushed her hair behind her ear. "Just like with you today."

This time Dan paused before answering. "I guessed it was Josh and that's what I told him.

I know Liz has been having problems and you were trying to help."

"You knew?"

"Joyce."

"I see." Libbie shook her head. "No, it's me, Dan. Jim sees me as someone who is needy, self-focused. Not someone he can deal with when other things are going wrong.

"Maybe I am sometimes. Regardless, I want a partnership. Not someone who thinks I want or need them to do all the heavy lifting." She rubbed her temples. "I thought Jim was different. That he understood, respected who I am. But I forgive that. With time, we can work it out. What I can't accept is the suspicion. It's a deflection. An excuse to cover his own fears."

She stood abruptly. "How he could think— and don't deny this—he DID think something was going on between us today. You and I. Did you set him straight? What did he say? I hope he was ashamed."

Dan, with his lovely dark eyes, met and held hers. "He wasn't wrong, Libbie. Not entirely."

Libbie gripped the railing. Her lips felt glued together. Surely there were words to be said, but she didn't know what they were.

He paused for one brief moment, as if waiting for a response, then nodded 'goodbye' and left.

****

The snow melted quickly, as snow in Virginia often did. Snow this early in the season always did.

Here she was, almost back where she'd started. Almost. She had Max and now there was the cat, too. And Joyce lived nearby. How had Libbie thought she could leave Cub Creek? Even for Jim.

And yet....

Jim had made the choice to give up on them. What about her and her choice?

Despite so much negativity happening in her life, the welcome at Cub Creek was unmistakable. As she turned onto the Loop and slowed by her driveway, she felt it again. But this welcome was brief.

A sedan was parked in the driveway. Barry Raymond stood on her porch. Waving.

Libbie jumped out of the car. She strode up the walk and stomped up the steps. "What is the deal with this porch? Margaret. Adam. Now you. What are doing here?"

Barry opened his mouth, then closed it again.

"What? Speak."

"What do you mean? What about the porch?"

"Every time I come home someone is on it, waiting for me, and usually not with good news."

He shook his head. "It's a long way out here. If they come for a reason, they wait. As for me, I've been staying up in the DC area. It's quite a drive down here. I came to apologize and to say goodbye. And so I waited."

"What?"

"That's what you want, right? For me to leave?"

The spark that lit his eyes angered her.

"I want to know why you came here in the first place."

He stared at her. "I never expected to see you again, Libbie."

"How can you say that?" She waved her arms. "You found out where I lived. You tracked me down."

"I mean when I left before." He pressed his hands together, finger aligned to finger. "When I saw you in Sicily, so many unexpected memories rushed back. About you. About the life I used to live."

"Explain that, too. Why did you act like you just happened to stumble across me in Sicily?"

"I did. I—"

"Don't lie, Barry. I saw you in a photograph taken before Jim left. You saw me there. You saw Jim there." She slapped the railing. "Then you pretended you hadn't. Explain that."

"You've grown hard, Libbie. One of the

things I remember most clearly was your vulnerability. You tried to be strong and pretend everything was okay. It was sweet and brave. Endearing."

"If you found me endearing, then you were the only one who ever did. And you discussed my business, my confidences to you, with my aunt and cousin." Libbie shook her head. "I didn't understand back then, that when you said you'd betrayed a client's confidence, you were actually talking about betraying me."

"I tried to tell you. You didn't want to know. I wanted to apologize, to take you away from those people. They had no idea who you were, the real person. I did and I valued you."

"You wanted to apologize? Really? You didn't have the guts to do even that small thing right."

He shuffled his feet and his face flushed. "Won't you sit down? Maybe we can go inside or somewhere else. We can sit down and have a reasonable talk."

"No." A strangled noise came from somewhere down in her throat. She breathed in twice. When she spoke, she lowered her voice. "I'm done with betrayals. I'm done with being victimized. You betrayed more than me. Yourself, too. You are a pathetic excuse for a psychiatrist, and as a friend? Well, you suck."

"What do you want from me, Libbie? I don't

want to hurt you. I never have. Anything I have done has been motivated by…because I care about you, then and now. I left. I did the right thing."

"Why didn't you stay away? You valued me? Yet you went behind my back and talked about my feelings, my secrets. I trusted you."

"That was long ago. I meant well." He shrugged and spread his arms. "I told you then and I'll tell you now. I was wrong."

She stared at him. "Why was it so wrong then but okay now?"

He paled. His jaw tightened. "I've been up in DC. I had some idea of maybe setting up practice again, but that last time I was here, waiting, and you didn't arrive, and I began to realize a few truths about myself. Not very attractive truths. Libbie, I owe you more than one apology, but I wouldn't do anything to hurt you."

"Then why do you continue to interfere? Why are you the judge of what's right for me? Like talking to Jim? You did, didn't you? Trying to drive him away from me?"

"Libbie. Please sit down. Please. I promise when I leave this time, I'll stay gone."

"No! Haven't you heard a word I've said?"

His voice went low and soft. "She kept in touch with me."

She could hardly hear him over the thudding

of her heart and the roaring in her ears.

"What did you say?"

"When I left, I didn't encourage her. I responded out of courtesy. She told me you were troubled about me sending the postcards. So I stopped. I didn't want to be your stumbling block. You were doing so well. The help I'd given you, the progress we'd made, I didn't want to subvert that out of...because of my feelings for you." He paused and looked at his hands. "I hadn't received a note from her in a long time until she wrote to tell me you were coming to Sicily."

Her face felt warm. Flushed. "Margaret stayed in touch with you...told you...."

"No, Libbie. Not Margaret."

Lightheaded. Disoriented. She scrambled to make sense of what he was telling her.

"No. I don't believe you. It doesn't make sense. In fact," she leaned forward and pointed her finger at him. "When I moved here, Liz asked if I'd seen you recently."

He frowned. "Why?"

"She was worried about the decision I was making. It was a big one, moving from the city to the middle of nowhere, alone and on my own. She thought I should see someone, you know, like a therapist." She shook her head. "Why would she mention you if she'd been in contact with...." Her words trailed off, uncertain.

"Maybe she had genuine reasons for suggesting you see someone for emotional help. Or maybe she was fishing, wanting to know if I'd been in touch with you. If I'd told you about her."

Libbie pressed her lips together, trying to think. Finally, she gave up, saying, "She told you I was coming to Sicily."

"She wrote me."

"If I believed you, I.... You waited until Jim left before you approached me."

"She didn't give me many specifics like hotel and such. I don't think she knew them, but I was able to track you down. I was curious, Libbie. I admit it. I was eager to see you again. You coming to Sicily... I thought maybe that meant something." He looked at the pastures across the road. "To my credit, I didn't respond to her. I never acknowledged receiving her message."

Libbie felt like her head was splitting apart.

"Why should I believe you? Honestly, why? I know you talked to Margaret back when...back then. And you interfered with me and Jim. You talked to him behind my back. You must've. Who else...."

"I didn't talk to him."

"Dan told me. He said someone's been talking to Jim about me."

"Liz?"

Aghast—the air was wicked from her lungs

328

and the pain was intense. She pressed her hands to her chest. Max whined. Other than the ringing in her ears, she could hear that and nothing else.

He put his hands on her arms. His grasp was gentle.

Her hands moved over her eyes. She tried to shut the world out.

"Libbie," he whispered. "I am a friend. Not perfect, but your friend. You're shaking. I know this is difficult. May I hug you? As a friend?"

He slid his arms around her. His hug was as gentle as his grip had been. Her forehead touched his shoulder. They held those pose for only a minute before she put her hands on his arms and moved him away. She did so kindly. Her anger with him was spent.

Libbie shook her head slowly. "Why? Why would she talk to Jim?"

"People interfere in the lives of others for many reasons. Good and ill. Usually all mixed up and somewhere in-between."

"To help? To hurt? Why would Jim listen to her?"

"If he listened. Remember, that part is conjecture, Libbie. Besides, it isn't unusual for someone who cares to listen to someone else they believe also cares about the same person. It's what he did with the information, whether he encouraged more breaches, that's the point.

And you'll only know that by asking him. If you can't ask him that, then your relationship isn't what you think it is."

"Liz told me she lied to Grandmother and her parents about me, about things I said and did when we were children."

Barry didn't respond. His hand stayed on her arm.

"She felt threatened by me… Or rather, that if they cared for me, they might love her less." Libbie shook her head. "That's the best I can understand it."

Libbie pressed her fingers to her temples. His hand fell away. "She keeps coming back, in and out of my life. Every time something big or exciting is happening—my move, boyfriends." She thought of Dan. Liz had talked to him, too, behind her back. At the time, she'd thought she was interfering…which she was…but because she cared. Libbie had been angrier at Dan for listening, than at Liz for speaking to him. "Now Jim."

She threw her hands out. "No, it doesn't make sense. She didn't want them. Why would she care if I did? Why would she interfere?"

"I doubt she could explain it if you asked her. She probably tells herself she's motivated by good will, by love." He stood and went to stand by the railing. "Neither of you can see it. I saw it before and it seems nothing has changed."

He shrugged, but his eyes darkened, his gaze intense. "Remember, back then I told you to build a life of your own, separate from your family, your aunt and cousin?"

"I tried, but they are the only family I have. I couldn't cut them out altogether. Besides, it's not fair to blame them for my failures."

"I'm going to say this plainly. Straight out. You can get angry now and think about it later, but listen to me. Liz is no more guilty than you. All of your lives, at least since you were old enough to be aware of each other, you each saw something in the other. Something you didn't have, that she didn't have—a lack of some kind. That partnership could've gone well. It could've made you closer if you were both healthy emotionally. You could've been like sisters, loving sisters."

"I felt like we were for many years, but then it changed over time. I thought we could get that back."

"I'm going to make a guess about Liz now. She was never my patient and never my friend, but I'm not blind. You represent her greatest fear."

"That's ridiculous."

"Failure. That she could fail, that the face she presents to the world could fail and everyone would discover she was flawed, or worse."

Libbie had thought something similar recently. Liz's confidence was covering a lack of belief in herself.

"Each time you make a move that threatens her status quo, it shakes her up."

"And she—"

"I don't think she consciously decides to sabotage you. She probably tells herself she wants to help you, to keep you safe, to help you succeed, whatever. But it's really about keeping the status quo—about maintaining her personal fiction of perfection."

When Libbie didn't respond, he said, "You can't fix them, people like that. They wouldn't thank you if you could. You can only improve yourself. The first step, is to recognize negative behavior in others and separate yourself from it. That's why I advised you to create your own life away from them."

She shook her head, confused. The words seemed to circle in her brain like wagons wanting to create a barricade, but the enemy was within. She wanted to argue her way out, but couldn't find the words. He'd told her....

Libbie threw the words at him. "You also told me that things would keep coming back until I dealt with them. I've done that over and over and it still goes on. I'm tired of it. I can't keep doing this."

He nodded. "Have you? Did you ever really

face them? Really? If you had, I don't think you would be shocked and bewildered by what I've said. You would already have seen the truth, accepted it, and moved on."

"All of my life I've been hearing about what's wrong with me. Most of my life I've been dismissed or rejected by the people who were supposed to love me. I'm done. I'm not hiding or accepting it anymore."

He nodded, his face still passive.

"I've forgiven Grandmother, my uncle, even myself."

A long pause and then he said, "You think so. You'll know you have truly forgiven them when you can say it without anger."

"Easier said than done."

"Always easier. That's what's so hard about it." He smiled, but his eyes were sad. "I'm sorry for letting you down before. I'm glad we had the opportunity to spend some time together again and I'm sorry I'm responsible for you having to relive bad memories. I'm sorry, but I'm also not sorry because this is my chance to make amends, at least in a small way. Do you know what I mean?"

When she didn't answer, he added, "Because facing them is the only way to know."

"Know what?"

"If you're really okay. That you realize how pointless all the angst, the guilt is, that it doesn't need to be that way."

"Maybe, but it doesn't change anything right now."

He nodded. "I think you may be right." He looked past her, considering, then he said, "It's time for you to truly face the unpleasantness and the unhappy things in your life. Think of it this way, Libbie. It's time to slay some dragons."

"What?"

"Face them and slay them. He smiled, then chuckled uneasily. "I don't mean that literally."

He stopped at the stairs. "One last thing? Something you can only determine for yourself. Perhaps there's a part of you that wants them to keep coming back into your life. Some part that depends on them, or is fearful of losing them forever. You have to face that question, Libbie. Face it, and accept that you must put an end to it, or you'll bear the burden of the past for the rest of your life."

****

Barry went, but there was no victory because there was nothing to be victorious of. Libbie told herself she wasn't slaying dragons, as he'd said, but rather she would tie up loose ends—the loose, dangling ends of her life that prevented her from being able to live via her strengths, and not at the mercy of her fears.

The same loose ends, the dangling threads

that bound her to a lifetime of hoping for better, for acceptance, for love. The hope was understandable, but she'd been looking in the wrong direction.

Libbie went out to the terrace and sat at the table. Max had returned and was stretched out nearby. On the other side of the table, the cat was curled up in a chair. Libbie could see her white fur and gray patches through the wrought iron between them.

Her life. Cub Creek. Her terrace. Her friends, such as they were, offered her companionship. The leaves rustled. The blue sky moved between white, fluffy clouds. The shadows among the trees and along the tree line hid no menace. She caught a glimpse of something moving among the trees and knew it was that buck. The rest of his family was somewhere nearby, no doubt.

Libbie checked her present world and found it good.

In her head she heard a soft voice whisper that things might be different tomorrow. And yes, they might, but each time she got knocked down, she'd get back up.

It was her task, a task only she could perform, to keep it good.

She found strength and determination by envisioning it in her head—facing down the dragons—the fears and memories from her past that haunted her present.

Liz had done things that wronged Libbie, but her mother had taught her, had groomed her daughter in how to effectively stunt her life. Similarly, Grandmother had never taught Libbie that her own life was worth saving.

A couple of hours north of here, depending on the traffic on I-95, and the traffic and stop lights on the city streets, Margaret reigned. Her house wasn't as big and shiny as Grandmother's, but it was big and still in that neighborhood where the address was as much a part of the value of a house as any other selling point. Maybe more.

White brick and wrought iron. Just short of ostentatious. But that was Aunt Margaret.

Libbie was going there in the morning. But before she did, she had another task to perform, a fear to face, something so important that if she didn't do it, and do it well, then the rest wouldn't matter.

****

She went upstairs and washed and fixed her hair. She put on a silky top, and nicer slacks than she usually wore. Even low heels. Because this was battle and, cosmetic or not, this was part of her armor. Each line of kohl on her lids, the dabs from her cover-up stick, the powder on her face, formed a part of it.

Libbie drove. She passed the concrete bridge at the north end of Cub Creek Loop and turned onto Rt. 522. She kept the door tightly shut on emotion and doubt. She cut across a back road to the elementary school and then took Rt. 33 east. She was so focused on reaching the Mitchell home she barely registered the white pickup truck that passed her going in the opposite direction. A few minutes later she sensed something behind her, then heard the sound of the engine. She glanced in the rearview mirror and saw the pickup. Saw Jim.

She must've wrenched the steering wheel because the car swerved and the tires kicked up the roadside gravel. She eased the car back onto the road. Her heart was pounding.

He honked, a short honk, no more than that. She looked in the rearview mirror again and he was pointing off to the side.

This wasn't going as planned. She'd envisioned herself in control, storming the Mitchell home on her own terms, not pulling off onto a winding, narrow road to nowhere somewhere along Rt. 33.

No house or driveway in sight—this was an access road ending at the South Anna River. No one was here, maybe due to the time of year. Libbie pulled up next to the one picnic table and then backed up to the river bank as she turned around, ready to move forward, perhaps preparing for a quick exit. But when Jim parked his truck, she surprised herself by driving forward to angle her car across the back of his, blocking him in.

Her door slammed. His door slammed. He looked at her, at her car blocking his truck, but he didn't move closer. Nor did she. The river was behind him. Only the sound of the water nearby and the leaves rustling above their heads, shared this space with them. That twenty feet of ground between them felt forbidden, maybe radioactive—a dangerous strip of dirt where anything could happen.

Libbie called out, "You owe me an apology, Jim Mitchell."

His hands went to his hips, then moved as he crossed his arms, then moved again to uncross and push up his sleeves. All of his energy seemed directed into his restless hands and his hazel eyes. "Do I? Tell me, Libbie, do you know what you want?"

"I do. You're the question mark. Why did you leave me hanging? Why did I have to run you down and confront you?"

"You've got it backwards." Jim took a step forward. One step into that dangerous space. "Every time I drove over to Cub Creek you either weren't home or you were in some man's arms."

"Some man?" How dare he? "Some man? You mean Dan?" She pointed at him, but saw her hand was knotted up in a fist. She shook it at him. "Don't blame him, Jim Mitchell, for your cowardice."

Did she say that? Out loud? She hadn't meant to say that. Didn't even know she was thinking it. She took a step back.

He rubbed his jaw as if he'd been hit. His eyes were bright and intent. Angry. She drew in a breath. If he wanted a fight she would give him one. No more hiding. But when he spoke, his voice was softer. She had to hold her breath to hear him.

"What about Dan? Tell me now if you want him, and be clear about it, Libbie."

"Dan?" she whispered.

She saw by the shock on his face that he'd misunderstood. Before she could say more, he crossed that dangerous ground. He put one arm behind her, and with his other hand touching her neck, her hair, he said, "I was going to abide by your wishes and bow out if that's what you wanted. But I'm not." He shook his head. "I stepped aside for you and Dan before. He already had his chance. Not again. Not this time."

He brushed his lips against her throat. She shivered down to her toes. He stopped and waited a long second.

"Open your eyes, Libbie. Tell me now."

She was confused. Were they talking again? She pulled his face forward until his lips touched hers. His hands were on her back, his arms tightening. She couldn't breathe. It was okay. She could breathe later. For now, she kissed him. When he moved his lips back to her throat, she sobbed.

It was a great gulping sob. It startled them both.

Jim pulled back, but didn't loosen his arms. "Are you okay?"

Libbie tried to control the gasping sound forcing its way out of her. Tears welling in her eyes. She didn't want to cry.

He pulled her close, tucking her face against his chest.

"Go ahead. If you're going to cry, do it here and do it now. I'm not letting you go. If I release you, if I give you a chance to think, you may evaporate again. Not this time. I've learned my lesson."

Libbie sobbed. She drenched his shirt with her tears. He held her more closely but with such tenderness, that she cried some more. When she finally lifted her head, she kept her eyes closed, afraid that if she opened them, the moment would vanish. Evaporate, as he'd said.

Gently, he kissed each of her tear-streaked eyelids and lashes. Libbie melted.

"Hold on." He supported her as they moved over to the picnic table. "Sit down."

She didn't sit. She leaned against the table but wouldn't release him.

He touched her chin. "Libbie. Listen to me. Some of it may have been unavoidable, I don't know, but we let too many things get into the way of us. Us. If you have doubts, tell me and we'll chase them away together."

His arms were on either side of her, but the angle was awkward. She wanted to be closer. She cursed the hard ground and the splinters in the table. Jim started speaking again.

"I had moments of doubt. I blame all of the things going on in my life, but mostly I blame myself. I will always regret I let this go on so long." He took her hand. "I guess we all have our dark moments. I was afraid you were looking for an excuse to break it off."

"Jim—"

"Seriously. When I stopped by that day and you accused me of not having a good opinion of you...I thought...you were looking for a way out."

He pulled her close again and with his free hand he reached into his pocket. "This went to Sicily with us, and I was on my way to Cub Creek today, one more time, when I saw you drive past." His voice sounded rough and his arm tightened. "I wasn't going to let you get away again." He opened the case. "Marry me, Libbie. Have some faith. Let's take a chance on us."

She touched his hand, wordlessly. He slipped the ring on her finger. It glittered through the tears on her lashes. "In Sicily, when you found out about the article and Joyce's interview, you never mentioned the part about the engagement."

"I intended to surprise you and that would've spoiled it. It was all arranged. I was going to propose at the trattoria, our café, our table, then Liz called. She'd seen the article, too. She said she was happy for us, but worried. That you couldn't leave Cub Creek, that you'd be miserable. She let it slip about your feelings for Dan."

"Jim, that was over a long time ago. Pretty much before it got going."

"She loves you, I know that. And she'd called overseas." He shook his head. "At best, I thought she was being overly dramatic. A busybody. But there was enough doubt...I didn't want to take the chance of spoiling the trip while we were so far from home."

"I don't understand why Liz—"

"Matthew's accident interrupted my plans, and then I was tied up with him, his surgery, his rehab. I can't regret that part. I had no choice." Jim shook his head. "Libbie, I don't care why she felt compelled to call when we were in Sicily. But later, I think she became worried that I'd tell you and so she called again and again while I was in California, always so pleasant, so concerned, so aggravating. I didn't want to worry and upset you, so I said nothing. I had too much to deal with already. I couldn't risk.... I promise you she won't be calling me again. About anything."

"How did you know she didn't mean well?"

"Libbie. It's the actions, not the words. Words are only the surface. The acts are the truth."

"Truth. Jim, I wasn't trying to lie about Barry Raymond."

He pressed his lips to hers and kept them there for a full minute. When he pulled back, he said, "I know. I had doubts, too. My own cold feet. Maybe Liz's calls played into that, but it's all on me. Remember, I've already proved I can fail at marriage. Then my pride got involved and I totally screwed it up."

Jim took her hands in his. "Now, before doubt can creep in again, we're setting the date."

"Okay, Jim, but I don't know when—"

"I do. The anniversary of the day we met. Right after you moved into Cub Creek."

"But Jim, I don't know what...how—"

"You don't need to know everything ahead

of time. Let's enjoy the trip, Libbie. We'll figure it out a step at a time, together, as we go along."

He held her hand, pressing her fingers to his lips. "We make the rules, Libbie. We do. We don't have to be conventional. We don't have to do what everyone expects. We don't have to be practical. We are blessed, Libbie. You and I together."

Libbie threw her arms around his neck. "Do you promise? Jim, this will sound crazy, but my aunt said I was bad luck for the people who cared about me…that I wasn't…healthy for them. I don't want any more injuries…not yours, not Matthew's…anyone's…on my conscience."

"You had a really messed up family. You can hardly do worse with the Mitchells. I guess we have our own brand of crazy." He ran his fingers lightly along her neck. "You and I have history. We bring baggage. But the bright side, in our favor, is that we aren't kids. We know who we are. I thought I was fine alone. Maybe I was until I met you. Now I don't want to live without you."

She let her happiness shine through. She wanted Jim to see it and believe it. Then she leaned close, pressed her cheek to his and whispered, "Yes, but—and please hear me—I will always believe you deserve better. That said, there's some baggage I must dispense with. When I've done that, I'll come to you. I'll hold out my hand and ask for this ring."

"Libbie—"

She saw the hint of hurt returning.

"I'm serious. I'm coming back to you. I have to slay a couple of dragons first."

His hurt turned to puzzlement. "Dragons?"

"Dragons or old baggage or just the crappy stuff from my past. Whatever you want to call it."

He put his hands on her cheeks. "I'll go with you. Let's do this together."

She nodded but said, "No. I am going to stand up for myself and come out better on the other side. I refuse to bring ugly memories into our life together."

He frowned. "You aren't in any danger, are you?"

It would be too extreme to say her sanity and future were at stake. Instead, she said, "I'll face them down and come back to you, to us, without fears and guilt that are too stupid to mention, but that have remorselessly dogged my life." Still dramatic, and it was, to her. It wouldn't be to her and Jim, as long as she took away its dark magic, its ability to hurt her.

"Someone once told me stuff keeps coming back if you don't deal with it. This time it will be dealt with." Libbie held out her hand. "I can't remove this, Jim. It would break my heart."

He took her hand and held it.

"I need you to take the ring and keep it for me until I return. I'll expect it back."

He kept his eyes on hers. "I don't like the idea, but I'll respect your choice. Understand, if you don't come back quickly, I will find you. I won't let you slip away again, no matter what."

Her finger wanted to curl, to prevent the ring from moving past her knuckle. She wanted to turn her hand into a fist. But she didn't. He held the ring and she pressed her hands around his, capturing the ring within their one grasp.

She said, "This is my promise to you, Jim." She kissed his hands. "I'll be back, and you'd better be ready because I will allow nothing, no power on earth, to stand in my—our—way."

He nodded. "I'll follow you back to Cub Creek."

"Cub Creek? Okay. Why?"

He smiled slowly and brushed her hair back from her face. "I believe I have a sweater to pick up?"

Chapter Fourteen

Barry, back when she'd called him Dr. Raymond and she'd been his patient, had told her, "Things will keep coming back until you deal with them." Libbie knew personally they often came back anyway.

Today that stuff would be dealt with once and for all.

As she sipped her morning coffee, it ran through her mind that Liz had confessed her lies and destroyed what belief Libbie had left in them, as family, probably because she knew she'd overstepped with Jim. She knew she would be exposed.

Shame on Liz. It was no reflection on her, Libbie. It was all on Liz.

She paused at the front door and called Max's name. He must've been nearby because he came running to the porch and straight up the steps. She didn't know where the cat was and didn't have time to wait. She expected to be gone for the better part of the day, but to be back home before nightfall.

It was a long ride to Georgetown. She

should've been tense, but mostly she was simply determined. And a little tired, too. She yawned. Jim had returned to Cub Creek with her and stayed late into the evening. He was probably telling his mother and son, perhaps at this very moment, about their plans.

She took the cross-country route through the Lake Anna area, the same route she'd driven less than a year ago that had brought her to Cub Creek. It was a beautiful drive until one reached the city, and the city grew bigger every year, spreading farther out, the population becoming denser and the traffic heavier.

First, she went to Grandmother's house. Not her grandmother's home for more than ten years, but forever hers in Libbie's brain.

It looked no different from the outside.

Libbie climbed the curved steps to the front door. The railing, as it slid lightly beneath her fingers, felt no different than when she'd last been here. The massive wooden door was perfectly appointed with a heavy knocker.

Of course, it would look the same. Brick townhouse in a fashionable, historic neighborhood—historic preservation committees and watchful neighbors would ensure continuity of appearance.

Libbie knocked.

A young woman answered the door.

"Hi. Sorry to bother you. I lived here a long

time ago. I was curious."

She smiled, fresh-faced and upbeat, but spoke softly. "I'm the au pair. Can't invite you in. You understand."

"Of course." Was Libbie disappointed or relieved?

"Sorry for the whispering. The children are napping. If you'd like to come back later, the owners will be home. Or you can leave your number and they can call you?"

"No. I don't want to bother anyone. I was passing by and stopped on impulse. Sorry to have disturbed you."

The girl smiled and nodded as she closed the door.

Libbie walked down the street, observing and remembering. She was about to return to her car when she remembered the passageway between the houses. The gate should be locked. She could try it. She would find it locked and then feel free to go on her way.

It was a tall, heavy wrought iron gate. She pressed her hand against it, and the other against the latch. It wasn't locked. Careless people. She pushed it open, listening for the sound of a watch dog. All was silent, except for the traffic on the road behind her.

Libbie walked down the narrow passage. The brick walls rose high on either side. The windows were set well above her head.

Dim light. Moss growing. Cracked walkway beneath her shoes. The low windows, almost unnoticeable at her feet, were filthy. They barred the way to the old, unused coal bins in the basement. Everyone, every place had a dark and dusty secret.

At the end of the passageway was the lure of daylight. A promise or a warning?

Neither. It was just different.

Grandmother's wrought iron table was long gone. Some of the gardens remained but most of the space was occupied by benches and children's toys. A playhouse. Some sort of climbing thing molded in big, colorful plastic. A toddler's plastic bike with tires well-worn from being ridden on the brick patio. In the silence, she heard the echo of children's voices laughing, arguing, pretending, as if the brick patio, the walls, the trees, had absorbed them through the nearly two centuries that this house had existed. The Havens family had made up only a fraction of that time.

Not a ghost of Libbie's history remained.

Elizabeth Havens had been erased. What little there had been of her husband, Kader Havens, was gone. Her sons, along with their joys and tragedies, were as nothing.

The world had moved on. Seeing it with her own eyes brought the truth home. She had harbored the past in her heart and in her brain. Although they were nothing more than ghosts of memories, Libbie had given them refuge and sustenance, and kept them prisoner.

Liz had memories, of course. And Margaret. But their memories were theirs and different from hers. They had continued to build their lives. Neither of them had made a life out of hosting memories as she had. And the bad ones had been given the greatest portion of her energy and devotion. How crazy was that?

Libbie pressed her hand against the brick and stayed in the shadows. She stared, taking in this homey scene of colorful, familial disorder. Quite the antidote. She let it filter into her brain easing out the uglier memories and reducing their strength until the scene, the current reality in front of her, began to appear commonplace and boring. A homey scene and one that had no connection to her life. Maybe proof that bad could be superseded by good.

That the bad didn't have to last forever.

She backed away from the patio view, then turned and went to her car.

The hardest part was yet to come.

Tension ratcheted up her back and into her jaws. She gave herself credit that she'd stayed the course thus far and hadn't turned back. She stood on Aunt Margaret's elegant, understated porch and lifted the knocker.

She stood waiting, but when no one answered, she pressed her hand against the flat of the door and leaned her cheek against the painted wood.

There was nothing. No sensation, no color here for her.

She heard a noise and stood back as the door opened.

Libbie didn't recognize the woman. A maid?

"Is Mrs. Havens here? My Aunt Margaret?"

"Come in, please." She stepped back to allow Libbie in, then nodded toward the living room.

As she stood in the foyer staring at the open double doors, the maid vanished down the hallway.

Aunt Margaret was standing by the front windows. The curtain sheers filtered the sunlight and created a soft effect around her. She turned toward Libbie. "What do you want? Why are you here?"

Libbie thought she sounded more exasperated than harsh, as if she wanted to appear cold and remote but was really shaken.

"You'd like me to go away."

Margaret nodded.

"You'd like me to go away from not just your door, but your life."

"I gave you an envelope with information about your other family."

Libbie pulled it from her purse and waved it at Margaret. "You did. You gave it and ran. Now, you'll do it the right way."

"What does that mean?"

"We'll sit down together in a civilized manner and you'll open the envelope and explain what's in it and what it means, and anything else you know about it."

Margaret didn't laugh. She was, in fact, very pale.

"Why would I do what you want?"

"Because you owe me."

She was silent.

"You ignored a child in need. I was your niece. You left me there despite knowing what my life was like."

"You were safe, well-fed and lacked for nothing."

"Liar."

She turned away, toward the front window.

Libbie spoke to her back. "Liz is a liar, too. She lied because she couldn't be sure of her parent's love—that she might lose some of it to me—and you knew. You let her get away with it, and even encouraged it. So, you are both liars and you owe me for both of you—unless you want me to collect from Liz personally."

After a long pause, Margaret asked, "You'll leave us alone?"

"No promises. Remember, I don't owe you

anything."

Margaret shook her head and looked at her empty hands before turning back. "Where is it?"

For a moment, Libbie went blank.

"The envelope."

Libbie hesitated. Afraid? Not sure? Suddenly, she wanted Jim with her. Coward, she scolded herself. This is what you came for—to slay the past. It only works if you wield the sword yourself.

She passed her the envelope.

Margaret looked at it, clearly noting that it was rumpled, but unopened. She slipped her finger under a loose edge and took about a year to draw her nail across and open the flap.

"Tea or coffee?"

The maid. She broke the tension. It had been sucking Libbie in, almost hypnotizing her. Suddenly, she saw Aunt Margaret. Really saw. A woman, alone in this mausoleum, with only a niece who despised her and a maid who surely had no particular fondness for her. Margaret was comfortable in society and had taught Liz that skill, but home, alone, she was stripped of that...that veneer? More like a disguise. Without it, she looked smaller. Diminished. Shorter than Libbie remembered.

Both women were staring at Libbie.

"Nothing for me."

Margaret pursed her lips. "We'll have tea."

"Yes, ma'am." The maid vanished again.

"Have a seat, Libbie."

"I'm fine."

"Please take a seat. I feel the need to sit."

Margaret seemed a little breathless. It wouldn't serve Libbie's purpose if her aunt collapsed.

Libbie pulled a chair out and sat. Margaret did too, but more slowly.

The envelope had vanished below the table, still in her hands. "Liz told me you were getting married."

"That's not what I'm here to discuss."

"She spoke highly of your fiancé."

"That's nice."

"She was only a child."

What? Oh. "As was I."

Margaret sighed. Her hands reappeared above the table and she slipped papers out of the envelope. "It was my job to protect her." She opened the papers, looking at them. "It wasn't any one person."

"What does that mean?"

"Not Liz. Not me. Elizabeth was loathe to let you go. Your uncle thought it was because she missed your father, but missing someone doesn't mean they can be a good parent. Still, you should know that Elizabeth was determined to keep you. To keep you under her control. Thus, it wasn't that hard to resist Phillip when he suggested you come to us. He was the only one who thought it was a good idea."

It hurt. Even after all these years. *Slice and dice my heart, Aunt Margaret, yet again.*

"Control? Of me?"

"Of your fortune."

"She had so much already."

"Can one ever have enough? Some cannot. But it wasn't greed. It was about control." She added, "It has always seemed to me that the people who are the most insecure, the most fearful, are those who are the most determined to control others."

Libbie arched her eyebrows in disbelief. "Is that a theory or you own practical experience when it comes to managing your life and the lives of others? If so, you taught Liz the lesson well."

The maid returned. Margaret looked up as the woman placed the tea and a plate of cookies on the table. Oatmeal Raisin. Libbie stared at them.

"Don't be cruel, Libbie. It doesn't become you." Margaret closed her eyes, breathing in the aroma of the tea. When she opened them, she continued, "Did you know that your mother and I were friends in college?"

No, Libbie hadn't known, but Margaret wanted a reaction so she tried very hard not to give her one.

"Well, if you're not interested...."

"I am." Libbie said. "What was she like?"

"That's not the point. The point is that while I never met her family, I knew there weren't many of them, and then her parents, your maternal grandparents, died in the same accident."

Libbie opened her mouth but there were no words in her head. Her brain had suddenly gone empty and all she could do was gasp for air.

"At the time, when we realized you didn't understand the full extent of the loss, it was decided not to tell you. You were a young child. There was no value to adding to your grief. It was expected that you would be told later, but you didn't ask and Elizabeth decided not to do anything that would prompt you to ask questions. If you'd asked, she would've told you, I'm sure. Did you never want to see your parent's obituary? A newspaper article about the accident? No, apparently not."

"I–I...."

"In part, I can't blame you, but it also seemed to me to be unnatural. Think about it. Your parents, your mother's parents, the people who cared the most about you–"

"Dead because it wasn't healthy to be close to me, to love me."

"Well." She shrugged. "It was true. I never

said it was your fault."

Libbie heard Margaret's voice and Liz's all wrapped up together. Not Libbie's fault, but she was punished, anyway, over and over. But never again. She placed her fists on the table because they needed to go somewhere and the table top was better than Aunt Margaret's face. Violence burned in her veins. She saw red and it had nothing to do with her special senses. This was rage. Her calves tightened as she began to rise from her chair.

Margaret continued, her voice dispassionate, not looking at Libbie, "I've said before that I know you'd never deliberately hurt my daughter. But, it is equally true that you have never understood her. You always expected…not the right word. You believed she was someone she wasn't. You put your own expectations upon her. Your almost-sister. Your best friend. She could never be those things for you. I understood her. You never did."

Her aunt left the papers, still folded, on the table. She walked over to a side table and opened a drawer from which she removed another, smaller envelope. "The envelope I gave you before contains items I found among Elizabeth's papers, including the copy of your parent's wedding license, which you would already know if you'd looked. I thought you might like to have them, so when I was going through Elizabeth's personal items, I found and saved them for you. Also, in this smaller envelope are your mother's and grandmother's wedding and engagement rings." She stared at the small red envelope in her hand and seemed to forget Libbie for the moment. She shook her head slowly, saying, "I should've insured them." She looked at Libbie directly. "I put it all in a safety deposit box to save for you. I was waiting until you seemed more stable emotionally. I didn't know it would take so long."

Perhaps Margaret wanted to hurt her again, to get another dig in, but her rage was abating. Margaret looked small, old, and confused. Where was the evil aunt? The woman who had frightened Libbie almost as much as Grandmother had?

Margaret said, "I was only protecting my family."

Had she read Libbie's mind?

"Too bad no one was protecting me."

Her aunt nodded. She tipped the red envelope into her palm and extended her hand. "Here."

Libbie opened her hand and Margaret dropped the rings into it. Her heart twisted and tried to tear itself open.

Aunt Margaret touched Libbie's hand. When had she ever touched her? Libbie couldn't think. She curled her fingers back into a fist, but this time over the rings.

"You can read the letter and the clippings later." Margaret pushed the papers across the table toward her. "In short, your mother's great-uncle contacted Elizabeth regarding your care. He was coming to meet with her. I remember how threatened she felt. Tried to rally me and Phillip. She was expecting a fight, because she was certain he was after your inheritance from your father. It was a significant portion of the Havens' fortune."

Margaret added, "I understand his health was poor and he died before he could make the trip."

"Yet another person who cared about me who died." It wasn't trauma that spoke, but sarcasm.

Margaret rose slowly, as if every joint pained her. "Liz and the children are all I have. Let Liz have her...her self-image. It's good for her and for the children. Please stay away from them. I see them little enough as it is, and I've never been good at sharing."

"Or loving," Libbie added.

As far as Libbie was concerned that could be Aunt Margaret's epitaph. It made no difference to Libbie. Margaret had nothing worthwhile to offer, nor any weapons left with which to hurt her. Only the people you cared about could hurt you, right? As for the rest? It was up to you as to whether to allow them to give hurt, or accept it as such. Aunt Margaret no longer held that power because Libbie didn't care. She could feel a little pity for her aunt.

"Wait," Libbie said.

Margaret turned in the doorway. "What else?"

"Dr. Raymond. When I was seeing him after Grandmother's death, he spoke to you about my treatment. He betrayed my confidence. Why did you push him to it?"

She frowned, but it was an expression of confusion. Bewilderment. "Why would I not? I was the closest thing you had to a relative, someone who cared enough to bother. Still am, I guess, at least as far as the relative part applies."

And that about summed it up.

Margaret touched the door frame, then pulled her hand back and straightened her posture. "One more thing. There is something I've wanted to say to you for many years. It wasn't all Elizabeth's fault. Part of the problem between you and Elizabeth was that you were too much alike. Neither of you would give an inch, or offer a breath of kindness to the other."

Libbie's shock must have shown on her face because Margaret's expression showed satisfaction.

Margaret added, "Make better choices.

Don't find yourself alone and unloved at the end of your life as she did. Please excuse me now. Mary will see you out."

Libbie was alone in the room.

She remembered she was clutching the rings when she felt them biting into her flesh. She opened her fist and stared at them. Bits of gold and diamonds. On one level they were no different from any other engagement-wedding ring sets sitting in glass cases, in jewelry stores, around the globe. Nothing special.

On the other hand, these had been on the ring fingers of her mother and grandmother. Libbie's father and grandfather had slipped the rings onto the fingers of each of their beloveds. That understanding made all the difference.

She reached across to where her aunt had sat and pulled the letter, the wedding license, and the newspaper clippings toward her. The suspicion and intimidation was gone. Forcing a little daylight between herself and Aunt Margaret had been worth it.

Bold letters on one of the clippings caught her attention. Funeral services planned for.... She put them back in the envelope and secured the envelope in a zippered section of her purse. She'd read them later when she was in more positive surroundings. She put the rings back into the little red envelope, sealed it, and put it into her purse, too.

She, Libbie, wasn't like Grandmother. Not at all. The concept was too bizarre to consider.

The tea sat untouched on the table. Libbie took one soft cotton napkin and wrapped two cookies in it. Oatmeal raisin was her favorite, so it seemed Aunt Margaret and she did have one thing in common.

"Ma'am? I can put those in a container for you."

"No, need. I've taken care of it."

"Yes, ma'am."

As Libbie sat in her car, waiting to pull out into traffic, she considered confronting Liz with all of the things she should've said but hadn't. If it had only been Liz, then maybe. She certainly deserved it. But confronting Liz would risk upsetting the children's lives again and nothing, including Libbie's own feelings, was worth that. In that, she also agreed with Aunt Margaret. Liz would be allowed to keep her self-image, at least for as long as she could keep it intact, anyway. Libbie wouldn't do anything to destroy it.

****

Driving south. Leaving the city behind and then the interstate, too, Libbie headed back the same way she'd come, via Lake Anna and the scenic route.

That day, less than a year ago, when she'd

taken a wrong turn and ended up on Cub Creek Loop, she saw and bought the property on impulse. The moving van had completed her move within two months. It went to show how much good could come out of an accidental turn of fate.

Not a year later, here she was again, sailing uphill and down and taking the curves, but carefully, and always with an eye to other traffic, wildlife or life less wild, but nonetheless valuable. She was almost giddy with relief.

"Jim," she thought, "I'm on my way. Next stop—our future."

Jim had suggested the day they met as their wedding date. That would be March. It was still several months away.

Such a short time that she'd been at Cub Creek, yet how much life and living these months had held.

A breeze blew leaves across the road. Autumn. Did they really need to wait until spring? Carpe Diem. Seize the day. No time like the present. Waste not, want not. Well, that hadn't been referring to time, but it still applied. Waste not the days; life is short, and the opportunities for happiness are rarer still.

Libbie had to slow down for lights and traffic going through Mineral. She was heading home first to tend to Max and her cat. After she attended to the needs of her furry dependents, she'd take the time to primp a bit and then ask Jim where he'd like to meet so that he could propose properly. Soon the traffic and stop lights were behind her and she was free again. It was clear sailing until she reached Cub Creek Loop.

Another gust of wind shook the cypress trees along the roadside. They'd already had an early taste of winter. They'd have the real thing before long.

She slowed the car where Cub Creek Loop branched off to the left. The first concrete bridge over Cub Creek was around the curve. Already moving back up to speed, she must've eased her foot off the gas as she remembered how, when coming from the opposite direction only months ago, the foliage had shivered, and Max had jumped out. It had been a close call for more than her and Max. She would never forget the sound of her car hitting the concrete railing or the taste of blood.

The branches shivered again. Libbie was confused, still stuck in the memory from before.

A tan body leapt in a graceful arc from the woods, across the ditch, apparently intending to land on the road. The windshield filled with a wide swath of tan color. The glass fractured in slow motion like jagged strings of lace, growing and spreading, then the glass bowed inward beneath the weight of the animal.

She saw hooves at the same moment that the sound returned, and the screaming, rending and exploding began.

Chapter Fifteen

Her arms covered her face. Something pressed against her, suffocating. It dropped away, but then there was more screaming.

Screaming. Her or the deer? Maybe both. Some part of her was shrieking while the other part, detached, heard the screeching of friction as the car flew, and noted the sensation of something immovable hitting the passenger side of the car, the tipping feeling, and a sickening lurch.

When it stopped, she didn't know. She was unaware. Whatever had happened, she was cozy, snug, and she refused to open her eyes.

Keep them closed, she told herself. Rest. Then her feet grew cold, a cold that crept gradually up her legs. As it climbed her calves and neared her knees, she felt the eddy of the current. She opened her eyes and panicked.

The screaming tried to start again, but her side hurt. She couldn't drag in enough air to scream without needing to scream about that. She tried to slow her breathing and swallow the panic. She was pressed against the car door, her arm pinned. She couldn't move her legs. Her other arm seemed to be free, but was unable to help. Branches full of leaves filled the broken windshield.

Colorful leaves. No expanse of tan blocking her view. No deer now, but she knew it had been there. She could see patches of hair and hide, and blood smeared across the broken edges and on the dashboard.

No lights on the cracked and dented dashboard. Her head hurt. Front and back. She tried to take stock, but the tally scared her. She closed her eyes again hoping it was a nightmare, wanting to find that cozy, safe place.

Instead, she was stuck in reality. Her legs were cold. The waters of Cub Creek were in her car where they didn't belong. The forest occupied her windshield and the passenger seat and side window. The leaves and branches filled in where the glass had been.

Libbie tried to look toward the side window, but pain sliced across her head and her vision turned red. Like when she'd been so angry at Aunt Margaret. How long ago? Not long. No more than a couple of hours probably. But it seemed forever.

She'd been out again. Unconscious. For how long? This time she listened without moving. She heard the gurgle of the creek. There was no color to it, only cold. Libbie hadn't seen another car, and since she was still here it was obvious that no one had seen the accident. Had the car left evidence above? Would someone see wrecked vegetation or the deer, and investigate? One thing she knew was that having come to rest in the creek, her car wasn't easily visible from the road. The leaves rustled. Her car seemed to be camouflaged. And she was trapped.

She moved her eyes without moving her head. Her arm, the passenger side arm, was okay. She could move it now. Bloody, but not badly hurt. Her purse and cell phone had been in the passenger side seat. If she could reach into the seat, feel around, she might snag the purse and the phone.

Mostly leaves and tree debris, and in the midst, it looked like the remains of an airbag.

Libbie wasn't aware of going out again, only of returning. How long this time?

Someone would eventually miss her. Maybe not before tomorrow. Even then, how hard would they look? Jim would assume she'd had the world's worst case of cold feet, or was still busy doing battle with the past, and give her space.

Her legs weren't totally numb, but neither were they so cold now. Not warm, but warming. That scared her more than the relief from the cold. Her side hurt. She had to control her fear and her breathing.

If it got dark enough, someone might see the lights from her car. Except the dashboard was dark, dead, and that didn't bode well for the headlights or tail lights.

Months ago, back before Jim and Sicily, when she thought she was falling in love with Dan, she'd had some kind of nifty gift wherein if she thought of someone, they would come. Mostly that was Dan, but also Mitchell's Lawn and Landscaping. And Liz. Liz had always sensed it when something went badly wrong in Libbie's life and she'd usually call.

Liz wouldn't call this time. Nor did she truly believe she could summon Dan or Jim or anyone by thinking of them, but she tried anyway. She might hear colors and feel emotions by touching walls and rocks, but this time she needed a genuine superpower. A true superpower. And she was fresh out of inspiration.

She thought she dozed off, as opposed to going unconscious this time. A tiny noise, a tinkling noise, but flat sounding as with tempered glass breaking off, woke her. She almost resented it. If she could sleep, rest and wake up later when it was all over, safe and warm in a hospital bed....

A cat. Her cat. She was peeking in through the leaves and branches filling the broken windshield. The cat perched in the middle of it, one gray paw, dainty and delicately touching here and there, picking out the best place to step. Libbie watched her choose and then with graceful motion, she landed on the passenger seat only to be lost again amid that foliage. With a furry paw, the cat softly tapped her arm. It was the arm she could move and she turned her palm up. The cat touched Libbie's flesh with her cold, wet nose, then meowed.

No rescue here, as far as she could see. Merely a curious cat. Chills raced up Libbie's torso and she shivered.

The cat, Libbie's cat, climbed with tentative, precise steps over the center console, past her arm, and settled on her lap. The water had stopped at her knees, but it seemed the chill had spread upward, more than she'd realized, until the warm cat's body curled against her belly. The cat felt like banked coals against her body.

Libbie's pinned arm was numb, but not painful. She tried to speak, and that pain wracked her side again, so she whispered, "Hi, kitty."

Her eyelids were growing heavy again. She wanted to sleep. The cat butted her head against the good arm. Libbie tried to pet her. She should stay awake. She knew she should.

It wasn't night yet, but hidden down here in

the creek in the shadow of the bridge and in her cave of trees, the light was failing. Libbie stroked the cat's tail. She purred. Libbie was glad not to be alone. She'd never been one to rely on prayer. It hadn't rescued her during those years with her grandmother, had it? Those loveless years. But Libbie tried. It was a mostly wordless prayer. A supplication. A memory of a candle and a message about looking for the light when lost in the dark came to her. It had been a gift from someone. Gladys? On her mantle, that's where she put it. It seemed a long time ago. With the purring on Libbie's warmish lap, she must've dozed because she heard a noise and turned to look at the passenger side seat.

Elizabeth was sitting there. Grandmother. The branches and leaves framed her face and shoulders. Annoyed, Grandmother reached up and snapped off a small twiggy branch that was caught in her silver hair and brutally tossed it aside.

"Grandmother." Libbie knew she was dreaming. She was also annoyed. If she was going to dream of someone, it should be Jim. Maybe her mom or dad. She must have some memory of them to draw on, somewhere lost in her brain cells.

"What have you done now?" Grandmother asked.

"It was a deer. Not my fault."

The woman who couldn't be there shook her head. "We bring these things on ourselves."

"I deserved this. Is that what you're saying?" Libbie's words were slurred. Her jaw felt tight.

Grandmother touched Libbie's leg. The cat didn't stir. Her sweet face stayed tucked under her paw, despite Grandmother's fingers vanishing into fur, apparently reaching through the cat, to pat Libbie's thigh. Grandmother said, "You go to sleep. I'll sit here awhile."

Libbie was okay with this dream passing on without her. As she drifted away, she heard her grandmother say, "Don't find yourself alone at the end of it all." It sounded like Margaret's voice.

Scratching. The sound started at the side of the car, against the paint, then near the window. Libbie opened her eyes again, frantic. The deer. It was back. Stupid thought, but even as she told herself the idea was crazy, she imagined the deer had returned to finish the job. For revenge. Pain tore through her head, her arm, as she struggled.

"Ma'am?" It was a man's voice. He yelled, "Hey, Dave. She's alive. I saw her move. Not much, but I saw it. Get back up on the road. I'll stay here."

Time stretched and yawned. It seemed ages before he spoke again. "...where he can get a signal. Hold tight. I can't get you out on my own. I won't leave."

The man was doing something near the windshield. The branches shook and moved aside. Orange cap. Orange vest.

"How're you doing? Miss?" He peered in through the broken windshield.

Libbie looked at him. The cat was gone. So was Grandmother. Dreaming? It was a thin line between dreams and nightmares. And hope, too. But hope was real, she knew because it hurt. As Libbie began to hope, her heart quickened and her muscles awoke, and the pain overwhelmed her.

The man stepped back, and the branches rushed in. When they parted again, someone else reached through the broken windshield. His hand touched her cheek. No orange cap, this time. Tan shirt.

"Dan." Libbie said, but she couldn't hear her own voice.

"Hold still, Libbie. Hold tight. We can't get you out yet. The car is wedged in down here."

Barking. Agitated. Almost ferocious. The barks were interspersed with howls that filled the low area, bounced off the trees, the concrete of the bridge, and boomed around the car.

Dan yelled, "Keep the dog up there." He spoke to her again, his tone gentle again. "You might have to rename Max. We're going to start calling him Lassie."

"Max," she echoed.

Dan smiled. "Libbie, listen to me. You are going to be okay. I know because someone called out all the angels. There's a host of them on your side, so you hang in there. Don't let us down." He yelled again, "Other side." Then turned back to her. "You'll hear chainsaws. We have to cut some of these branches away, so we can see what's what."

The saws roared and spit out wood. She heard but saw little. The passenger side door creaked. It opened mere inches, and Dan wasn't a small guy, but somehow, he made it in.

"Glass," she warned.

"Libbie," Jim said. "What hurts? Let me know." His head bowed forward, and his hand disappeared into the black creek water.

The pressure was faint, but she could feel his fingers against her legs and fluttering down by her feet.

"Jim." she said.

He smiled. His eyes were wet. The lashes glittered around his hazel eyes. "Can you feel that? Does it hurt?"

"I can. Not much."

"I think your legs are wedged in. You've got an injury on your forehead. I can see that. What about your arm?"

Thoughtlessly, Libbie tried to turn her head toward him, to see him better, to answer him, maybe to smile a bit, and the pain took her away.

When she opened her eyes again, Libbie said, "Jim." But it wasn't him touching her arm, it was a stranger checking her pulse. Someone was touching her neck and abdomen and asking her what hurt. Libbie closed her eyes.

Chaos surrounded her. Chain saws. Loud wrenching grinding noises that somehow connected to the excruciating movements of her car. The descent had been fast and hard. The ascent was slow and careful and tortured. Every time Libbie tried to leave the present, the car jolted and brought her back. Max had barked until he didn't. He wasn't barking now. Someone must've taken him away.

A stranger said, "Ma'am, was that your cat? We tried to catch her, but she got away."

Someone else said, "No one cares about a danged cat right now."

"Well, she might. Cat came through it okay, ma'am. I expect she'll find her way home."

Libbie's cat. She opened her eyes and peeked at the passenger seat. No cat. No Grandmother.

Men's voices. One close to her window said, "You're a civilian. You need to step back and let us get this done."

It was Dan's voice.

But then another voice said, "Get out of my way and give me the coat. You do what you do best, and I'll do my job. I'll take care of Libbie."

Jim. That was Jim's voice.

"It's dangerous, Jim. And when we release the pressure...."

"She'll need me there and that's where I'll be."

She opened her eyes and he was there beside her again.

"I'm going to put this over you, Libbie. Hold still. They're going to cut the car away." He was wearing a fire helmet.

Libbie felt like she should make a joke about Jim joining the fire department. The idea was fleeting, and the words couldn't come together, still, being able to have an actual, coherent thought about someone else seemed an improvement.

Jim draped the fabric, a heavy garment, over her head and tucked the edges gently behind her shoulders. It smelled of exhaust and soot. He reassured her, "I'm going to stay here beside you."

Under cover, still she sensed him hovering over her, protecting her with his body. Metal twanged, and something shifted. The water drained from around her legs and the pressure eased. Libbie moved, and then she began to scream. At least her mouth was open, but the shrieking might have all been in her head because she couldn't hear anything except the chaos and then everything stopped.

****

Jim. Libbie caught his scent, or rather the color of his scent, over the stink of the antiseptic hand wash and the sterile hospital odors. To her, he seemed blue. A soft hazel blue-green like his eyes. It comforted her. Hospital. Jim. Marriage. It hit her in a rush. How many pieces was she in? She struggled to open her eyes. The eyelids seemed stuck.

"Took long enough." It was an old woman's voice. A grumpy, moody old woman.

"Joyce?"

"Hah. See, she said my name. Couldn't hardly hear her, but it still counts. Spoke to me first, she did." A clang against the bed rail. Her cane. The bed moved. "Libbie! Can you hear me?"

One of Libbie's eyes opened. Joyce's face swam slowly into focus.

"Just so you know, I didn't walk here." She cackled. "Jim Mitchell had one of his nursery trucks pick me up. Took two people to lift me up into the seat." She rattled the bed rail. "I told 'em to go for it. Just toss me in. I have to go see my friend."

Libbie's other eye opened. Jim was standing beside Joyce.

"I called him, you know." Joyce pointed a finger at Jim, then at Libbie. "You can thank me later when you're feeling better. I didn't dither about it. Soon as Alice tole me you were in trouble, I insisted the matron call 9-1-1 but she wouldn't, that stubborn mean-spirited jailer. But I kept at it until she called the sheriff's office."

Jim said, "You weren't answering your phone, so I was already on my way over when Dan called. I checked the house first. Max was going crazy trying to get through the door. Joyce told me where to find the key. As soon as I opened the door, Max took off running, barking back at me to keep up."

Angels. Lassie. Dan had said that, right? Were these her angels?

Jim explained. The hunters had come across the injured deer and recognized the signs of a vehicle hit. They didn't have to look far before finding the car lodged at the bottom of the slope, nose-down in Cub Creek.

Libbie hadn't seen any angels, just people...friends. Her friends. Plus, she seemed to recall another disturbing visitor, but one that hadn't been unkind.

It occurred to her that, maybe, that's how angels preferred to work. Through those you loved, or will come to love and appreciate.

****

The verdict was cracked ribs, a concussion, broken arm and various cuts and bruises. Miraculously, the damage to her legs was minimal, yet those and her ribs hurt the worst. It would all heal given time and rest.

Jim drove her home. The headache was troublesome, but the ribs hurt the most. Breathing, walking and sitting were painful. But Libbie was well medicated and so, despite the pain, she smiled a lot. Jim smiled back.

"I'm hard on cars," she muttered.

"What?"

"The last time I hit that bridge I had to buy a new car."

"Bridge wins every time. This time, though, you avoided hitting most of it. Only grazed it."

"That's a good thing, I think." She touched his arm. "Not hitting it, I mean."

In the driveway, he leaned over, careful of her hurts, and kissed her gently on the lips.

"Wait here while I unlock the door."

Max shot out as soon as Jim opened the front door, and rushed to the car. Libbie hurt all the more anticipating his boisterous greeting, but Jim said firmly, "Stay. Sit."

Max did.

He sat as ordered, but fidgeted as if his butt

was situated on an ant hill. Libbie wanted to tell Jim to release him from the command, but then remembered Max's usual manner of greeting her. He'd probably try to jump into her arms. A little restraint wouldn't hurt him. Not this once.

Jim put his arm around her, keeping away from the troublesome ribs, to support her as they walked to the steps and climbed to the porch.

"Matthew wanted to be here. Said he had experience with injury and recovery. Mom made soups and casseroles and she'll bring them by later."

"Nice."

"I found your door already unlocked. Joyce is inside. She said to tell you she didn't walk. Dan dropped her off. Said she wanted to sit with you while you napped."

Joyce was in the corner chair under a blanket, snoozing. Apparently, Max's excitement hadn't disturbed her.

"Looks like she got a head start."

"I'm going to settle you here on the sofa. Do you need something to drink? Anything?"

"Thank you. I need you to not hover. I'm not an invalid."

"Glad to hear it." Jim walked over to the fireplace mantle and lined up the prescription bottles. "Here's your meds, right next to the candle. That's the one Gladys gave you, right?

What's this?" He picked something up off the mantle. He held it between his thumb and finger and turned toward Libbie. "A souvenir from our trip?"

The coin.

"100 Lire. A souvenir and reminder, to cherish the good memories and let the rest go."

Jim gave her a longish look, then returned to the coin to its place. He dropped a kiss on her forehead. "You relax while I'll go out to the car and get my bag."

Libbie frowned.

"Who else is going to stay with you?" He nodded at Joyce and shook his head. "Dan? Not a chance. Not Liz. Maybe my Mom? I know she wouldn't mind."

"Get your bag."

He paused in the foyer. "By the way. Your purse is wrecked. It fell into the floorboard. Got soaked."

A memory tugged at her. "My purse? At the hospital, you did say you retrieved my things from the car, right? It's all pretty foggy."

"You remember right. I went through your purse and tried to dry the stuff out. Some of it's ruined, but you can decide what to throw out. It's all in my duffle bag. I'll bring it in."

The rings. If they washed out of the purse, they were likely lost in the bottom silt of Cub Creek...and the letter and clipping and whatever else Margaret had crammed in there, were surely destroyed. A marriage license, hadn't she said? Could they have survived the soaking? Tears welled in her eyes. She'd gotten to the point where she could look forward to reading them, and the gift of the rings...it was all she had from her mother.

Joyce snored. Libbie stared at her. What had Aunt Margaret said? Or had it been Grandmother? Don't find yourself alone and unloved at the end?

Things. Rings were things and didn't matter. Still, a tear rolled down the curve of her cheek.

"What's wrong?" Jim knelt at her side. He touched her cheek and stopped the tear with his finger.

Libbie reached up and took his hand. "Must be a convalescent phase." She tried to smile. "I was remembering what's important."

"Are you sure you're okay?"

She kissed his hand. "I am."

Her purse had been replaced by a paper bag.

"Oh," she said.

He opened the bag and pulled out the red envelope. "These are safe."

"Oh," she said again. She wouldn't cry. She wouldn't. She held the envelope in her hand. It was stained and bubbled, but it had stayed in her purse and the fastening had held.

"And this. I apologize in advance. I laid the pages out to dry. Couldn't help noticing. Read some. I hope you don't mind. They came through the wetting pretty good. Lucky, they were in that zippered pocket in your purse. Not quite waterproof, but it did give some protection."

"I didn't know anything about your other family, Libbie. It was interesting reading. You'll have to tell me more about them." He grinned. "I admit, as difficult as your childhood must've been, your grandmother and aunt and uncle never seemed quite real to me. Liz is the only one I ever met." He pointed at the letter and clipping. "I'd like to get to know these people."

Jim reached into his pocket. "One more thing. Now that you're out of the hospital and we're both here, I'm not taking a chance on losing another opportunity." He was already on his knee, so he opened the little black box.

"Libbie, will you marry me?"

****

It was inevitable that Jim would need to start spending more time over at the nursery and his own home. He didn't push Libbie to move over there, but they both understood that she would.

Max would get accustomed to a new patch of woods. The cat? Libbie figured she'd be happy so long as the food dish was filled regularly, and she had a soft place to sleep. Jim said they were both welcome. Libbie wandered the rooms of her home, staring, touching a wall here, or a fixture there. In her own way, she was assessing the state of things, wondering what would happen to this house, Cub Creek, when she left. Because leave, she would. This time, Jim and she would stick together, even if it broke some part of her heart.

"Libbie? What are you doing?"

She turned to smile at him. "Walking. Remember what the physical therapist said."

He studied her face and came closer. He touched her cheek. "How are you feeling?"

"Better all the time." Libbie laid her hand on his arm. The ring on her finger glittered with promise.

Jim left for the nursery and she resumed her walk. Room to room. What would she take and what would she leave behind? What could she store? What should she sell? Panic began to tighten her chest. She breathed in slowly and deeply and held her breath for a few moments before releasing it.

This wasn't going to be easy, but stuff worth having, rarely was.

Libbie pressed her hand, her cheek, against the wall. The warmth was still there. She closed her eyes.

Liz was wrong to say those things to Jim, but

she wasn't entirely wrong in what she'd said. Leaving Cub Creek was going to be difficult, but Libbie had done harder things and this time she wouldn't be doing it alone.

Jim returned in the afternoon. She heard his car in the driveway and was expecting to hear the front door, but nothing. Libbie waited, listening, then got up from the chair and walked to the front window. His car was there. She went to the back door. He was standing on the terrace and facing the woods.

She opened the storm door. "Jim? You okay?"

He turned and smiled in reassurance. "Thinking. Doing a little remembering."

"It's chilly out here." Libbie gripped the rail to ease her steps down.

Jim said, "You're moving better all the time."

He met her on the last step.

She said, "I'm fine now. All but recovered. The rest is a matter of time." She draped her arms over his shoulders and he put his around her waist. He lifted her down from that last step to stand beside him on the terrace.

"Will you take a short walk with me?" he asked.

"Anywhere, Jim. I'll follow you anywhere."

He kissed her lips. "I'll hold you to that."

With his arm around her, pretending he wasn't steadying her, they walked across the terrace and stopped near the concrete pad.

Libbie said, "Did you know that Dan suggested, not so long ago, that we should use this as a dance floor at our engagement party?" She wouldn't repeat the rest of the nonsense Dan had spouted that day.

"A party? I think we can do better than this. For one thing, it needs to be much larger. Also, I'm not waiting for an engagement party before we get married. We can have a post-wedding party. How does that sound?"

"Sounds lovely."

"We'll have it in the spring as soon as the weather warms up, but we won't wait to hold the wedding because I'm not taking a chance on losing you again."

"No chance of that, Jim."

"So, I was thinking about it, but this," he pointed at the concrete, "is too small for a party."

"We can rent a hall or something. Do you have someplace special in mind?"

"I do." He nodded.

Jim continued staring at the concrete pad. It made Libbie curious and a little uneasy. He said, "Remember when you found out I'd planned to buy this property? Before you bought it out from under me?"

"Well, it wasn't exactly like that. But, yes, I do recall that."

"You may remember I'd planned to store equipment here, to have it on this side of the county?"

"That's right."

"Of course, it's your property. I don't mean to tell you what to do with it."

"What are you talking about? Jim, I'm confused. You can keep whatever equipment you want here, any time you want. But if I'm leaving here, I presume I'll sell the property, or rent the house out or something like that."

He pointed this way and that and said, "We could enlarge the garage area. Might have to take out one or two of those trees. How would you feel about that?"

"Jim. I don't understand."

"I could add a small office. Make this a satellite office, sort of, for the lawn care business. I think I could handle the commute."

"From clear across the county, Jim? Everyday? I don't think so."

"No, Libbie. I mean the commute from there," he pointed to the back door, "to here."

"Are you serious?"

"Would I joke about this?"

"We can live here?"

He smiled. "We can live anywhere. I think that Max and Buttercup like it better here."

"Buttercup? Who's that?"

"If you don't name that cat, that's what I'm

going to call her. I won't continue calling her "cat" or "the cat."

"Never mind the cat, Jim." Libbie was almost breathless with anticipation. She told him silently, *Say the rest.*

"I thought this would make a perfect location for Mitchell's landscaping on this side of the county. I was hoping you hadn't gotten your heart set on leaving. We could stay right here."

"Stop speaking, Jim. Enough words." She kissed his lips, then pressed her face into the crook of his neck.

"Is that a yes?" Jim said.

"Yes."

"There's one thing still standing in the way of us getting married."

"What?"

"We need a marriage license."

"Oh, Jim. Not funny."

"I'm serious. Once we have that the rest is easy." He led her back to the terrace and the wrought iron table. "Did you know, Libbie, that the Sheriff can perform the service?"

She stepped back. "No."

"Yes."

"No, that's not what I meant. I mean *no.*"

Jim laughed. "For several reasons, I agree with you. No to the sheriff, then. I happen to know a pastor who'd be happy to help us out."

She sighed. "I like that idea. But small. A

very small service."

"You've got it. Just us and the pastor."

Libbie stepped back and looked into his beautiful eyes. "Your mother and Matthew, too. I'd like them to be there. I think they'd like that? Your sister? Joyce, of course."

Jim coughed. "I think they would like that very much." He pulled her close again. "When should we do it?"

"I'm ready when you are. Now and forever, Jim."

Epilogue

"Day trip," Jim said. "Got your camera, Mrs. Mitchell?"

"I do." It was her third very expensive camera in a few, short months. Libbie held up the little point and shoot she'd purchased in Sicily. "Got the backup, too. One never knows." She smiled.

"One never does, that's for sure."

"Where are we going? Why so mysterious? Are we taking a honeymoon trip, after all?"

"I believe we already did that." Jim opened the car door and waited for her to climb in and get settled.

The ribs were still twingey, but no longer painful.

"Thanks, Jim."

"My pleasure."

He looked like he meant it. In fact, that whole grinning persona was getting annoying. Surprises weren't always nice for the recipient. Libbie knew that for a fact.

He climbed into the driver's seat and before she could get too frustrated, he pulled a map from the center console and handed it to her.

"What's this?" she asked.

"Take a look. See that red circle?"

Yes, someone, presumably Jim, had drawn a bulls-eye around a small town named Preston.

"That's the town mentioned in the letters. That's where were going?"

"Yes, ma'am. We're headed to Preston with that camera to see what we see, and while we're there, maybe we'll find some people we'd like to meet." He reached into the console again. "And I brought this along in case we need it." He handed her the long, white envelope from Aunt Margaret.

She accepted it, held it, but could only stare. "Suppose...."

"No worries, there, Libbie. We can afford to be choosy about who we invite into our lives." He squeezed her hand. "We have each other. So long as we stick together, the rest of the world is interesting, but optional."

"On with it, then. I'm apprehensive, but wherever you go, I go, and vice versa. We'll enjoy today, and take on the future as it comes, together.

THE END

ABOUT THE AUTHOR

Stories of heart and hope ~ from the Outer Banks to the Blue Ridge

USA Today Bestselling and award-winning author, Grace Greene, writes novels of contemporary romance with sweet inspiration, and women's fiction with romance, mystery and suspense.

A Virginia native, Grace has family ties to North Carolina. She writes books set in both locations. The Emerald Isle, NC Stories series of romance and sweet inspiration are set in North Carolina. The Virginia Country Roads novels, and the Cub Creek novels have more romance, mystery, and suspense.

Grace lives in central Virginia. Stay current with Grace's news at www.gracegreene.com.

You'll also find Grace here:
http://twitter.com/Grace_Greene
https://www.facebook.com/GraceGreeneBooks
http://www.goodreads.com/Grace_Greene

Other Books by Grace Greene

A STRANGER IN WYNNEDOWER

(Virginia Country Roads ~ Single Title Novel)

<u>Book Description:</u>

Love and suspense with a dash of Southern Gothic... Rachel Sevier, a lonely thirty-two-year-old inventory specialist, travels to Wynnedower Mansion in Virginia to find her brother who has stopped returning her calls. Instead, she finds Jack Wynne, the mansion's bad-tempered owner. He isn't happy to meet her. When her brother took off without notice, he left Jack in a lurch.

Jack has his own plans. He's tired of being responsible for everyone and everything. He wants to shake those obligations, including the old mansion. The last thing he needs is another complication, but he allows Rachel to stay while she waits for her brother to return.

At Wynnedower, Rachel becomes curious about the house and its owner. If rumors are true, the means to save Wynnedower Mansion from demolition are hidden within its walls, but the other inhabitants of Wynnedower have agendas, too. Not only may Wynnedower's treasure be stolen, but also the life of its arrogant master, unless Rachel can save them.

THE MEMORY OF BUTTERFLIES
(Lake Union Publishing ~ Single Title)

Brief Description:
A young mother lies to keep a devastating family secret from being revealed, but the lies, themselves, could end up destroying everything and everyone she loves. Hannah Cooper's daughter, Ellen, is leaving for college soon. As Ellen's high school graduation approaches, Hannah decides it's time to return to her roots in Cooper's Hollow along Virginia's beautiful and rustic Cub Creek. Hannah's new beginning comes with unanticipated risks that will cost her far more than she ever imagined—perhaps more than she can survive.

THE HAPPINESS IN BETWEEN
(Lake Union Publishing ~ Single Title)

Brief Description:
Sandra Hurst has left her husband. Again. She's made the same mistake twice and her parents refuse to help this time—emotionally or financially. Desperate to earn money and determined to start over, she accepts an offer from her aunt to house-sit at the old family home, Cub Creek, in beautiful rural Virginia. But when Sandra arrives, she finds the house is shabby, her aunt's dog is missing, and the garden is woefully overgrown. And she suspects her almost-ex-husband is on her trail. Sandra needs one more change at regaining her self-respect, making peace with her family, and discovering what she's truly made of.

KINCAID'S HOPE

(Virginia Country Roads ~ Single Title Novel)

Book Description:

Beth Kincaid left her hot temper and unhappy childhood behind and created a life in the city free from untidy emotionalism, but even a tidy life has danger, especially when it falls apart.

In the midst of her personal disasters, Beth is called back to her hometown of Preston, a small town in southwestern Virginia, to settle her guardian's estate. There, she runs smack into the mess she'd left behind a decade earlier: her alcoholic father, the long-ago sweetheart, Michael, and the poor opinion of almost everyone in town.

As she sorts through her guardian's possessions, Beth discovers that the woman who saved her and raised her had secrets, and the truths revealed begin to chip away at her self-imposed control.

Michael is warmly attentive and Stephen, her ex-fiancé, follows her to Preston to win her back, but it is the man she doesn't know who could forever end Beth's chance to build a better, truer life.

Thank you for purchasing

LEAVING CUB CREEK

I hope you enjoyed it!

Please leave a review where this book is sold.
It helps authors find readers and helps readers
find books they'll enjoy.

I hope you'll visit me at www.gracegreene.com
and sign up for my newsletter. I'd love to be in
contact with you.

Books by Grace Greene

Stories of heart and hope ~ from the Outer Banks to the Blue Ridge

Emerald Isle, NC Stories
Love. Suspense. Inspiration.

BEACH RENTAL (Emerald Isle novel #1)
BEACH WINDS (Emerald Isle novel #2)
BEACH WEDDING (Emerald Isle novel #3)
BEACH TOWEL (short story)
BEACH WALK (A Christmas novella)
BEACH CHRISTMAS (A Christmas novella)
CLAIR: BEACH BRIDES SERIES (novella)

Virginia Country Roads Novels
Love. Mystery. Suspense.

KINCAID'S HOPE
A STRANGER IN WYNNEDOWER
CUB CREEK (Cub Creek series #1)
LEAVING CUB CREEK (Cub Creek series #2)

Single Titles from Lake Union Publishing

THE HAPPINESS IN BETWEEN
THE MEMORY OF BUTTERFLIES

www.gracegreene.com